Seduced by the Pharaoh

By

Sheniqua Waters

Seduced by the Pharaoh by Sheniqua Waters

TheWorldsBestBook.com

ISBN: 978-0615827131

Thank you for purchasing this book.

This book is dedicated to:

Burt Vialpando

For being my husband and my hero

Chapter One

Nubia – 852 B.C.

A piercing scream reverberated over the waters of the Nile shattering the calm tranquil morning. A shiver coursed down Latifa's spine as she turned her gaze from the water to retrace the route of the shrill sound. Her eyes scanned the top of a wheat field and skimmed the thicket of trees some distance away. Suddenly, she noticed black smoke rising above the trees and billowing grimly toward the sky. A moment later, she saw two girls exit the line of trees then she lost sight of them when they ran into the tall stalks of wheat. A minute later, the girls emerged from the rows of wheat and ran toward her. Though they were some distance away, Latifa realized she knew the youngsters and ran to meet them. As she neared the girls, she saw their faces were smeared with trepidation and that a sheen of perspiration glistened on their black skin. The smell of sweat mingled with musk filled Latifa's nose when the young girls came to a hastened stop before her.

"What is the trouble? What's happening?" she questioned.

"They…he…here! They've come…and…and attacked the fortress! You must run for your life!" the older of the two girls panted.

"Who's come? Who's attacked our village?" Latifa asked.

"The Egyptians!" the girl announced.

"That can't be!" Latifa protested even as her heart began to pound in her chest.

"They deceived us! Now they're taking captives!" the youngest girl exclaimed.

Latifa grabbed the hand of the older girl when she moved to commence her escape. "My sister, Tanesha. Where is she?"

"The Egyptians got her! I'm sure of it!" came the reply.

"Oh my God!" Latifa released the girl's hand and covered her mouth in horror. "I've got to find her!"

5

"It's not safe! You ought not go back!" the older girl advised before dashing into a sprint.

"Come with us," the younger girl urged a moment before she continued her flight as well.

"I must find my sister!" Latifa called out.

As she watched the girls race away, Latifa shook her head in disbelief. The fortress was being attacked by Egyptians? How could it be? Just the night before, word had come that her father, King Rassom, signed a peace treaty with the newly appointed Egyptian King. To celebrate the new era of peace, the villagers had gathered around a large bonfire. Game had been roasted, songs had been sung and the jubilant crowd had danced the night away.

Now it seemed, a new era of peace would not be a reality. A very different reality was taking hold. Egyptians were raiding the fortress which meant her father and those with him were dead. If that was the case, her younger sister, Tanesha, was all she had left. But where was Tanesha? What had become of her? At the thought, Latifa ran to the mule she used as transportation. The animal which was nibbling on a stalk of wheat seemed annoyed when she collected the reins and climbed on its back. Clicking her tongue to the roof of her mouth, Latifa pressed her knees into the animal's flanks.

The animal stood still ignoring the nudge.

Latifa dug her knees into the animal's flanks once more. But as before, the mule remained motionless.

"Damn mule!" Latifa hissed and leapt off the animal. Hastily, she tugged on the reins in an attempt to pull the mule forward.

The obstinate mule stood its ground.

"Stubborn beast! I hope you get eaten by a leopard!" Latifa huffed then not wanting to waste another second, she dropped the reins.

Ignoring the dirt path that led to her home, she ran toward the wheat field which was the faster route. Wind swept against her face as she ran into the plush pasture of wheat. The tall stalks of wheat scratched at her skin as she sprinted through the field.

When Latifa exited the wheat field, screams of panic and moans of defeat mingled with the desperate yodel of basenjis and invaded her ears. As she neared the fortress, the pungent smell of charred wood stung her nose. Blindly, she ran toward the wall of thick dark smoke that spewed through the open gates of the fortress. As she raced past the gate and into the fortress, the pernicious smoke drenched her. Through the black haze, she saw crimson flames devouring nearby huts. Weaving to her right, she dodged a stampede of horses, cows and chickens spooked by the blistering flames billowing from the roofs and windows of doomed huts.

A flurried mass of people darted past her. She watched her tribesmen race about like hapless prey while Egyptians brandishing blood stained swords were in deft pursuit of them. Latifa scanned the faces of those running by in search of her sister. Through the menacing haze of smoke, she spotted a welcomed face.

"Kofi!" she yelled out the name of her intended only to find her voice drowned out by shrill screams and shouts of fright which seemed suspended in the air.

Her brow wrinkled with horror when she saw a tall Egyptian wearing a pleated *schenti* secured with a red sash advance unobserved behind Kofi.

Latifa began to run toward the disparate pair and called out to Kofi again. She watched Kofi look around as if in search of the person who shouted his name. She yelled out his name once more and frantically waved her hands in an effort to catch his attention.

He caught sight of her.

"Behind you!" Latifa hollered as she watched the Egyptian extract a dagger from the sheath that hung from his sash.

Kofi's brow wrinkled and he opened his mouth to speak.

"Behind you!" she yelled desperately and pointed to the towering Egyptian at Kofi's heels.

She watched as comprehending her words, Kofi spun on his feet a moment before the Egyptian let out a menacing roar and swung the knife. Kofi leapt backwards to avoid being sliced by the blade. Latifa sprinted to his side.

"Latifa get out of here!" Kofi hollered then acting quick shoved her away from him.

Unprepared for the shove, Latifa lost her footing and fell to the ground. She spat out the dirt that filled her mouth and raised her head to look at Kofi. He had backed several steps from the Egyptian who was advancing forward. She watched the Egyptian draw close. When the Egyptian raised his leg to step over her, she grabbed his boot. The tall man stumbled slightly then glowered down at her with an agitated glint in his black eyes.

Kofi howled in an effort to reclaim the man's attention. The Egyptian refocused on Kofi and swiped his dagger at Kofi who remained slightly out of reach. The Egyptian lifted his leg to take a step but Latifa pulled on his boot preventing him from moving forward.

Suddenly, the Egyptian reached down and pushed Latifa's face into the ground. Dirt once again filled her mouth. She spat out the dirt along with a curse. However, she did not release her hold on her prize. Obstinately, she held on to the Egyptian's boot as she thought about the fact the Egyptians had taken all of her relatives from her. Somehow it was important that this Egyptian not take anyone else from her life.

The Egyptian snarled, ran his free hand through his hair which was cropped close to his scalp then he lifted his dagger over his head. Dark smoke snaked around the knife's silver blade and swirled against the brass handle. In the next instant, mercilessly, the Egyptian brought his hand down and smashed the brass handle against the side of Latifa's head causing her head to slam into the ground. Pain exploded on the side of Latifa's head and the tangy taste of blood coated her mouth. An instant later, everything went black.

⚃

Latifa's eyes fluttered open to the silver light of the moon. Immediately, a cascade of memories flooded her thoughts. The image of gleaming flames and billowing smoke flashed in her mind. The sound of earsplitting screams and anguished groans echoed in her ears. She recalled the menacing Egyptian with the sinister glower. A shudder coursed through her as she remembered the brutish man pushing her face into the ground, clenching his dagger then callously slamming the brass handle against the side of her head. Latifa looked up at the moon shining from its place in the sky. How long had she been lying as she was? Where was the Egyptian? Afraid he was still close, she closed her eyes and listened for an answer to her fear.

Quiet crackled in her ears. Was there no one left alive in the fortress? Silence answered threatening to explode into a crescendo of distress. Unable to stand the stampede of calm, Latifa's eyes snapped open. Shifting her gaze, she saw the form of a male. Her eyes focused on the hapless male body prostrated face down on the ground beside her.

"Kofi?" she whispered.

There was no response.

Cautiously, Latifa lifted her head and saw a small number of huts stood untouched among smoldering ones that had been burnt to the ground. She spied a few Egyptian soldiers near the entrance of the fortress. Grateful they were unaware of her, she rose to her knees. Something sharp pricked her leg. She lifted her leg and saw the dagger that belonged to the tall Egyptian on the ground beneath her. She pushed the dagger aside, brushed dirt from her face then reached out to touch the man lying beside her. When she placed her hands on the male's shoulder, she felt a sappy substance under her palms. She lifted her hands and saw the crimson stain of blood covered her palms and fingers. An uncontrolled scream ripped from her throat. The scream of terror was immediately followed by regret when she heard the raised voices of the Egyptian soldiers who were at the entrance of the fortress. She looked up and saw their daunting figures rushing forward and realized the scream was leading her enemies to her. Acting quick, she grabbed the dagger from the ground, ran behind a stockpile of wood then into a nearby dwelling.

Latifa's heartbeat sounded in her ears as she listened to the Egyptians' hasty approach. The enemy soldiers advanced on her hiding place. Her knees began to shake. When the men ran past the dwelling, her knees buckled underneath her and with an exasperated sigh she slid to the floor. Recalling the events of the day, the memory of all she had lost flooded back to her. She lowered her head in anguish. Everyone she cared about was dead. She had nothing left to live for and it was all because of one man – the Pharaoh of Egypt. The Pharaoh was a treacherous man. He was a liar who was no doubt amused at his cleverness in deceiving and decimating the Nubians. She gripped the dagger. Oh how she wished she was a female warrior! If she were, she would track down the Pharaoh and plunge the dagger into his heart.

When she was young, she had dreamed of being a warrior. After all, she came from a long line of female Queens who ruled Nubia brilliantly and led raids into enemy territories. Her grandmother had regaled her with tails of Nubian Queens and the female warriors who fought in battles beside them. She had been awed by stories of how the women warriors refused to let their smaller size or lessened physical strength be a disadvantage when fighting against men. According to her grandmother, the women warriors used their wit to outsmart their opponents on and off the battlefield.

The tall tales of spectacular victories and improbable combative triumphs had spurred her imagination and taken root in her mind. She admired the female warriors she knew and tried to model herself after them. When she asked her grandmother to tell her the secret to becoming a great warrior, her grandmother responded by saying great female warriors followed the lead of Nubian Queens of old and never involved themselves with men. She explained being with a man eroded a woman's focus and caused her to lose her militaristic supremacy. After hearing her grandmother's words, Latifa decided she would adhere to a self imposed vow of chastity. She promised herself she

10

would focus on training to be a warrior and avoid being involved with a man.

When she told her father of her intent, he responded by conceding the idea was a courageous one. But, he said, she was not the type to be a woman of war. According to him, she should think about getting married because she would be happiest in a relationship with a man. In response to his assertion, Latifa declared she had no desire to marry and pleaded with her father to let her live life the way she chose. However, her words had not persuaded him. He insisted she forget her misdirected sentiment and accept a marriage to Kofi who was sure to be a good provider and a caring husband. Latifa had continued to protest. But, despite her objections, her father betroth her to Kofi.

One day, while she spoke with her father about ending her betrothal to Kofi so she could keep her vow to be a warrior, a message arrived from the new Pharaoh of Egypt. According to the message, the newly appointed Pharaoh wanted to negotiate a treaty that would end Nubian raids in his kingdom. When the contents of the letter were announced, there had been much debate by all of the tribesmen as to whether a treaty should be made. A few of the elders recalled attacks by Mamelukes from Egypt and warned against any negotiations with their enemy. Some people said signing a treaty meant the subjugation of all in the land of Kush. Others declared Nubia should unite with Makuria and form a single federated kingdom to stand against the Egyptians. In the end, her father decided to meet with the Pharaoh.

As her father put on his crown and prepared for the journey to meet the Egyptian Pharaoh, he had announced he would consider retracting her betrothal so she could begin training to be a warrior. The timing of his change of heart was not lost on Latifa. She knew her father was finally considering her request because once the treaty was signed she would not have an occasion to participate in a raid or step on a battlefield. Even though this was true, Latifa had been happy at her father's possible change of heart and had been anxiously anticipating his return. For her, if her father conceded to her request, it meant the beginning of a new phase in her life. Now, however, her new life meant nothing because her father was not coming home.

At the thought of never seeing her father again, tears streamed down Latifa's face. She lifted her hand to the base of her neck. Relief eased her sorrow when she felt that the thin chain her father had given her was still around her neck. She let her finger sweep across the pendant of a cobra that hung from the chain. She was glad it still hung around her neck because now it was all she had in the world and she felt strangely reassured by its presence.

Latifa willed the tears that swelled in her eyes to remain unshed. She told herself she could not succumb to her heartache. Though her father was dead, there was a chance her sister was still alive. Since there were only a few soldiers left in the fortress, she reasoned any people of her village who had been captured must have been taken to the Egyptian camp. She had to get to the Egyptian camp and look for her sister. She could cry later.

Using the moonlight that slithered through the window as a guide, Latifa stood and walked to a table that held a wide brimmed clay jar. The jar was filled with water which she used to wash her blood stained hands. Once her hands were cleaned, she wiped her pendant and the dagger clean. Latifa peered out of the window and saw the soldiers' forms receding beyond the gates of the fortress and into the darkness. She reasoned the Egyptian camp was close by since the men did not mount any horses. Latifa gripped the dagger and exited her hiding place. Careful to stay a safe distance behind the soldiers, she slipped past the fortress gates then ran into the knot of trees and followed them.

After a brief walk, the soldiers arrived at their campsite.

From her vantage point in the thicket of trees, Latifa scanned the encampment for captives. She saw several virile men walking between large tents and saw others sitting around pits of fire which dotted the campsite. A dog's bark sounded from somewhere within the camp and Latifa knew she needed to be cautious lest the animal pick up her scent.

The rustle of leaves blowing in the wind met Latifa's ears a moment before she heard the snap of a fallen tree branch under the stomp of heavy feet. Spinning on her heels, she barely managed to catch the scream that rose in her throat when she saw an Egyptian soldier standing behind her.

"How did you come to be here?" the soldier inquired.

Latifa's answer was to lunge the dagger toward the soldier's throat and pray she hit her target.

Chapter Two

"May Petbe damn them!" Tariq bellowed as he pushed aside the flap at the entrance of his tent and stomped inside. "The Nubians were attacked! The attack undermines everything I worked to achieve! Who could have done such a thing?"

"It was done by someone who knew the Nubians' defenses were down," Jabari, the Lieutenant of the Army, explained as he followed Tariq into the tent. "It appears it was a surprise attack that happened a few hours ago. Most likely the perpetrators knew King Rassom had left the fortress. They must have known he had gone forth to meet you and sign the peace treaty."

Tariq began to pace the confines of his tent. "When the King returns to his home and sees the decimation, he shall think I planned the attack. He shall think the treaty was just a ruse."

"Whoever did this cannot have gone far. I am certain they are traveling at a slow pace...encumbered by the Nubians they snatched. Scouts have been dispatched to try and pick up their trail."

"Tracking the perpetrators was a prudent decision," Tariq stated. "When they are found, I shall be torn between pursuing the culprits and waiting here to speak with the King when he returns. We should help him rebuild."

"I am sure the best course of action shall come to you, Sire."

Tariq stopped pacing and turned his dark brown eyes upon his close adviser. "Sire? When we are on military campaigns, you have always called me Commander. That does not need to change."

"As you wish. When we are on military missions, I shall continue to call you by your military title. When we return to Egypt and you are leading us as Pharaoh, I shall then call you Sire. I shall make sure all in the platoon do this as well," Jabari promised.

"I thought military service was all there would be for me. I never expected my father to name me Pharaoh over Narmer."

"It was unexpected to be sure. It is proof your father loved you very much...just as he loved your mother. He married Narmer's mother out of duty...to seal an alliance."

"And now the son of a concubine is ruler over all of Egypt."

"Just as on the battlefield, the direction of one's destiny can never be assumed. Your path is still unfolding before you. I sense you are tiring of war and now yearn for peace. If you didn't, you would have never tried to make peace with the Nubians. When hieroglyphs are etched on the wall of The Temple, your name shall be inscribed. For generations yet to come, you shall be known by the name 'Peaceful Warrior'."

"Your words are kind, Jabari. We have been through many perilous predicaments together. Your dedication has not gone unnoticed. You have been as a Vizier to me. It is only fitting that I appoint you *Tjaty* when we return to Egypt. Think upon it."

"You honor me with such a thought. But, I am just a soldier and shall always be a soldier with only one goal. To serve Egypt. Now that you are Pharaoh, you are Egypt."

Tariq nodded and walked to the table in the corner of the tent. "I must perform my duty and decide the next course of action."

"You have decided fitting resolutions to tenuous quandaries before. I leave you to your deliberations, Commander." Jabari nodded then exited the tent.

Tariq sank on the stool behind the table. After many weeks of travel, his legs ached and he was grateful to relax them for a moment. He looked into the flame from the lamp on the table and began to rub his right leg as he thought about his conversation with Jabari. He was indeed growing weary of war. He had hoped signing a treaty with the Nubians would usher in a period of peace and prosperity for both nations. But, as Jabari reminded him, life was unpredictable and now due to the provocation on the Nubian village peace seemed further away than ever.

Tariq's thoughts were interrupted when the flaps of his tent were pushed aside and Jabari reentered the tent. He dropped his hand to his side as Jabari began to speak.

15

"Apologies for the interruption but it is necessary. An intruder has been apprehended."

Tariq waved his hand dismissively toward the Lieutenant. "You know what we do with intruders."

"Ah... This is not any intruder. I think this is someone you'll want to see."

"Bring him in," Tariq directed.

The seasoned soldier turned and disappeared out of the tent.

A few moments later, the quietness of the night was shattered by a boisterous squeal. The raucous sound of a scuffle ensued followed by a string of curses from what sounded like a female voice. Tariq raised his eyebrow as the tumultuous commotion advanced upon his tent.

"Don't let her get away!" Jabari's voice bellowed a moment before he along with a second soldier and a female burst through the opening of the tent.

Tariq's eyebrow wrinkled as he viewed a petite female sandwiched between the two burly men. Long thin braids imprisoned her black hair and framed her oval shaped face. Her nose was wrinkled in protest, her lips were closed in a confrontational pout and her dark brown eyes blazed with ire. As she pulled against the grip of her captors, Tariq could not help but notice the way her sullied kaftan yielded to her delicate curves.

Tariq stood to his feet after the threesome came to a bumbling stop. Looking from the female to the soldiers, he belted out, "What is the meaning of this?"

"This is the intruder I was telling you about," came Jabari's response as he worked to keep a hold on the trespasser.

Tariq stepped forward so that he stood in front of the female.

"This girl?" he questioned.

"Yes, Sire...Commander. She was found lurking around our camp. Show him what you found on her," Jabari instructed the soldier who also had a hold on the uninvited arrival.

"She tried to kill me!" the soldier screeched then held up a dagger.

16

Tariq's brow crinkled when he saw the dagger. He took the dagger from the soldier's hand and examined its steel blade and brass handle for a few moments before slipping the knife under the leather strap that hung around his waist.

"You are dismissed," he said to the soldier who had given him the knife.

The soldier released his hold on the female, saluted sharply then made his exit.

Tariq turned his attention back to the female. Impulsively, he leaned forward and reached out to touch her. Instantly, her dark eyes locked with his and the venom within them gave him pause. Instead of touching her, he reached for the necklace that hung around her neck. He heard her inhale sharply and saw her body stiffen when his finger grazed the figure of a cobra that dangled from the thin chain.

He straightened himself when the ache in his legs clamored to recapture his attention. Remaining silent, he shifted on his feet and looked into the female's eyes once again. Finally, he spoke. "So you are the intruder? This is unexpected I must admit. What is your name? Why were you following my regiment?"

Her answer was an insolent glare.

"You were there when the Nubian fortress was attacked, were you not? Did you see who led the attack?"

Silence met his inquiry.

"Speak when I speak to you!" he commanded authoritatively.

She remained silent.

Suddenly angry, Tariq reached out and yanked on the gold chain ripping it from her neck.

"Give that back to me!" the female shouted indignantly and lunged forward.

"So the Nubian speaks," Tariq quipped as he watched Jabari maneuver the female's arm behind her back to prevent her from escaping his grasp.

She fell silent.

Lifting the necklace toward the flame that flickered from the lamp on the table, Tariq studied it. "It's becoming clear why this necklace is of importance to you. It's made of gold.

How did you come to possess such a costly piece of jewelry?"

His inquiry was rewarded with silence. He cast his gaze on the girl and spoke again. "If you do not speak to me, I shall keep this necklace. ...You can talk to me. I am your friend."

"You are not my friend! You are an idol worshiping heathen who attacked my village!" came the reply.

Tariq saw the girl wince indicating Jabari had tightened his grasp on her arm. Motioning for Jabari to loosen his clutch, Tariq admitted, "It was not my intent that your village be attacked."

The female continued to glare insolently at him.

"Do you know who I am?" he asked her.

"You are a liar! An Egyptian murderer and thief! An invader in our land! You take innocent women like my sister prisoner! Release my sister!"

"Your sister is not here. There are no females here. Only men. A female among these men is assured discord. That is why it's prudent of me to release you forthwith. But, before I do, I want to know what you know about the attack on the fortress."

"I know only one thing! Egyptians cannot be trusted. Now release me! I command you release me!"

"You command? Who are you a Nubian Queen?" Tariq inquired.

"My father was King Rassom. I suggest you release me or retribution shall fall on your head!"

"You say you are King Rassom's daughter? The King spoke of a daughter who wants to be a warrior. You expect me to believe you are she? You are but a defiant child. You are no warrior, little one."

"If your Centurion wasn't holding me, I would show you just what kind of warrior I am! Release me! I demand to be released!" the girl snapped peevishly.

"You demand? I give the orders around here. I am the decider. I am the..." Not yet ready to reveal the truth, Tariq let the word Pharaoh die on his lips. "I am the Commander and I give the orders. You shall find I have no tolerance for insolence. So, I suggest you change your attitude forthwith."

"Or what? You'll torture or kill me? You get thrills out of killing, don't you? Well, I am not surprised. You Egyptians are all the same. You don't have a drop of kindness in you. You are all murders, just like your Pharaoh!" she hissed.

Anger flared in Tariq at her words. Then, as suddenly as the feeling surfaced, it dissipated. He realized he was more impressed by the girl's boldness than affronted by her impertinent manner. She was surrounded by battle hardened men yet she stood her ground. If everyone in his contingent showed such courage, the unit would never face military defeat. But, courageous or not, no one could be allowed to speak to him in such a way and get away with it. The girl needed to be shown her place. However, attempting to tame the feistiest female he had ever encountered could prove to be a challenge. On the other hand, every woman fell easily under his spell. If he chose to do it, bringing this girl to heel would probably prove to be unchallenging. At the very least, it could prove to be entertaining. As Jabari said, he had decided fitting resolutions to tenuous quandaries before. He was sure he could come up with an amicable resolution for the current situation.

"You are brave but you must learn how to treat your superior," the words were out of his mouth as he thought them. "You have no home to go back to. As long as you are in my camp, you shall show me respect. You shall do as I say when I say."

Tariq watched as the girl's eyes blackened with increased animosity. He slid her necklace in the pocket of his *schenti* then walked to the table and sat down on the stool. "Come here," he instructed firmly.

Jabari released his hold on the intruder.

Her response was to fold her arms and remain where she stood.

"You have until I count to three to come to me or I shall act like the Pharaoh you despise so much. One..." Tariq said calmly. "...Two..." he paused when he saw Jabari capture the girl's gaze and menacingly pat the sword encased at his side.

A second later, the girl unfolded her arms and stomped to where he sat.

Leisurely, Tariq lifted his right leg and placed it on to the table. "Massage my leg," he directed.

Bewilderment showed on the girl's face at his request. For a moment, it appeared she was not going to do as she had been told.

Slowly, Jabari began to pull his sword free.

Tariq watched as the girl promptly pushed the material of the *schenti* up his leg.

Jabari slid his sword back into its leather sheath.

"Proceed," Tariq ordered after she laid her hands on his flesh.

Any thoughts he had of tender hands soothing his aching muscles were quickly vanquished when the disgruntled intruder began to brutally knead his leg. Tariq almost yelped as her hands continually twisted his skin. After a few moments, he was sure he would have no feeling in his leg if he did not stop her. "Softer!" he barked.

"You ordered me to massage your leg. This is the way I massage," came her stiff reply.

The girl continued kneading his skin...her touch even harder than before. Just when he thought he could not take it any longer, she dropped her hands to her side. "There. You got what you wanted. Now, I am done," she declared.

Tariq raised his thrashed leg from the table then lowered it to the ground. Surprisingly, it felt much better than it had before she massaged it. Maybe her harsh technique was exactly what his achy muscles needed.

"Your work is not done," he remarked when she began to turn from him. "I have two legs," he noted.

The girl exhaled loudly when he lifted his left leg on to the table. However, without a word, she pushed the material of his *schenti* out of her way and once again began to rub his leg.

Despite her efforts for failure, Tariq realized her course method was actually soothing his achy muscles. He looked at her hands on his skin as she went about her task. Her

20

black hands on his bronze leg looked tantalizing. He moved his leg slightly and her hip touched his inner thigh. Suddenly, Tariq felt an unexpected stir in his loins.

Not realizing the effect she was having on him, the girl continued her chore. As she worked, Tariq studied her face. Thick black lashes shrouded her almond-shaped eyes. Now that she was not pouting, he saw she had full inviting lips and that a pretty nose enhanced her face. As his examination progressed, he could not help but notice how the two small globes of her breasts yielded to the pull of her clothing while her shapely bottom pressed against the confining material to provoke a stare. Upon completion of his close inspection, it was clear his initial assumption was incorrect. She was not a girl but was a desirable young woman. If by some miracle she dropped the brazen attitude, having her in his bed for the night was certain to be very enjoyable. As he thought of it, his member stiffened and hardened.

"Jabari, leave us," he said to the Lieutenant.

"Commander, are you sure?" Jabari asked perplexed.

Tariq shook his head affirmatively.

Jabari paused a moment then said, "Keep a watch on her. She's the spawn of Apep's daughter."

Tariq grabbed the young woman's arm when she took a menacing step toward Jabari. "I can handle her," he assured chuckling at her antics.

"I'll be right outside if you need me," Jabari stated then backed out of the tent careful to keep his eyes on the ornery intruder.

When Jabari was gone, Tariq released his hold on the young woman's arm, lowered his leg then stood to his feet. "We began our acquaintance in an unpleasant manner. I think we should begin anew. I would like it very much if you would tell me your name."

"My name is Latifa," came the response.

"La-tee-fa. That's a pretty name. Well, Latifa, I must admit, I am impressed by your boldness and courage. If we were to settle our differences, it could be pleasant for both of us."

Latifa eyed him suspiciously. "What do you mean by that?" she inquired.

"Am I to assume you are not a seasoned warrior woman as you claim? If you were, surely you'd understand my meaning." He stepped toward her.

Latifa examined the man who advanced upon her. He had piercing brown eyes, sun-kissed skin and a shaved head. The lines of his lips, nose and ears looked sculpted as if they had been chiseled from stone. A thin band of hair framed his mouth and chin and covered the ridge along his jaw. As she examined him, she realized she was looking at a very virile man. She took an uneasy step backward and bumped into the table behind her.

With one step, Tariq dissipated the space between them. Without speaking another word, he reached out and pulled Latifa to him. Pressing his body against hers, he leaned down and caught her lips with his.

The moment the Commander's lips touched her lips, it seemed a rousing flame scorched Latifa's entire body. She felt her legs buckle beneath her causing her to lean into him. She put her hands out to steady herself and found them pressed against the solid wall of his muscular chest. Any resistance she harbored treacherously evaporated under the touch of his lips. He slid his arms around her waist tethering her to him causing the awakening of a craving she could not name. When his hand touched her bottom, a euphoric feeling so unexpected and new engulfed her. It seemed to Latifa she was in a dream and she found she did not want the dream to end.

The bliss of the dream evaporated into reality when she felt his hardened member through the material of her kaftan. Latifa scolded herself. How could she let this man keep his arms around her? How could she betray the promise she made herself? She had vowed she would not find enjoyment in the arms of a man. Men were off limits. Especially an Egyptian. This man's kiss was depleting her strength just as her grandmother foretold. She needed to maintain her concentration even more now that she was in the enemy's camp. Summoning all of the strength that had so easily retreated, Latifa pushed away from the Commander.

"Keep your hands off of me you filthy Egyptian!" she hissed. "I am of royal blood. It is beneath me to consort with a barbarian. I'd sooner consort with a Philistine!" she assured.

"Your lips tell a different story." The Commander grinned then pulled her against his chest once more.

Incensed at the truth of his words and ashamed that she had succumbed to his kiss, Latifa slid her arm around the Commander's waist and reached for the dagger secured by the leather strap. Grasping the handle, she hoped for success as she pulled the knife from under his strap. In the next second, she attempted to shove the blade into him.

Reacting to the nick of pain, Tariq bumped Latifa's arm with his and knocked the blade off its course but not before it pierced his linen tunic and punctured his skin. Reaching out, Tariq clenched Latifa's wrist in a vice like grip and squeezed. Unrelenting, he tightened his clutch until she groaned, unclenched her fist and dropped the dagger to the ground.

"Wildcat!" Tariq shouted in outrage. "You cut me!" he fumed when he viewed a red stain collecting around the marred material.

In the next instant, Jabari appeared and indignantly jerked Latifa from Tariq's grasp.

"I wish to God I had killed you! You and your Pharaoh shall be driven into the sea!" Latifa hollered at her victim as Jabari dragged her to the opposite corner of the tent.

Tariq peeled off his damaged tunic revealing a bronze chest which rippled with muscles. He wiped the tunic over the laceration on his side then tossed the garment onto the table. When he looked at Latifa, his brown eyes were filled with a grim expression. In an eerily calm voice, he said to her, "You shall receive a fitting punishment for your deviousness. Jabari, take her out of my sight while I decide what is to be done with her."

Jabari pushed Latifa toward the entrance of the tent.

"One more thing," Tariq's voice halted Jabari's steps. He picked up the dagger from the floor and balanced it in his hand. After a few moments of silence, he said, "Make sure Latifa is washed up. If I kiss her again, I want to know I am kissing a female and not a burnt offering."

Latifa had only a moment to gasp in outrage at the Commander's words before Jabari dragged her from the tent.

CB

Anger boiled in Latifa as she plucked at the knot on the rope that bound her leg.

"What are you looking at?" she barked at two soldiers who stopped to stare at her.

The men, like the soldiers before them, sidled away without uttering a word.

Latifa now knew, just as the Commander said, she was the only female and the only captive in the camp. A steady stream of soldiers intrigued by that fact had stopped to gawk at her. Now that a couple of hours had passed, the flow of men had slowed considerably. She hoped she would not see any more soldiers for the rest of the night because she did not want any of them to look at her let alone touch her. At the thought, Latifa rubbed the back of her hand across her lips as if to wipe away the Commander's kiss. That kiss should have never happened. It would never happen again. She had to find a way to free herself before the Commander sent for her. Who knew what punishment he would mete out after her attempt on his life. After all, he was the Pharaoh's hired killer.

Latifa scanned the ground for something she could use to free herself. A small rock caught her eye. A plan began to formulate in her mind. If she could slice through the rope, she could free herself and escape from the enemy camp. She surveyed her surroundings. The young guard assigned to secure her had long since lost interest in her and wandered off with another soldier who walked by. Seeing no one else near, she leaned from the cot she was sitting on, picked up the rock and began to rub it against the thick rope that bound her limb.

As she swiped the rock over the rope, her thoughts turned once again to the events of the day. There had been death, anguish and pain all due to the deception of one man – The Pharaoh of Egypt. It was because of the Pharaoh's deceit that her father was dead and her home destroyed. Now, Kofi was dead and in order to find out if her sister was alive or dead, she had to escape from the Egyptian camp. Her sister, Tanesha, had probably been with Aren when the fortress was overrun due to the fact the couple was happily betroth and spent every waking moment together. If Tanesha had been with Aren at the time of the invasion, Latifa knew Aren had done all he could to protect her sibling. But, even though he was young and capable, there was no way he could withstand the might of the Egyptian invaders. More than likely Aren was dead which meant the Egyptians had taken yet another person she knew and loved. She promised herself, if she ever had the chance, she would make the Pharaoh pay for his guile.

Latifa continued to swipe at the rope as the night deepened and quiet settled over the camp. The quietness was intermittently broken by a dog's vigilant bark somewhere within the rows of tents. Latifa lifted her head and peered into the darkness to see if she could spot the sentries that stood watch along the perimeter of the campsite. All she saw was the glow of torches staked around the perimeter of the camp. It seemed everyone had settled in for the night and had forgotten about her. Though no one was in sight, she reminded herself, she must remain vigilant in case one of the soldiers or the burly brute named Jabari happened to appear. Hoping to work undisturbed, she continued to hack at the fiber of the rope.

During the deepest part of the night, in the distance, the eerie cackle of what sounded to Latifa like a band of hyenas pierced the air. Latifa shivered as she thought about the pack of hyenas and the other nocturnal animals beyond the camp's border. For a moment, she was glad there were soldiers standing watch – even if they were Egyptians.

The night wore on and her pace slowed as fatigue spread through her body. When it seemed she could not go on, she touched the base of her neck where her necklace used to rest. Her necklace had been taken away and she would never get it back. She would be damned if she lost her freedom as well. Obstinately, she willed herself to persist at her mission. Despite increasing exhaustion, she continued to work until the rope began to fray. Rejuvenated by the small success, Latifa renewed her efforts to wear through the rope.

Latifa realized she had worked through the night when the black sky began to lighten with grey. The grey slowly evolved into indigo only to be enveloped by tawny colored light. As birds began to chirp their morning song, Latifa rested her arms by her side and once again let her eyes scan the camp. At any moment, the golden glow that now crept across the welcoming sky would raise the men from their slumber. That thought spurred Latifa to grind the rock into the rope. She did not stop until the worn threads that comprised the rope finally gave way beneath the force of her effort.

Latifa sighed with relief and pulled the frayed rope apart. Quickly, she looked around to ensure she had remained unobserved and was still alone. Spying no one, a smile creased her lips. Clutching the rock in her hand, she rose from the cot and stood to her feet. Stealthily, she shimmied to the back of a nearby tent. After a moment, she gingerly peered around the canvas and looked about for the best escape route. Spotting an opening between the tents, Latifa prayed she would remain unseen then she darted into the light of the early morning sun and ran behind another nearby tent. Once there, she stopped and listened for the shout of alarm from someone who had spotted her. The smile on her face evaporated and her heart began to thump wildly when she heard not a shout but the sound of heavy footsteps headed in her direction.

Latifa flattened her back against the tent to more effectively meld into the dark shadows that lingered against the canvas in disapproval of the morning light. The footsteps approached. She realized she had been holding her breath after a soldier strode past the tent unaware of her presence. Latifa took a deep breath to stave the pounding of her heart then silently continued to the back of the next tent.

Chapter Three

Tariq opened his eyes and looked around his tent. The lingering shadows in the confines of his quarters revealed the light of the sun had not kissed the sky. He knew he could not sleep due to the myriad of thoughts traipsing through his mind. With a grimace, he recounted the events that recently unfolded. He had always assumed he would meet his end on the battlefield. It was impossible to believe he had almost been sacked by a fiery female...using his half brother's dagger no less! His half brother, Narmer, was back in Egypt. So, how had Latifa gotten the dagger? He would have to question her again but next time he would be more careful. After all, if it had been up to her, he would have found permanent sleep in the Valley of the Kings. Tariq gingerly ran his hand over the shallow wound on his side. A lesson had been learned. Never underestimate a Nubian.

Tariq closed his eyes. An image of Latifa glaring at him flashed in his mind. Her string of curses rattled in his ears. Suddenly, the sight of her dark hands on his skin flickered in his mind followed by the sight of her breasts and bottom straining against the thin material of her kaftan. He thought about the moment he pulled her against him. Her body soft and supple melded perfectly into his.

Tariq opened his eyes. What was he thinking? Latifa obviously hated him and wanted him dead. He should be thinking of ways to punish her and not thinking about how pleasing her body felt pressed against his. Obviously, it had been too long since he had been with a woman. He needed to conclude things in Nubia and head back to Egypt where he knew a willing female with generous curves awaited him.

He sat up in his cot and turned his thoughts to the last night he spent in Egypt. He remembered how the scent of lilacs filled his nose when he kissed the back of his companion Selma's neck. He recalled hearing her moan as he pushed himself inside her sheath. Pressing his chest against her back, he had reached under her arms and caressed her plump breasts with his hands.

"My Tariq, my love, my King, don't stop," Selma had purred wistfully.

Her exuberant sighs had increased as he fondled her jiggling breasts which in turn instigated an increase in his own fervor. Repeatedly, he entered Selma's hot warmth. He remembered moving his hands to her hips then guiding her hips to meet his steady rhythm as he plunged in her over and over again.

"You're sweeter than honey," he acknowledged when it was over.

"It's always good between us," Selma admitted softly.

"We are very compatible," he had affirmed and swatted her bottom.

"If we were married, you could have me anytime day or night," she had teased.

"I can have you anytime I want now. I do not need the title of husband and you haven't needed the title of wife for us to enjoy ourselves."

Selma's response to his words had been a frown. "Now that you are King, you are going to have to choose a wife. I may not be of royal blood but my father is High Priest. No one would object if you chose to marry me."

Tariq remembered sitting on the edge of his bed and saying, "The gods are unpredictable. Their ways are not easy to understand. Destiny foretold I would be Pharaoh. So, I must take a wife. Presently, however, I am far too occupied with my duties to think of marriage. The campaign into the South to meet with King Rassom and the Nubians has all of my attention. Who knows how long I'll be gone. It could take a prolonged time to decide terms that both nations can agree on."

"Take me with you," Selma had pleaded after she sat on the bed beside him.

"Traveling with a regiment of men is no place for a woman. Besides, I need you to be my eyes and ears with The Council. Who knows what Narmer shall be up to while I am away? He shall try and use his position as Chancellor to his benefit."

"Of course, Sire. I shall do as you request. I shall make sure all is well while you're away. I shall be nothing but a benefit to you," Selma promised.

"You prove yourself valuable in bed and out," he acceded.

"My Tariq, I love you," she blurted out and wrapped her arms around his neck. "Tell me you love me," she added then stared expectantly at him.

"Love? What is love but the reverie of poets? Warriors such as I have no desire for love."

His words had been met with silence. Abruptly, Selma removed her arms from his neck and ran from the room leaving the sound of a muted sob in her wake.

Women! Tariq mused as he swung his long legs over the side of his oversized cot. He did not have time to continuously ponder thoughts of them. Deciding to take a walk around the campgrounds to clear his mind, he stood to his feet. Stretching his arms in the air, he yawned and walked to the entrance of his tent.

He pushed back the flap at the entrance of his tent and the dim glow from the rising sun greeted him. By the light in the sky, he knew the men would awaken soon. He looked out at the quiet camp. Ashes still coated the fire pits and men still stood guard around the perimeter of the camp. As he surveyed the men at their posts, a quick movement caught his eye. He focused on the movement and realized it was a person maneuvering along the back of the tents.

Tariq's brow wrinkled. Why would one of the soldiers lurk in the shadows like a thief in the night? He watched the person dart toward another tent. When the person dashed into the morning light, Tariq realized the person was not a soldier at all but his unruly prisoner Latifa. Letting out a low growl, he stomped after her. He had to stop her before she made her escape.

ᗅ

Unaware that she had been spotted, Latifa moved quickly on her feet and made her way to the row of tents at the edge of the encampment. Once there, she cautiously peered around one of the tents to look for soldiers. She spotted a sentry a short distance away then she let out a ragged sigh of relief that his back was to her. Sure of a successful escape, she raised her foot to leap into a run. A loud scream of panic left her lips when the Commander's daunting form suddenly appeared before her.

"Where do you think you're going?" the Commander's deep voice rumbled.

Several soldiers, including the sentry bolted to the scene.

"What is the cause of the disturbance? Who screamed?" Jabari lumbered up wiping sleep from his eyes.

"I have this well in hand," the Commander announced to the men.

The soldiers looked at Latifa curiously but compliantly turned and walked away. However, Jabari remained standing behind his superior.

The Commander shifted his attention back to Latifa.

"I asked you a question. Where do you think you're going?"

"Speak when the Commander speaks to you!" Jabari bellowed.

Latifa shook her head in defiance.

Jabari stepped forward and lifted his hand to strike her face.

Acting quick, the Commander caught his arm. "That won't be necessary," he predicted.

"I don't need mercy from you, you Egyptian pig dog!" Latifa spat.

Before the Commander could respond, the sound of hurried hooves pounding on the earth filled the air.

In unison, the trio turned toward the sound and saw a few soldiers run out to meet a man who approached on horseback. A minute later, the rider dismounted and one of the soldiers who had run out to meet the new arrival scurried toward the Commander.

"Pardon. May I speak?" the young soldier inquired.

The Commander looked at the young man and shook his head affirmatively. "Speak Kwame."

31

"The raiders' trail was found. The place where they must have camped last night was spotted."

"That is good news."

"How far is this camp?" Jabari questioned.

"About a half day's journey. It should be easy to overtake them because it appears they are laden with a bounty of slaves."

"I shall ride out and take a look," the Commander said.

"I'll go with you," Jabari announced.

The Commander's lips became thin lines as he turned his attention once again to Latifa.

"Stay away from me!" she ordered when he took a step toward her. "I mean it!" she yelled then stepping back raised her hand and showed him the rock she held.

Jabari laughed. "What are you going to do with that little stone? Don't be foolish, girl. You're in a camp full of soldiers dedicated to our Commander. You harm him and you shall breathe your last breath."

As Jabari's words settled in her ears, Latifa realized the precariousness of her position. She was sure the Commander was furious at her for cutting him with a knife. If she hit him with a rock, he would be even more livid. In truth, how much damage could she possibly do with such a small rock? She would probably just irritate him further which would not help her case when he made a decision about how she was to be punished.

"Drop the rock," the Commander ordered.

Dropping the rock was probably the best course of action, Latifa surmised. But, if she dropped the rock then she would be submitting to him. There was no way she wanted to capitulate to the Commander. So, she obstinately held on to her weapon.

Suddenly, the Commander reached out and placing his hands on her hips pulled her to him. The masculine scent of him met Latifa's nose. Unexpectedly, an addling feeling made her knees want to buckle. Angered by her bodies response, she used her free hand to push against his chest. She lifted her eyes to his. Anger was replaced by surprise when she saw intense desire idling in the dark depths of his gaze. Her whole body suddenly felt flush. Flustered, Latifa dropped the rock.

"That's better," the Commander muttered. Then, stepping away from her, he said to Jabari, "Take her to my tent. I shall deal with her later."

Jabari stepped forward ignoring the slew of curses that littered the air and used his superior strength to drag Latifa to the Commander's tent. Once they made it to the tent, he shoved her inside the structure.

"You should be punished and thrown from this camp," he snarled.

"You can't keep me here!" Latifa shouted.

"Oh yes I can!" Jabari declared then exited the tent and called out a name.

Latifa rushed after him but stopped in her tracks when she saw a large dog with a burnished golden coat scurry to the front of the tent. Unblinking, the dog trained its incandescent eyes on her causing fear to creep up her spine.

"Sit," Jabari commanded the dog.

Obediently, the dog sat.

"This hound has been trained to attack. Try to escape and you shall see the results of that training."

Latifa hoped Jabari did not see the shiver that went through her at his words. Without further protest, she stepped back into the tent and angrily closed the flap behind her. She gritted her teeth and looked around. The space was sparse with only a table, stool and several satchels varying in size in the corner next to a cot. There was no way to know how long she would be in the confining quarters before the Commander returned or what punishment he planned to mete out. Whatever punishment he ordered, she was sure she would get through it. Her hatred for the Egyptians would sustain her. The day would come when she would have a chance to get her revenge and get revenge she would.

Latifa began to pace the tent. The dull hum of the camp slowly coming to life floated through the thin canvas. The smell of antelope being roasted over a fire drifted to her nose. Latifa's stomach growled reminding her that it had been many hours since she had eaten. She walked to the entrance of the tent and pulled back the flap. Bright sunlight now filled the sky. She looked at the path before her and saw the dog was still there. She eased back into the tent and searched it for food. Finding none, she told herself to ignore the hunger pangs that needled her stomach. Eventually, however, the rumbling in her stomach drove her back to the front of the tent.

The dog had lain down but rose on its haunches when it saw her. Latifa waited until she saw a soldier walk near the tent then she called to the man. When he drew near, she recognized him as the soldier she had seen earlier that morning named Kwame. She told him she needed food. The young soldier nodded then continued on his way. Latifa stood where she was for several minutes waiting for the food.

After a while, she walked back into the tent. This time, she sat on the stool behind the table. Lowering her head, she rubbed her forehead. She had made a mess of things. There seemed no way to escape her jailers.

Her thoughts were interrupted when Kwame entered the tent with a plate in one hand and a goblet in the other. He unceremoniously plopped the plate and goblet on the table in front of her.

"The Commander, Jabari and a few soldiers are gone. But, don't get any more ideas about attempting to escape. Even though they are not here, they left me in charge of watching you. The Commander said you need to bathe and he is right. Water shall be brought in for you to clean yourself," Kwame explained.

Too hungry to reply, Latifa watched the young man make his exit. When she was alone, she began to eat the food in front of her. Just as she finished eating her fill of the antelope on her plate, two situlas of water were brought into the tent. When she was once again alone, she shed herself of her sullied garment. Bending over, she splashed water over her face. Noting the water was tempered with natron and moisturizing oil, she picked up the loofah floating in the water and rubbed the fibrous sponge along her arm. She dipped the loofah in the water again then ran

34

it over her chest and stomach. Methodically, she began to remove the layer of soot and musk from her body. When her body was cleaned, she dabbed undiluted natron on her tongue then slid her tongue over her teeth to clean them. With this done, she looked through the satchels and selected a tunic from one of the packs. She pulled the garment over her frame and found it fit loosely and hung well below her thighs. Redressed, she walked to the second bucket and washed her braided hair. After which, she washed her dirty kaftan then laid it out to dry.

When she was done with the situlas, she carried them to the front of the tent so they could be carted away. The dog watched intently as she placed the buckets on the ground. Noting the intimidating dog and the intense heat from the sun which was now high in the sky, Latifa backed into the coolness of the tent. Sitting back on the stool, she once again began to plot an escape.

CB

From her place by the gates of the fortress, Latifa smiled as she watched her father and the contingent that followed him draw near. She listened to shouts of her father's name ring out from those gathered by the gate to witness his departure.

"King Rassom! Peace be unto you!" she joined the chorus of voices. Hoping to catch her father's eye as he rode atop a black stallion, Latifa lifted her arm and waved to him. Happiness filled her when he spotted her through the host of admirers, returned her smile and waved back at her.

In the next moment, his horse pranced past her and the crowd surged forward in pursuit of the departing travelers. Due to the host of raised arms, Latifa lost sight of her father. Wanting to get another glimpse of his face, she began to nudge her way toward the front of the crowd. With each step forward, it seemed more bodies appeared to block her advancement. Desperation began to claw at her as she jostled her way through the throng of bodies. Anxiously, she began to shove people from her path. Unable to break free of the horde surrounding her, she began to yell her father's name. Suddenly, there was a break in the crowd and she saw her father about to disappear in the distance. Putting one foot in front of the other, she began to run in an effort to reach him. However, she soon realized the distance between she and her father was not diminishing. Picking up her pace, Latifa kept running. However, the faster she ran the further her father seemed to move from her.

"Father! Father! Don't go!" she shouted and flailed her arms in an attempt to catch his attention again.

In the next moment, the crowd of people closed around her once again cutting off her view of him.

Dejectedly, Latifa fell to her knees and lowered her head.

"Your father is dead. He was killed by the Pharaoh," a voice sounded in her ear.

Latifa grimaced and glanced up to see who had spoken to her. Seeing no one, she looked over her shoulder. Her eyes widened when in the distance she saw a group of her tribesmen standing before a newly built tumulus. A somber expression was etched on each of their faces. Slowly, she rose to her feet and began to walk to the small group.

As she approached, those gathered lowered their eyes and pointed to the tumulus. Feeling she had to know what was in the tumulus, she walked to the structure. A sense of foreboding gripped her as she entered the tomb. Immediately, darkness eroded her view slowing her ascent up the ceremonial ramp. At the top of the ramp, a sense of dread paralyzed her. She peered through the darkness ahead of her and anxiously eyed the crypt at the foot of the ramp.

Fear scratched at her heart urging her to flee but an ominous curiosity compelled her to proceed down the ramp and to the crypt. When she stepped through the entrance of the dimly lit chamber, coolness touched her skin and a malodorous smell scorched her nose. She looked around for the source of the smell and saw a stone coffin in the back of the chamber. Not wanting to but unable to stop herself, she shuffled to the coffin. When she came to stand over the coffin, she felt all of her strength drain from her body. A moment later, her resolved returned. Inhaling lightly, she reached out and pushed back the stone lid covering the sarcophagus. Slowly, she lowered her eyes to view the contents within the stone casket...

Latifa opened her eyes and sat upright with a start. Breathing deeply, she realized she had fallen asleep and had been dreaming. The dream that started off so joyously had turned into a nightmare. Would she ever be able to enjoy a peaceful sleep again? She wished she could talk to her sister about the way she felt so they could comfort each other.

The smell of spicy meat caused Latifa to look down at the table. Another plate filled with antelope meat and dates had been placed before her and her goblet had been refilled. Looking around the room, she noticed shadows gathered in the corner of the tent to reveal the sun was setting for the day. Latifa was sure the Commander would be back soon which meant she needed to get dressed before he returned. She walked to where her kaftan lay and touched it. It was still damp so she decided to eat her dinner. After walking back to the table, she ate the savory meat and washed it down with fruit juice from the goblet. When she was full, she walked to the entrance of the tent and saw the dog still dutifully on guard. As she bent to place the plate on the ground, the dog lifted its nose into the air.

"You want to get this food, don't you?" she spoke to the dog.

The dog cocked its head inquisitively and licked its chops.

Latifa picked up the bone she had left on the plate. The dog's ears perked up and its tail began to wag back and forth.

She tossed the bone to the hound and the canine began to chew its prize.

"So, you like bones. That's good to know," she mused realizing the dog did not look quite as menacing when its tail was wagging.

Noting the dog's reaction, Latifa wondered if feeding the dog could lead to winning its trust. If so, she could distract the dog with food and make her escape.

Latifa looked up at the moon now resting in the sky and noticed how its silver light illuminated the camp. She watched some of the soldiers mill about the campground while others sat in small groups playing games such as *senet, mehen* and *pwer.* Guards stood as dutiful lookouts around the edge of the encampment seemingly oblivious to it all.

As Latifa studied the scene before her, her eyes began to feel as if they were weighted with sand. She knew the events of the previous days were catching up to her. Not wanting to sleep less she have another nightmare, she willed herself to stay awake. But, as the moon crawled over the sky, her eyes started to close. As sleep beckoned her, she thought about the Commander. He had not returned as she expected. Drowsily, she looked over her shoulder and into the tent. The bright light of the African moon slipped past her to swathe the cot and create an inviting scene.

Deciding she needed to shut her eyes, Latifa stepped into the tent and closed the flap behind her. Immediately, a cloak of blackness filled the confines of the tent. Though it was dark, she walked the few steps to the cot and sat on it. Her eyes closed for a moment before she pried them back open. Knowing she would be unable to stay awake much longer and now sure she would be alone until morning, Latifa pushed the blanket that covered the cot out of her way then stretched out on the cot with an exhausted sigh.

As she lay on the cot surrounded by darkness, she recalled all that had happened over the past two days. Never could she have guessed that she would end up a prisoner in an Egyptian camp. What gruesome fate now lay before her? She did not know. What she did know was there was no escape from whatever was going to happen next. Since the Commander had not returned, she would have to wait one more day to find out her punishment. As it turned out, waiting was just fine with her because now all she wanted to do was sleep.

☙

A thin cloud staked its claim over the moon obscuring the moon's celestial light when Tariq and his small contingent rode back into camp late that night. After the long hard ride, Tariq was grateful to finally be back at camp. Tired and exhausted, he quickly washed himself to rid his body of dust and grime from the grueling ride. When his body was cleaned, he left the men who washed beside him and made his way to his tent.

Entering the dark chamber, he walked through the darkness to where he knew his stool to be. Carelessly, he dropped his dirty clothing on the seat and letting out a light groan stretched his arms upward. Without lighting a lamp, he walked to the space where he knew his cot was and lowered himself on it. To hedge against the coolness that had claimed the night, he reached for the blanket at the foot of the bed. As he pulled the blanket over his body, he noticed the form of a person lying next to him.

"What the..." Words died on Tariq's lips as he peered through the darkness and realized the person beside him was Latifa. What was she doing in his bed? He straightened to a sitting position and attempted to recall the events of the day.

Suddenly, he remembered ordering Jabari to confine Latifa to his tent. After everything that had happened that day, he had forgotten the order. If it had been any other female, he would have enjoyed having her in his bed he was sure. But Latifa? After such a long day, he was not certain he had enough energy to get into another sparring match with her. Due to her barbed disposition and the fact she spat curses like a plebeian fisherman, he was sure she would drive a stake through his heart if she woke up and found him asleep next to her.

As he looked at Latifa a thin streak of moonlight, now absolved of clouds, slithered through a slight opening left at the entrance of the tent. The streak of light danced in the black strands of her braided hair, caressed her mahogany colored face, kissed her mahogany neck and hugged the curve of her hip. Surrendering to the effect of the silver light, he let his eyes peek beneath the loose material of the tunic she wore. His eyes rested on her small breasts which were round like melons with chocolate colored cherries at their tip. He had to admit, Latifa did look very inviting as she slept. Dare he say it...almost angelic. Enticed by the vision before him, he reached out and lay his hand on her hip.

When his hand touched her, Latifa stirred and her eyes opened a sliver. Suddenly, she shot to a sitting position and gaped at him. "What the hell are you doing?" she shrieked.

Chapter Four

"What the hell are you doing?" Latifa demanded of the Commander.

"Quiet your voice less you wake the whole camp," came the order.

"What are you doing here? When...when did you get back?" she sputtered as she pulled the blanket to her chin.

"I returned to camp a short time ago."

"Get out of this bed!" Latifa ordered.

"I have no tunic on. Are you sure I have a *shendoh* on?" her bedmate queried.

At his words, Latifa noticed the ripple of muscles on his chest and wondered if he wore anything beneath the blanket bunched around his waist. Petrified dismay enveloped her face. "Oh my God!" she shrieked.

"A lot of women call me god. Especially after they spend a night with me."

"There is no way I am sleeping in the same bed with you! Put your *shendoh* on and get away from me!" she instructed.

"As you wish." The Commander slowly began to push the cover from his body.

"No!" Latifa yelled waving her hands in front of her face. "I don't want to see!"

"Amun give me strength!" the Commander groaned exasperated. "How do you expect me to do as you order if I can't get out of bed?"

"Fine. I won't look. Just...just get out of this bed," Latifa pleaded then turned her face from him and closed her eyes.

When he did not make a move to exit the cot, she opened her eyes and looked at him.

"Well? What are you waiting on? Get out of here!"

The Commander speared her with a disgruntled look then said, "I told you, I give the orders in this camp. I am the decider and I have decided I am not going anywhere."

"What!" Latifa exclaimed flabbergasted.

"I don't take orders from domineering women who don't know their place. This is my bed and if you are displeased with the idea of me in it then you leave."

"How dare you!" Latifa screeched as she watched him make a big deal of fluffing the blanket around him. "So you're not leaving?" she questioned when he finally finished prepping the covering.

His answer was to lie on his back.

When Latifa's eyes became thin slits in response to his actions, he grinned. "It's been a while since I've had an attractive female in my bed. I supposed you'll do even if you do act like a she-cat."

Latifa inhaled sharply too angry to say a word.

"You clean up quite well. You have a nice body on you but do not assume you can seduce me with it because believe me I've seen better."

"Why you presumptuous...pompous...barbarian!" Latifa spat and lifting her arm swung her hand to slap him.

The Commander caught her wrist. "Settle down now," he instructed placidly.

Latifa pulled against his grasp then pushed forward in an effort to free herself from his clutches. At that same moment, her bedmate released his hold on her causing her to fall forward and her breasts to flatten against the massive wall of his chest. Instinctively, the Commander attempted to steady her. His hand inadvertently slipped under the oversized tunic she wore and slid over her soft skin before coming to rest on the silky flesh at the base of her spine. Upon feeling the Commander's strong hand against her skin, Latifa lifted her eyes to look at him. She gasped when in the next moment he grasped her shoulder, pulled her downward then captured her lips with his.

cg

The moment the Commander's mouth pressed against hers, just as before, molten heat bolted through Latifa stealing her breath from her. She tore her lips from his and gulped for air. He held her firmly against the solid wall of his frame causing her body to fold neatly against him.

"What...what do you think you're doing?" she stammered.

"I'm kissing you," he replied lightly.

"I...I..." Latifa's thoughts fled as her mind centered on the fact she was still sprawled on top of his muscular male form.

She attempted to roll off of her perch. When she did, the inside of her thigh brushed against the Commander's middle. In response to her movement, she felt his member harden. Without warning, he circled his leg around hers and tightened his hold on her shoulder, plastering her against him. In a flash, he rolled their bodies so that she lay beneath him and he hovered above her. Once more, he touched his lips to hers sending an uncontrolled moan from between her lips. Encouraged by her response, he pushed his tongue between her lips in a move so surprising Latifa moaned again.

"Let this happen," he whispered as his lips moved to brush her neck and his hand glided over the front of the oversized tunic she wore.

Latifa drew in a soft breath when his fingers cupped the material covering her breast. Impulsively, she arched her back to him even as she told herself to ignore the tentacles of pleasure that weaved through her entire body. Fervently, she tried to gather enough strength to extract herself from the Commander's embrace but found little energy to do so. Weakly, she pushed against his shoulders.

"Don't fight this. Just give yourself to me," his words sounded hoarse in her ear.

Latifa shook her head in objection and once again tried to garner enough strength to extract herself from his hold. When his hand slid under the tunic and to her belly, she found the impetus she needed to break free from him.

"I do not want a quick turn in the bed with you," she breathed, pushed away from him and sat up.

"It shall be anything but quick," he assured.

"I don't even know your name."

"My friends call me Tariq," he replied.

"Well Ta-reek, you and I are not friends. Since you are not going to leave this cot, I shall," Latifa announced.

"There's still the matter of you being punished."

Tariq's voice stopped her from stepping off of the cot.

She looked at him as he rose to a sitting position.

"You did try to kill me, did you not? You then tried to escape before justice could be rendered. You don't think I can let you get away with that, do you? I am known as a great leader. How would I look in front of my men if I were to ignore all that you've done? I have no choice but to say you are not free to leave."

"I am of royal blood not a slave to be done with as you will. I demand you set me free," Latifa insisted.

"Did I not tell you, you are not in a position to demand? I say you drop your demands, bridle your tongue and share my bed."

"I would rather be eaten by a crocodile than be with you."

Her words were met with laughter. "Women back home would swoon at the chance to make love to a god."

Latifa snorted. "You are no god. You have no special powers."

"There are plenty of women who would disagree with you. After you experience my power to bring you pleasure, you'll soon change your mind."

"That shall never happen."

"Don't be so sure," Tariq hedged as he folded his arms and looked at the female in his cot. He had never had to work to get a female to be nice to him let alone bed him. Every woman he had known tripped over themselves to please him. He was sure many did so because he was royalty. It would be interesting to see how long it took to subdue Latifa since she knew nothing of his royal lineage or his true identity as the Pharaoh of Egypt. Yes, taming Latifa could be an entertaining distraction from a tedious trip.

"I say we settle this with a wager," Tariq said the next time he spoke.

"A wager?"

"A wager with a prize I know I shall win."

"And what is the prize?" Latifa inquired.

"Your maidenhead," he stated matter-of-factly.

44

"What?"

"I wager before we see the light of the next full moon, you shall give yourself to me."

Latifa laughed. "Truly you jest."

"I do not jest. I wager I can make you beg me to make love to you before the next full moon. I shall forget your attempt on my life in exchange for your agreement to my terms."

"What do I get as a reward for not giving myself to you?"

"Your freedom of course."

"Until this wager is concluded, I suppose you plan on trying to keep me detained against my will. Earlier you said having a female in your camp was not a good idea."

"Having a female in camp is usually a bad idea but I've decided to make an exception. I must admit, it sounds to me like you're afraid because you know it is inevitable that I'll be the victor."

Latifa sniffed. "I am not afraid of you. Fine. I accept your wager."

Tariq held out his hand.

Latifa reached out and shook Tariq's hand to seal the terms of the wager. She was confident not giving herself to Tariq before the next full moon would be an easy wager to win.

A grin spread across Tariq's lips. "Then our deal is sealed. I am a warrior and you claim you are a warrior as well. We are now two warriors with one wager between us."

"I am a warrior who shall win this battle," Latifa assured and rose from the cot.

"Where are you going?" he asked her.

"I am not staying in the same bed with you. I am going to sleep in the corner."

"On the ground?"

"Yes."

"I wouldn't do that if I were you. Poisonous snakes have been known to slither into tents at night. I've known hardened soldiers who were bitten then died a slow painful death because they weren't careful."

45

Latifa froze in place upon hearing Tariq's words. Rethinking her plan, she squealed and quickly jumped back on the cot.

Tariq chuckled.

She climbed over his rock hard frame then turning her back to him lay as far away from him as possible.

"I suggest you don't get out of bed during the night. There could be a snake slithering on the ground," Tariq whispered.

He smiled when in the next instant Latifa pulled the blanket to her chin. It looked like he would not have to worry about her trying to escape or harming him...until morning at least.

ɔ3

Latifa pushed back the thin curtain that covered the litter she was riding in and peered out at the military men trudging around the transport. She looked around to see if she could spot Tariq but did not see him. Early that morning, she had been awakened by the sound of a shofar to find he had already left the tent. After she slipped into her kaftan, Jabari appeared and told her it was time to break camp. He revealed they had picked up the trail of those who attacked the Nubian fortress and the regiment was setting out to catch up to them. Upon hearing the news, Latifa decided she would not try to escape but stay with her current companions until they caught up with the other band of Egyptians. She had to know if her sister was among the captives taken by the band who decimated her village. Not wanting to draw undue attention to herself, she had not argued when Jabari told her to stay out of sight of the men and ride in a litter.

Looking beyond the men who walked beside the litter, she saw the regiment was now traveling along the Nile River. She watched a herd of gazelles running on the opposite side of the riverbed. As she watched the scenery pass before her, thoughts of the previous night unexpectedly crept into her mind. She could not believe she had fallen asleep. The surprising fact was she had not had a nightmare about losing her family and home. Even more surprising still was the knowledge she had felt comfortable enough to relax when she was laying next to Tariq.

Unexpectedly, thoughts of his kiss filled her mind. She recalled his hand against the small of her back and the rugged feel of his body beneath hers. Suddenly, a wave of remorse washed over her. She had never thought about kissing Kofi or Kofi's touch. In truth, she had not thought much of the man she had been betroth to since the attack happened. Despite the fact she had not been eager to marry Kofi, he had been nothing but kind to her. He had been a caring man who had tried to protect her even at the end. She had not loved him in life but she told herself he did not deserve to be forgotten.

The order to halt sounded and Latifa sighed with relief. She had been in the litter since the sun began to rise and now that the sun was setting she was happy at the thought of getting a chance to stretch her legs. Restlessly, she watched the soldiers come to a halt in response to the order they had been given then disperse and begin to prepare camp for the night.

Latifa braced herself for the brambly movement of the camel as the animal knelt to its knees. When she stepped out of the litter, Jabari appeared and led her to a tent that had been quickly erected. Once she was inside the tent, she stretched out over the cot for a moment to rest her achy body.

Sometime later, Jabari arrived with her dinner. She walked to the table and sitting behind it began to eat the food on her plate. As she ate, she thought of her sister, Tanesha, and wondered if she was alive and what she was doing that very moment. She wondered when she was going to see Tariq. There were a lot of questions she wanted to ask him. One thing she needed to know was how long it would be before they caught up to the other band of Egyptians. She contemplated going in search of him. But, the truth was, she did not feel entirely comfortable being the only female among an army of blood thirsty men. Staying out of sight of the men was an instruction she

47

agreed with. So, she stayed in the tent. However, as the evening wore on, boredom began to creep in and Latifa once again began to contemplate seeking out Tariq.

The sound of the dog barking outside her tent drew her to the entrance. When she looked out, she saw the hound she had seen before sitting close by and knew Jabari had once again left the canine there as a deterrent so she would not leave the tent. Latifa walked back to the table that held the plate with the remnants of her meal. She picked up a bone that had shards of meat left on it and returned to the entrance.

She looked around to make sure no one was watching her. Seeing everyone occupied with their duties, she held up the bone. "Nice dog," she cooed softly.

The dog looked at the bone with interest.

Seeing she had the dog's attention, Latifa peeled off a thin slice of meat and tossed it to the animal.

"Go on," Latifa coaxed. "Take the meat," she said then held her breath as she watched the large dog before her.

The dog cocked its head to one side as it continued to eye the meat on the ground. After a moment, the canine lowered its head and snatched the meat between its teeth.

"Good boy!" she exclaimed.

The dog swallowed the meat then turned its attention back to her.

She held out the bone and the dog began to whine. She tossed the bone away from the entrance of the tent and smiled when the canine ambled to its prize. As the dog began to chew on the bone, Latifa stepped out of the tent and took a few steps away from the dog.

"Going somewhere?" a deep voice sounded.

Latifa spun around and saw Tariq standing on the side of the tent cleaning a sword.

She flipped a few of her braids from her shoulder and muttered, "What exactly am I supposed to do for the rest of the evening?"

Tariq looked up at the moon that was beginning to glow in wake of the fading sun. "There is no full moon tonight which means I can think of one thing you won't be doing."

Latifa sighed exasperatedly and turned to retrace her steps.

"Would you like to go for a walk?" His words stopped her.

Latifa quickly thought about the boredom she had begun to feel. Not wanting to return to the tent just yet, she walked to where Tariq stood and said, "I would like to go for a walk."

"Anubis must like you," Tariq ventured after they began their walk.

"Anubis?" Latifa looked at Tariq. Her eyes followed his gaze to see the hound trotting happily behind her.

Tariq stopped to pet the dog. He motioned for her to do the same. She did and the dog began to wag its tail.

"What kind of dog is this?"

"This breed is called a Pharaoh Hound. Her name is Anubis after the god of the underworld."

"Her?"

"Yes. She's a female who's normally reserved with strangers. But, it seems you are an exception. She's a trained guard dog who can be ferocious when necessary."

"She doesn't seem vicious now," Latifa admitted of Anubis who followed them as they exited a row of tents.

When they walked past one of the men standing guard, Anubis ran ahead of them and into the night. A cool breeze brushed the couple's skin as they approached the river and began to stroll beside it.

Tariq considered questioning Latifa about the dagger he had taken from her but decided it was not the best time to interrogate her. Instead, he let the silence remain between them. After they had been walking awhile, he finally broke the silence by saying, "It's a pleasant night."

"It would be a lot more pleasant if I did not have to spend it with you," came the reply.

"Your sharp tongue returns. I was beginning to think you decided to be nice to me."

Latifa eyed Tariq sullenly then picked up her pace and walked ahead of him.

"Dangerous animals come out at night in search of dinner. There could be a cheetah or lion watching us this very moment. Haven't you heard jackals howling late at night? The jackals could be watching too," Tariq called to her when she was a short distance away from him.

Latifa slowed her pace then came to a stop and waited patiently for Tariq to walk to where she stood.

"You are courageous as a lion and have a will of iron. I'm beginning to think you should be one of the soldiers in my regiment."

"In my heart I am a warrior. I fight to avenge the wrongs done to my family by you Egyptians."

"Tell me about yourself. What makes you hate all Egyptians?"

Latifa squared her shoulders and turned her back to Tariq. "If you think I am going to tell you about the destruction of my family you're touched."

Suddenly, a dark form came into Latifa's line of sight. Certain it was a leopard charging at her, she turned quickly and grabbed Tariq's hand. When the figure moved into the moonlight, she discerned the dark form was that of a soldier who had been following them. Realizing she had overreacted, she began to pull her hand from Tariq's hand.

Tariq gently closed his fingers over hers to prevent her from extracting her hand from his. "Can it be you don't hate me as much as you claim?" he questioned.

"Release my hand."

"You want me. Admit it."

"You think you can get me to swoon and beg you to take me. You're misguided if you think you can make me love you."

"Love?" Tariq laughed. "I am not asking for your love nor do I expect your love. A man in my position has no use for such fatuity because love is a triviality which makes a man weak, clouds his mind and makes him lose his focus. Someone in my position cannot afford such folly."

"Then we both are of one accord. A warrior has no time for love."

"That doesn't mean I can't enjoy the delights of your young body and you mine."

"I assure you, you shall never have me."

"So you insist on making this a true challenge."

"This is not a thing of merriment for me as it appears to be for you. I think it's time to head back to camp. Let go of my hand. ...Please."

Without further objection, Tariq unclasped his hand relinquishing his hold on her.

As they turned to retrace their steps, Anubis appeared beside Latifa and brushed her muzzle against Latifa's hand. Latifa pet the dog then the dog scampered ahead of them toward camp.

"When shall we catch up to the raiders?" Latifa question after they made it back to the encampment.

"It should be soon," Tariq answered after he walked her to the tent.

"You're not planning on sleeping in here are you?" she questioned when he started to follow her inside.

He remained silent for a moment and Latifa wondered if he really expected her to sleep in the same bed with him again that night. She could not. It was not proper and neither was the affect he had on her. There was no way she could spend another night in the cot alone with him. He might kiss her again and his hands might wrap around her again. Latifa felt her skin grow warm at the thought of his touch. What had come over her? Why did Tariq's touch affect her so? She did not want to think about the answer.

Instead, she said, "I want my freedom more than I shall ever want to share a bed with you. You understand that, do you not?"

Tariq looked up at the crescent shaped moon. "It could be a while before the next full moon. So, I shall let you have your way tonight. But, you are in my tent. Tomorrow I shall not be put out of my own bed. See to it that you change your mind before then," he instructed then turned and walked away.

☯

The next morning, just as before, members of the camp woke early and traveled all day beside the Nile River. Latifa once again road in the litter until the order came to make camp for the night. When she exited the litter, Tariq appeared riding atop a stallion.

"Join me on a horseback ride," he said and reached out to her.

"What?" Latifa looked at him confused.

"I said come with me for a ride."

Latifa lowered her lashes and looked at her hands not sure if she should do as Tariq instructed. However, after a quick assessment of her options, she decided going horseback riding was better than spending a long evening alone. So, she reached out and took his hand. He hauled her up so that she was seated on the horse in front of him. Purposefully, he clicked his tongue against the roof of his mouth and the horse trotted forward. As they left the camp, Latifa noticed two guards followed them on horseback careful to keep their distance.

"Where are we going?" Latifa called over her shoulder.

"You'll see," he answered cryptically.

Adeptly, he nudged the stallion into a sprint causing Latifa to slump against his chest. The horse sprinted along a path by the river for a short while. When Tariq pulled on the reins, the animal slowed. He guided the horse a short distance to the river's bank, dismounted then helped Latifa to the ground. The horse ambled to the water and began to drink.

"What is going on?" Latifa inquired.

Without a word, Tariq lifted a satchel from the horse along with the blanket they had been riding on.

"I thought you'd appreciate getting away from the troops for a while," he said as he led her to a large rock formation that jutted out over the river.

He climbed up the rock and Latifa followed his lead. Finding a smooth surface on the large boulder, he spread out the blanket then stretched out his hand indicating he wanted her to sit.

Latifa sat down on the blanket.

"I know you're hungry," Tariq said before he sat and opened the satchel. He pulled out antelope that had been seasoned with salt and a cruet of pomegranate juice.

Latifa smiled. "We're going to eat the evening meal here?"

"Can you think of a better place?"

Latifa looked out over the brilliant green water flowing calmly inside the river's banks. Pink and yellow streaks from the sun decorated the sky creating a serene setting. "I can't think of a more pleasant place," she admitted. "I just don't understand why you decided to bring me here."

"I am kind to you to show you your preconceived notions about me are misguided. You've judged me falsely."

"Have I? I think not."

"What makes you so sure?"

"You're an Egyptian, are you not?"

Tariq chuckled lightly. "I am an Egyptian you're beginning to like, even if you can't admit it to yourself."

He held out a piece of meat when she opened her mouth to speak. Obligingly, Latifa let her words evaporate from her lips and she accepted the meat from Tariq.

As they began to eat, Latifa saw a small herd of ostriches in the distance. Their small flat heads bobbed atop their long necks and their black and grey plumage flopped as they waddled across the plain. Tariq pointed downstream to a vervet monkey swinging from a tree branch. Latifa smiled at the sight. To show she appreciated his efforts at kindness, she asked him about his military service.

Tariq began to recount stories of military battles. Despite her initial hesitation, Latifa found herself intently listening to his tales.

He finished his story as dark clouds began to sweep across the sky causing the breeze from the Nile to cool considerably.

"Looks like a storm is coming," Latifa announced after she finished the last of her food. "Maybe we should head back."

"We shall head back but not before you tell me your story."

Latifa's brow wrinkled with uncertainty.

"Yesterday, I asked you to tell me about yourself. You declined. I repeat my request and ask that you tell me about your life."

Not sure she could speak of the events that had occurred in her life without crying, Latifa said, "Your tales of military victories are captivating. But, I find I feel guilty for enjoying listening to them."

Tariq's brow wrinkled. "Why?"

"We Nubians have a long history of warrior Queens and women warriors who have fought for the Nubian Kushite Empire. My mother was one such woman. She used to fight alongside my father. Five years ago, after losing a battle to the Egyptians, my mother along with many of the people from our tribe were captured and taken from us."

"Five years ago?" Tariq quickly recalled the offensive he had led on the Nubians five years prior. He had defeated them in battle and collected one hundred and fifty people who were taken to Egypt and sold as slaves. Was Latifa's mother one of the people who had been his spoils of war?

"What is your mother's name?" he questioned.

"Her name is Akela. I miss her so much." Tears crowded in Latifa's eyes which she tried to blink back.

Tariq reached out and touched her cheek. "It fills me with distress to hear what happened to your mother. If I can make it right, I shall."

"What can you do?" Latifa turned her face away from his touch embarrassed he had seen her display of frailty. "Besides, it happened long ago."

"It should not have happened."

Latifa shrugged her shoulders. "With mother gone, I tried my best to be a mother to my sister Tanesha. She's younger than me and I feel it's my duty to protect her. I do not know what's become of her. She may have been captured during the assault on the fortress a few days ago. She's all the family I have left. I've got to find her. My family is very important to me. That is all I am going to tell you."

"You have been through much at the hands of Egyptians."

"You don't have to act like you care."

Tariq touched her chin and turned her face back to his. "I find I do care," he admitted.

Latifa was taken aback by Tariq's words of sympathy. They seemed like something Kofi would say not the words of a battle hardened warrior. She lifted her eyes and looked at Tariq. It was as if she was seeing him for the first time. He was very different from Kofi. Not just in the way he talked and acted but also in the way he looked. For instance, he had a smooth bronzed colored face, no hair was on his head and his light beard and goatee divulged only a hint of grey. As for Kofi, his dark face had started to crease with wrinkles and his hair was splattered with grey. Latifa did not consider him attractive while Tariq looked appealing…almost handsome.

A drop of rain landed on Latifa's forehead ending her inspection of Tariq. She squealed as another cold drop hit her cheek followed by a drop on her nose.

"We'd better head back," Tariq remarked a moment before the skies opened up and rain poured down in sheets.

The pair quickly picked up the items lying on the blanket and shoved them into the satchel. Tariq gathered the blanket then the couple ran to his stallion. They rode back to the camp in near blinding rain which soaked their clothes.

When they arrived at the encampment, Tariq directed the steed to his tent. He climbed off of the horse and helped her to the ground before they both ran into his tent.

"Thank you for the ride and the meal. I must admit I enjoyed it all. It was very nice," Latifa acknowledged.

"Yes, it was very nice indeed," Tariq agreed.

When Latifa looked into his eyes, she realized he was not speaking of the meal as she had been. "I think you'd better go."

He nodded and took a step toward the entrance of the tent. Latifa turned her back to him and walked toward the table. She heard the flap of the tent open then close announcing Tariq's departure. Idly, she shed herself of her soaked kaftan and lay it on the stool to dry before stepping toward the cot.

"Beautiful," Tariq's voice sounded low and husky.

Startled, Latifa turned to see he had not left the tent but stood near the entrance with a clever grin on his face. She watched dumbfounded as his eyes leisurely inspected her body. When his eyes found hers, motion came back to her and she reached for the blanket on the cot and hastily wrapped it around her body.

"Get out of here!" she screeched.

Tariq shook his head as his tongue clicked the roof of his mouth several times. "Tiss...Tiss. There you go again demanding things." Slowly, he walked toward her. "When are you going to learn, I am the one who gives the orders and I order you to let me stay."

"But...but you can't stay."

"And why not?" Tariq questioned as he came to a stop in front of her.

When she did not answer right away, he reached out his hand and his fingers caressed the silky skin on her shoulder then slid down her arm.

"I think you like it when I touch you," he said when she did not immediately push his hand away.

"I...I..."

Tariq placed a finger in front of her lips. "It seems you're having trouble speaking. So don't speak. Just feel."

In the next instant, his body pressed against hers and his lips confidently claimed her lips. For Latifa, the moment his body and lips touched hers, it was as if lightening entered the temporary shelter and struck her causing her entire being to explode in a torrid heat. She felt Tariq's hand glide back up her arm and caress her shoulder before sliding to her chest. His hand then followed a path down the valley between her breasts to her flat stomach. Tariq's hand gently slid over her hip and down her right leg. Still seeking its treasure, he guided his hand up her left leg. Cool air nipped at the drops of water that clung to her skin chilling her and reminding her she was nude beneath the blanket. Latifa knew she should extract herself from Tariq's hold. However, the sound of rain hitting the tent seemed to conspire with Tariq to soothe her and lull her into compliance.

Thunder crackled in the sky as Tariq lowered himself to his knees. A bright flash of light illuminated the tent for a moment snapping Latifa out of her haze and she opened her mouth to protest. Knowingly, Tariq reached up and caressed the material that covered her right breast luring a moan from her lips. As the tent fell dark again, he kissed the cloth covering her belly. Inhaling softly, Latifa closed her eyes and tilted her head back as his lips made their way across the smooth material that veiled her stomach. In response to sensations she could not name, she dropped her hands so they curled around the back of his head betraying her desire and beckoning his lips lower.

Sensing the rise in Latifa's ardor, Tariq rose to his feet. He saw Latifa part her lips a moment before his lips met hers yet again. He slid his left arm around her waist cradling her in a secure embrace. The water from his wet tunic soaked through the thin material of the blanket scandalously revealing the ridge of her thick nipple which he teased with his fingers.

Latifa's moan of entreaty was accompanied by a sigh of pleasure when Tariq thrust aside the cloth and his lips deposed his fingers to claim her needy nipple. Suddenly, Tariq stepped away from her and pulled his damp tunic over his head before dropping it to the ground. He stepped back to her, encircled his arms around her waist and began to guide her downward. Sanity returned to Latifa when she realized she was being lowered onto the cot. When he lay her on the bed, she admonished herself for not being able to lift her weightless arms and push away from Tariq sooner. Hastily, she pushed against his shoulders as his lips found hers once more. Abruptly, he stopped kissing her, grabbed her wrists and pinned them against the cot.

Latifa lifted her eyes to look at Tariq as the tent illuminated with light from a flash of lightening. Her eyes met his and she glimpsed desire so poignant it caused her to tremble uncontrollably. The light faded and darkness returned. She felt him lower his head then felt his lips press on her neck causing a salacious yearning to slither through her. Latifa whimpered at the feel of his hard tower against her leg and again when his tongue settled over hers. Tariq removed his hands from her wrists and as if they had a mind of their own her arms circled around his neck.

"You shall be mine now. Tell me you want me," his voice was a whisper.

At his entreaty, Latifa groaned in revolt. She knew she had let things go too far. She also knew if she did not put a stop to the way Tariq was touching her, she would be his. She could not be his. He was an Egyptian. He and his men slaughtered her tribesmen. How could she have let things get so out of hand? How could she be so affected by his kiss? He had wagered she would give herself to him before the next full moon. Was the reason he made the wager because he sensed she would easily succumb to him? Well she wouldn't. There were many reasons why she couldn't. Not now. Not ever.

Gathering her courage and self restraint, she breathed, "No! No! This can't happen."

"It can and it shall. You want to make love to me. Confess."

Latifa shook her head but found she could not speak to deny his words. Dear God. How could she find enjoyment in the arms of her enemy? Why had she made a wager with him in the first place? Why was she so willing to risk giving up her freedom? Surely, she had made a wager with the devil himself. Finding pleasure with Tariq had to be the same as partaking of a sweet treat offered by the devil. In the end, the sweet would leave a bitter taste in her mouth.

"There are so many reasons why I can't be with you," Latifa explained.

"Don't worry about the reasons. Just live in the moment. Focus on the way you feel right now," he instructed softly.

Latifa covered his roving hand with hers to still it when he touched the inside of her thigh. "You must stop touching me in such a way. Please, honor my request," she managed to say.

"Are you ordering me out of my own tent? It's raining out there. Where would I go?"

Latifa found she could not respond.

A moment passed. His hands left her skin. She felt the cot sag as he stood to his feet.

"You're leaving?" she questioned.

Tariq reached for one of the satchels and pulled a dry tunic from it then said, "Unless you are willing to give me your maidenhead, me being near you is not a good notion right now."

"Are you sure?"

"I am sure of only one thing."

"What is that?"

"You shall give yourself to me."

"Impossible," Latifa objected.

"After tonight, I know it won't be long before you do," Tariq assured. Then, he exited the tent leaving Latifa alone to listen to the sound of thunder in the sky and the composed beat of the rain as it pelted the top of the tent.

Chapter Five

The next morning donned clear blue skies and a bright sun that did not divulge a hint of the previous evening's rain. As usual, the soldiers began to break camp in the early morning light. Latifa watched the men loosen ties secured around thin wooden beams, remove the canvas that covered the beams then lower the beams and stow them for travel. Tariq appeared and asked her if she knew how to ride a horse on her own. When she replied she did, he asked her if she would like to ride beside him to hunt prey for the evening meal.

Latifa felt flushed as she remembered the events of the previous night. Hastily, pushing those thoughts aside, she spoke. "I'm not certain it's a good idea for me to go horseback riding again."

"And why not?"

"I was told to stay out of the sight of the soldiers," Latifa responded.

"No one shall accost you if you're with me. Besides, riding on a horse has to be more entertaining than riding in a litter all day."

Latifa thought about the time she had spent riding a horse the day before. It had been enjoyable. "I did have a good time riding with you yesterday," she admitted. "But, aren't you afraid I'll escape if you let me ride a horse alone?"

"You wouldn't get very far without food. I told you about the wild animals that lurk about ready to devour a tasty morsel like you. You must remember, it is not only the big ones you have to worry about. There are spiders and snakes—"

"Ew. I can't stand the sight of those cursed creatures," Latifa snorted and flailed her hands about.

Tariq smiled at her antics then led her to an awaiting horse. He helped her onto the steed. After she was safely seated, he climbed on his stallion and prodded the horse into a walk away from camp. Latifa gathered the reins of her mount and followed in Tariq's wake. Anubis' bark sounded and Latifa glanced over her shoulder and saw the hound running to catch up to them.

Latifa smiled as she urged her horse into a brisk walk in order to keep up with Tariq and the handful of soldiers who were a part of the hunting party. During the ride, she found it taxing to keep up with Tariq and the expert riders. When she began to fall behind, Tariq guided his horse alongside hers. They talked leisurely together as their horses slowly trekked forward. Several times, the couple had to prompt their horses into a gallop in order to catch up with the hunting party. After a while, Tariq suggested they leave the hunt and ride on their own. Latifa agreed.

Warmth from the sun cradled the pair who with Anubis at their heels directed their horses into a sprint to the Nile. Once the couple made it to the river, they stopped for lunch and a brief rest. After the respite and after their horses were watered, the pair climbed on their mounts and continued their excursion.

The day went by extremely fast for the duo who raced their horses beside the river.

"I am triumphant! I won the race!" Latifa exclaimed leaping from her horse after the last race of the day.

"That's because I let you have that success," Tariq affirmed after he climbed from his horse.

"You wish." She nudged him playfully then smiled in response to his smile.

Taking her hand, Tariq led her to the top of a small hill that was shaded by an acacia tree. Anubis wagged her tail and barked happily as she followed the couple. Tariq spread a blanket under the tree and lay out fare he had taken from the satchel on his horse.

They began to eat.

Latifa looked around and saw the guards who had been trailing them had dismounted and were eating a meal as well.

"Are we camping here for the night?"

"It's still a bit early. My men shall make camp at sundown. We shall eat here then ride and catch up to them," Tariq revealed. "So tell me, are you glad you

61

decided to come riding with me?" he inquired changing the subject.

Latifa nodded her head. "Today was wonderful," she admitted.

"Last night was enjoyable too. Don't you agree?"

Instead of answering, Latifa turned her attention to Anubis who lured by the smell of the food ambled near the pair. The dog sat on the ground, cocked her head and began to whine.

"Pesky hound," Tariq complained at the interruption.

"Here Anubis." Latifa held out a chunk of meat.

The dog snatched the meat from her fingers then quickly swallowed the fare. Once the meat was devoured, the dog licked Latifa's fingers causing her to giggle.

"You're a good dog," Latifa remarked as she pet the hound's glossy coat.

Attentively, the dog turned its head and looked downstream. Following the dog's lead, the couple looked toward the horizon and saw Tariq's regiment in the distance. As the contingent of men grew closer, the canine ran down the hill and rejoined the convoy.

Latifa examined the dog as it ran across the plain. It had powerful legs which moved gracefully, a long neck which arched as it ran and wide muscular shoulders crowned its lean slender torso. She noticed the hound's long tail, its nose, whiskers, nails and paws were the same burnished chestnut color as its coat which shimmered in the sun.

"She is as beautiful as she is good," Latifa remarked.

Tariq nodded his head and smiled. "I am glad I picked her from the litter. Like most of her breed she's independent. However, she has been a great companion to me."

"How much longer shall it be before we catch up to the raiders?" Latifa asked after Anubis disappeared within the ranks of the approaching soldiers.

"Any day now," Tariq answered.

The pair fell silent as they watched streaks of yellow, pink and orange light chase the sun beyond the horizon while soldiers, wagons, horses and camels passed below them.

After the last of the regiment disappeared in the distance, Tariq broke the silence between them and spoke again. "About the attack on your fortress...I am interested to know how you came to have the dagger with the brass handle in your possession."

"One of the Egyptians had it. He must have dropped it because I found it lying on the ground."

"Did you see the man who had the dagger? What did he look like?"

"He was tall. His hair was short...cut close to his head. He wore a red sash around his waist."

Tariq gritted his teeth as he realized the person Latifa was describing was indeed his half brother, Narmer. It seemed Narmer was not back in Egypt but was involved in the attack on the Nubian fortress.

Latifa continued to speak, "He had a fiendish look in his eyes...the look of a wild beast."

"You say he had a fiendish look and the look of a wild beast. You speak harshly of him but you haven't reproached me all day. I think that proves you are changing your mind about me," Tariq said.

Latifa chuckled. "There are some things that shall never happen. You getting me to change my opinion of you is one of them."

It was Tariq's turn to chuckle. "I almost got you to change your mind last night. As you experienced, I can be very persuasive."

Latifa found herself at a loss for words in response to the truth of his statement. Finally, she said, "What happened last night must never happen again."

"It shall happen again and I shall get what I want."

"No. You won't."

"We shall see," Tariq muttered knowingly.

The sound of horse hooves beating against the earth filled the air. Both Latifa and Tariq looked up to see the soldier named Kwame approaching them on horseback. Tariq stood to his feet and Latifa followed his lead.

"Commander!" Kwame saluted after he brought his horse to a stop and jumped from the animal.

"Speak soldier," Tariq ordered.

"We have overtaken the company that raided King Rassom's village. We made camp with them."

Latifa's heart began to pick up speed. They had caught up with the band of men who had taken her tribesmen. Was her sister among them?

"And Narmer? Did you see him?" Tariq inquired.

"He is in the camp," Kwame responded.

"Let's ride to the camp," Tariq suggested.

Quickly, the couple packed the items that had been lain out and climbed back on their horses. The remaining light from the sun dimmed then disappeared from the horizon as they followed the soldier to the campsite.

When they entered the encampment, Tariq said to Kwame, "Take Latifa to my tent."

"I want to see those who were captured. I want to see if my sister is among them," Latifa responded.

"As you wish. I shall go find Narmer," Tariq said then dismounted and secured his horse.

Latifa watched Tariq walk toward the mess of tents and watched until she lost sight of him. Turning her attention back to her escort, she bridled her horse in deference to the young man then followed as he led her to the back of the encampment. Through the darkness, she saw shadowy figures sitting in a group near the place where the horses and camels were corralled. As they approached the group, Latifa scanned the people sitting before her and recognized the familiar faces of her tribesmen. Her eyes lit up when though his head was bowed low she spotted Aren. Latifa leapt from her horse.

"Aren!" she called out.

At the sound of his name, Aren lifted his head and looked to see who called to him. When he did, the person sitting behind him whose presence had been obscured from Latifa's view peered over his shoulder. Latifa's mouth fell open when she realized the dark faced person with short kinky hair and sullen eyes was her sister.

"Tanesha!" Latifa gasped ecstatically.

"Latifa?" Her sister sprang to her feet and a clinking noise sounded followed by a rattle.

It was then Latifa noticed that her sister's ankles were bound by chains. Ignoring the chains for the moment, she ran to her sibling. "Praise be to God! I found you!" she exclaimed then threw her arms around her sister.

ଔ

Tariq clutched the brass handle and held up the dagger he had taken from Latifa the first night he met her. "You lost your knife," he said in a low steady voice after he strode into his half brother's dimly lit tent.

"And you found it," came the response from the tall slender man who stood with his back to Tariq.

"Turn to look at me. When your King speaks to you, you must show respect," Tariq snapped.

A moment passed then another before Narmer turned to face his sibling.

"You were a part of the assault on the Nubian village," Tariq accused.

Narmer nodded, took the dagger from Tariq and placed it in its sheath which lay on a table. "Yes, dear brother. I have done as you say. It well could be said I led the mission. For without my influence, the skirmish would not have happened. "

"You acted against me and the interest of Egypt."

"Not true. The Nubians are raiders. They have pillaged our land and are an enemy of Egypt."

"Peace was made with King Rassom. The Nubians agreed to lay down their arms in return for lucrative trade deals with our kingdom."

"The Nubians agreed to peace? How was I to know?" Narmer shrugged innocently.

"You knew I was meeting with the Nubians."

"Of course I knew you were meeting with the Nubians. But, was I supposed to know an agreement had been reached?"

"You deliberately set out to undermine my authority!"

"I set out to defend Egypt!" Narmer slammed his hand down on the table in front of him.

"Don't think me a fool! You attacked the Nubians when you knew I was in negotiations! You invaded their fortress and captured their people because you do not want peace!"

"Why should we make peace with mercenaries? None of our people want peace with the Nubians. Since you have spent your whole life being a warrior, it's surprising that you do," Narmer snarled.

"It is because I have seen the results of war that I want the bloodshed to end. It is time for peace."

Narmer shook his head. "I have spent my entire life in Egypt. I am Chancellor of The Grand Council. I know what is best for the people. If I were Pharaoh—"

"But you're not! Father appointed me Pharaoh not you!"

Narmer folded his arms and leaning back on his heels stated, "I am well aware of the fact you were appointed Pharaoh. Your mother manipulated Father into making that mistake."

"It is what the King felt was best for our nation and now that I am Pharaoh my word is law," Tariq retorted sharply.

"True. But, does that law negate the power of The Grand Council? I know you would punish me for my act but you would have to risk alienating The Council to do so."

"In what way, Narmer?" Tariq's dark eyes glittered menacingly in the glow of the amber lamplight as he stared at his half brother.

"According to the law, any negotiations made with the Nubians cannot take effect until the Vizier writes them in the Book of Covenants. You have not appointed a Vizier. So, you see, I have the law on my side. When I fought the Nubians, we were still officially at war with them. What would The Council say if you were to punish me for indulging in a lawful act? I know you would love nothing more than to punish me and those who followed my orders. But, how would it look to The Council and the citizens of Egypt if the legitimate son of the Pharaoh who everyone loves and expected to be King was unjustly punished by the bastard son?"

Tariq was quiet for a moment as the sting of Narmer's words met their mark. Gathering his bruised pride, he responded in a steely voice. "The only reason you don't face harsher treatment from me is out of respect for our father. You know very well he made me promise to see that you are well taken care of and that no harm comes to you."

Narmer focused his disdainful gaze upon Tariq. With a smirk, he sneered, "You are right. I am well aware of the promise my father made you agree to before he resigned to pass to the afterlife. I also know the day shall come when you regret that promise."

 og

Latifa wiped the tears from her eyes as she walked to Tariq's tent. She was not sure how long she had spoken with her sister and the people from her village. What she did know was that the talk left her with a maze of jumbled emotions. She was happy that her sister was still alive yet sad to find her sibling and the others shackled like animals. Latifa knew she must speak with Tariq about having her sister and all of her tribesmen released.

When she made it to Tariq's tent, it was dark indicating he was not there. Making her way through the crepuscular hue that saturated the tent, she walked to the table and lit one of the oil lamps causing a golden light to blossom around her. She sat on the stool and tapped her foot anxiously as she waited for Tariq to return. As she waited, every moment that ticked by seemed like an eternity. When she was unable to wait any longer, Latifa left the tent in search of Tariq.

Unlike before, though it was late at night, the camp was alive with activity. As she meandered through the tents, she saw men whose swords clinked as they clashed their weapons together while others lounged around a fire and appeared to be gambling. She passed a small group of men standing in a circle around two other men. The two males in the middle of the circle spoke in raised voices and looked defiantly at each other. Unsettled by the commotion,

Latifa strode to a nearby tent and walked behind it in hopes of remaining unobserved.

As she stood behind the lodging, a familiar voice floated to her ears. While listening to the sound of the voice, she became convinced the voice she heard belonged to Tariq. She began to follow the sound of the voice which seemed to be coming from a tent a short distance away. Upon nearing the shelter, her brow wrinkled when she realized it was Tariq who spoke and he was speaking to someone in a cross tone.

Latifa slackened her pace then came to a stop when she made it to the front of the tent. Reaching out, she slowly pulled aside the flap at the entrance of the structure. Tariq came into view first. He was standing near the back of the temporary dwelling. Curious to identify the person he was speaking to, Latifa pushed aside the flap further. Her breath caught in her throat when she saw the face of the tall man standing beside Tariq. Though part of his face was drenched in the light of the flames from the lamp and the other covered by shadows, his piercing black eyes were unmistakable as was the pleated *schenti* with the red sash which he wore around his waist.

Suddenly, the sound of panicked screams echoed in Latifa's ears. The sight of red and orange flames flashed in her mind and her nose stung as if she could smell charred wood. She blinked to block out the memory of her village on fire. But, when she looked at the man with the short cropped hair before her, she could not help but be transported back to the day the fortress was attacked.

Kofi's face flashed in her mind. The man who stood talking to Tariq was the same man she had seen fighting Kofi. She released the flap and took a step backward. Latifa took several deep breaths and forced her feet to move. As she scurried back to Tariq's tent, memories flooded her mind. She remembered waking to the sight of the silver moon high in the sky. She recalled seeing Kofi's body prostrated beside her and the sight of blood dripping from her hands. Her entire body was trembling by the time she made it back to the tent. Wearily, she stumbled to the cot, lying face down she placed her forehead on her arm and began to cry.

Tears streamed uncontrolled from her eyes. She was not sure how long tears flowed from her eyes before she heard someone enter the tent. Instinctively, she knew it was Tariq. She tried fruitlessly to still the sobs that shook her body.

"Latifa?" Concern laced his voice when he called her name.

In the next instant, she felt the cot sag then felt his hand on her arm. She jerked her arm away from his touch.

"Latifa? What is troubling you?"

"How could you? How could you and your men attack my village and kill innocent people?" she cried.

"I know you think I had something to do with the destruction of your village. But, I promise you, things are not as they seem."

Latifa wiped her tears with the back of her hand then she sat up and faced him. "Things are not the way they seem? Don't tell me that when I saw you talking to one of the fiends you ordered to destroy my village. I remember his face. He killed the man my father wanted me to marry."

Tariq reached out to touch her but she moved away from him.

"Latifa, I'm sorry for all of the bad things you've had to go through. I didn't think I would ever see you cry. Now, that I have, I find it pains me to see you upset. The person you saw me talking to is my half brother, Narmer. He organized and attacked your village without my knowledge. He wanted to undermine me and my authority."

"Why? Why would he do that?" Latifa asked.

"It's a long story. A very long story. We were never close. Our mothers saw to that. Our mothers despised each other. I joined the military to travel and get away from the constant strife in our home. But, in the end, I could not escape it. Destiny brought me back to the people and the place I thought I left behind. Narmer has been and is still a thorn in my side. What makes it even more difficult, my father made me promise not to let any harm befall Narmer and make sure he always has enough to live comfortably."

69

Latifa was quiet a moment as she took in what Tariq said. Finally, she spoke. "The people Narmer captured from my village…one of them is my sister. She is chained like an animal. I can't stand to see her like that." A tear rolled down Latifa's face.

Tariq reached out and gently wiped all of the tears from her cheeks. "I shall see about the conditions of the captives in the morning."

"Really?"

Tariq smiled and nodded his head. "It is much too late to accomplish anything tonight."

"I must say, you don't act like a battle hardened warrior. You have been kind to me. More kind than I expected," Latifa admitted.

"That's because I find you to be a very intriguing person. I've never met a female like you before." He rose from the cot and rummaged through one of the satchels before pulling out a linen tunic and tossing it to her. "It's time to change for bed. You can sleep in that," he said then walked to the table and extinguished the flame in the lamp.

Latifa listened as he slipped out of his clothing except for his *shendoh*. She quickly slipped out of her kaftan and put on Tariq's oversized tunic.

"It's been a long day for both of us," she heard him say.

When he lowered himself to the cot and gathered her in his arms, Latifa did not pull away. Instead, she relaxed in his embrace.

"May your dreams be pleasant," he whispered when she lay her head against his chest.

Chapter Six

The amber glow of fire light illuminated the night coating the dark faces of the people sitting around the fire pit where a pig roasted. Her father sat in the shadows chatting with a group of men. Tanesha and Aren smiled happily while they watched dancers spin and sway to the dulcet sound of a beating drum...

Latifa's eyes fluttered opened. A frown spread over her lips when she realized she had been dreaming about the celebration that occurred the night before her father left the fort. She sat up in the cot as reality returned to her. She was not in her village. Instead, she was traveling with a band of military men who were no doubt breaking camp so they could begin their journey for the day. So, why did the sound of a drumbeat continue to fill the air? Latifa quickly slid off of the cot and hurriedly slipped into her kaftan. When she exited the tent, she was surprised to see the sun high in the sky and the soldiers leisurely milling about the camp. She looked around for Tariq and not seeing him headed to see her sister.

When she made it to the place where the captives had been held the night before, she was surprised to find they were not there. Puzzled, she followed the sound of the drumbeat. She came upon Jabari who was brushing a horse. He kept his back to her and continued to brush the horse without acknowledging her presence.

"When shall we head out?" she asked him after a moment.

He cast a stern gaze on her. "We shall not be traveling today. It seems the Commander did not want to wake you. It seems he thinks we should all take a day to rest...including the captives."

Jabari turned his eyes from her indicating he was done talking to her.

Latifa squared her shoulders and stepped away from him.

"I don't know what scheme you're concocting but I'm warning you it won't come to pass," he sneered over his shoulder.

71

"What scheme I'm concocting? I plan no scheme."

"Just don't get too amenable with the Commander," Jabari warned tersely.

Latifa cast a disdainful glare at Jabari's back before continuing on her mission to find her sister. Exiting a row of tents, she saw the source of the drumbeat was a swarthy middle aged man from her village named Mateo. She looked toward the Nile and saw other people from her village sitting a ways back from the water while a few daring souls frolicked in a shallow tributary. Setting a quick pace, she walked past the watchful eye of several guards and looked around for her sibling. When she spotted Tanesha sitting next to Aren, she called out her sister's name. Tanesha smiled, rose to her feet and scurried toward her.

"Latifa, I was so worried about you. Are you all right? Where are they keeping you?"

"I'm being treated very well. I am glad to see your chains have been removed," Latifa admitted as she hugged her sister close. When she heard a whimper, she looked and saw tears had begun to stream down Tanesha's face. Latifa reached out and gently wiped the tears. "Don't cry or you shall make me cry," she instructed then led her sister to a towering tree a short distance away. "I am so glad we're together again. Before last night, I wasn't sure I would ever see you again. I don't know what I would do if I lost you," Latifa revealed after the siblings sat on a patch of earth shaded by the thick leaves of the tree.

"Since the day mother was taken from us, you've been a mother to me. You could have continued your life with a lack of thought for your little sister. But, you didn't. You always made me feel like I was important to you," Tanesha sniffled.

"You are so very important to me," Latifa assured.

"I just wish I could have been with Father," Tanesha admitted.

"No. If you were with him then you wouldn't be here with me. We need each other now more than ever. I love you so much," Latifa hugged her sister once more.

"I love you too," Tanesha sniveled.

After their embrace ended, the pair continued to talk to each other until Aren interrupted them.

"To my angel and her sweet sister, I see you two are happy to be reunited."

The siblings nodded their heads in confirmation.

"Both of you have been crying for far too long. No more tears. It's time to celebrate." He reached out a hand to Tanesha and one to Latifa.

The sisters each took a hold of his outstretched hands and he pulled the pair to their feet.

"I want smiles on your lovely faces. Let's cool off in the water," he suggested and led them to the bank of the river.

The remainder of the day seemed to fly by for Latifa. She enjoyed splashing around in the water and reconnecting with her sister, Aren and the other people from her village. After a time of idling in the water, the joyous group decided to nap under a tree.

The next time Latifa woke, she realized she had been awakened by the sound of a drumbeat just as she had been that morning. Looking around she saw the few people who remained under the tree were being roused from their slumber by the drumbeat as well. Drawn by the sound, she made her way back to the camp. She spotted her tribesmen seated in a circle around a small bonfire and Mateo seated near a brazier filled with perch beating his drum. Latifa smiled when several people called out a greeting to her. She returned their greeting then sat down and began talking to the group about those of her tribe who were believed to have been killed or escaped the attack.

Eventually, the conversation turned to Egypt and what would happen once they made it there. Latifa assured everyone the Commander would release all of them soon. Her tribesmen seemed happy at her words and the group began to reminisce about events of the past. As they ate, the last of the sunlight disappeared beyond the horizon.

After the meal, several of the men decided they wanted to dance and began to form a circle around the gleaming flames. The beat of the drum which had ceased began again and the men moved in unison around the fire. When the first dance ended, the men laughed and slapped each other on the back. Jovially, they began to goad the women into joining the dance. Aren asked Tanesha to dance and in turn Tanesha asked Latifa to join in as well. Latifa agreed and when the drumbeat started once more she found a spot around the fire and swayed to the beat. As the beat continued, she gyrated her body and whirled with the tempo.

Latifa was not sure how long she danced but when the music stopped she found she was panting breathlessly. Looking around, she noticed several Egyptian soldiers including Jabari had meandered over to watch the merriment. As her eyes moved past them, she saw Tariq standing in front of his tent. A euphoric tingle went through her when she realized he had been watching her.

Suddenly, Latifa wanted to thank him for his kindness in allowing everyone to take a day to relax and experience an evening of dancing. Deciding she should speak to him, she headed to his tent. When she approached the spot where Jabari stood, he stepped to block her path.

"You entered our camp as an intruder. Now you walk around as though you were Queen," he stated.

"If I walk around as if I were a Queen, it is because I am of royal blood. That is something no Egyptian can take from me," she replied.

"You wield an unacceptable amount of influence over the Commander and it displeases me. An entanglement with you shall bring him to ruin."

"I have no influence over the Commander," Latifa hedged.

Jabari nodded toward the captives who danced joyfully and talked freely around the fire. "Looks like you do."

Choosing to remain silent, Latifa stepped past Jabari and continued on her way. As she approached Tariq, she could not help but once again notice how handsome and virile he looked as he stood drenched in moonlight. He held a goblet in his hand which he tipped to his lips.

"Your people are enjoying themselves. I thought you would like that," he said softly when she drew near.

Latifa smiled lightly as she walked past him and entered his dimly lit tent.

74

Tariq followed her and stood behind her when she stopped at the table. Very aware of Tariq's closeness, Latifa busied herself lighting all of the lamps in the tent. While she lit the lamps, Tariq reached for an ewer and poured wine into his goblet along with a second goblet that was on the table. When all of the oil lamps cast a bright glow within the chamber, he picked up both cups and handed her one. He held up his goblet and waited for her to hold her goblet up before he drained the liquid from the vessel. Latifa followed his lead and drained the liquid from her cup. The tangy taste of over ripe grapes and honey kissed her tongue before the warm liquid coated her throat.

"Did you come to tell me of your appreciation for what I've allowed?" he asked as if reading her thoughts.

She nodded her head and sat on the stool. "Thank you for what you've done," she said as he poured more wine into her cup.

"You are saying something nice to me. Is the hardened warrior cracking?"

"Never," Latifa responded before taking a sip of wine.

He smiled.

Latifa smiled back. "You have shown me kindness and my people kindness and I am grateful. But, there is something else."

"And what is that?"

"My people need to be freed."

"Drink your fill," Tariq insisted. When she drained her cup, he said, "They are Narmer's captives. It is for him to free them."

"You are Commander, are you not? You can make him free them."

Tariq was silent as he added to her cup a third time. "If I do that for you, tell me, what shall you do for me?" he inquired.

Latifa drank more of her wine. Finally, she said, "How about I give you another massage?"

Tariq chuckled and sat his cup on the table. "I don't know if my legs can survive another bout of your crude method."

"If I recall correctly, you seemed to like that massage even though it was hard." Latifa grinned as she remembered her antics.

"There are some things that should be given hard and some things that should be given soft," Tariq stated cryptically.

Latifa puckered her lips. "What should be given soft?" she asked.

Tariq reached out and using his thumb traced the outline of her lips. "Do I need to answer that?"

Latifa shook her head which suddenly seemed hazy. She scolded herself for drinking the wine so fast.

"How about I just show you," he suggested.

"We need to discuss the release of my people."

"A discussion about your people shall take place tomorrow. Right now, I am not interested in them. I am interested in you."

"I…I told you I shall never make love to you," Latifa reminded him.

"And I told you, you shall. Do you think I am a boy naive enough to believe you won't make love to me?" Tariq paused a moment then pulled his tunic over his head.

His muscle carved chest gleamed in the lamplight.

Latifa found she could not take her eyes from him.

"Latifa, my little lioness, I am a man with desires. And at the moment, I desire you." He began to undo the strap around his *schenti*.

Latifa licked her lips nervously and sat her cup on the table. "If you think anything is going to happen between us tonight—"

Her words were interrupted when Tariq reached out and tugged her arm. He pulled her to her feet and locked his arms around her waist. "I don't think. I know what is going to happen between us tonight. The very first thing is a kiss," he whispered and lowered his lips to hers.

Latifa found her arms as if they had a mind of their own wrap around his shoulders.

"A kiss is something that should be given soft," he rasped when their lips parted.

"If a kiss should be given soft, what should be given hard?" she wanted to know.

Tariq smiled slyly, tightened his hold around her then swept her off of her feet. In a step, he made it to the cot and lay her on it.

"The people you care about are enjoying themselves. Now, it's time for you to enjoy yourself," he murmured as he stretched out beside her and pressed his solid mass against her yielding flesh.

His hand slid over the material that covered her hips and waist. Once his hand made it to her right breast, he fondled his prize. His lips touched her neck then moved to replace his hand on her breast. His tongue lightly stroked the material that covered her nipple causing pleasure to ooze through her.

Latifa shrugged her shoulders nervously and tried to pull away from him.

"Not this time," he muttered clutching her arm to prevent her escape. "This time you shall make love to me."

"I can't make love to you," she gulped.

"Maybe this shall change your mind," he whispered.

Reaching down, Tariq placed his hand on her leg. Cool night air kissed her skin in the wake of his hands as he pushed her kaftan up her leg. Then, his hand moved over her hips to the inside of her thigh. This time his fingers persisted on their quest and touched her moist folds. Though she began to form a word of denial, she found she could not utter a sound. Latifa was sure it was the wine that created the haze in her mind and rendered her mute. It must be the wine that made her moan and cling to Tariq as his finger slid along her slick folds.

"You want this to happen. Say you do," his words were a plea.

Unable to speak, she nodded her head. As a reward, he smiled and moved his finger into her treasure. Gently, he began to maneuver his finger. Masterfully, he created a fervor of need that solicited relief. Sitting up slightly, he pushed her kaftan upward and slipped it over her head. Placated into a daze by his touch, Latifa watched motionless as his eyes reverently devoured her naked form.

"Amun be praised. You look beautiful," she heard him say.

"I came to the tent to thank you not to—"

His look silenced her. "You came to the tent to thank me. This is how I want to be thanked."

Once again, he lowered his body next to hers. His arms circled around her and hungrily he kissed her. His finger returned to its exploration. Its every movement mounted sensations inside of Latifa which were evolving into something she could not name. Intensity built causing Latifa to move her hips in search of relief from the passion blossoming in her. Tariq's response was to slide a second finger inside her sheath.

"You shall be mine now."

His words settled in her ears and Latifa groaned. Never had she experienced the things she was currently experiencing. Maybe that was the reason she once again let things go too far. Maybe that was the reason she had some curiosity about what Tariq would do next. Who was she fooling? She knew the next step was her surrender to his addictive enticement. She knew she would give in to the intoxicating allure of his fingers if she continued to lay beneath him. It was as if she kept forgetting he was an Egyptian – an enemy of her people. Continuously, she let things get out of control because of his spectacular kisses and the enchanting touch of his hands. He had wagered she would give herself to him before the next full moon because he sensed she was easily affected by him and would surrender her body to him. Well she wouldn't. Not on this day or any day.

Gathering her strength she pushed frantically against him. "No! Stop!" she shrieked.

Tariq took a deep breath then stilled his hand.

An involuntary groan of protest sounded in Latifa's throat when he acceded to her command and pulled his fingers from her. Latifa found she wanted to cry out in objection that he had submitted to her request. Unfulfilled need galvanized every nerve ending in her body. Her hips wanted to continue to search for something that would sedate her yearning. Inexplicably, she found she felt intensely disappointed and extremely unrelieved.

"I can tell by the look in your eyes you don't mean a word you are saying."

Latifa did not speak to contradict Tariq's words.

He rolled from the cot to his knees, reached out, grabbed her ankles and pulled her to the edge of the cot. He pushed her legs apart.

Latifa found all resistance flee when Tariq returned his finger to her moistened sheath. She fell back on the cot and closed her eyes enjoying the sensational feel he created inside of her. Again, he slid a second finger in her and at the same moment she felt his lips on the inside of her thigh. Shocked, Latifa opened her eyes. Lifting herself onto her elbows, she tried to close her legs in an effort to shimmy away from him.

He placed a staying hand on her thigh. "Our enjoyment has just begun, little lioness," he remarked then nudging her legs apart he touched his tongue to her womanly treasure.

Latifa gasped at the rapturous feeling that immediately shot through her body as he hungrily ran his tongue across her maidenhead. He moved his tongue back and forth over her treasure. Surrendering to the exquisite sensation, she fell back onto the cot to marvel at the wanton desire originating at Tariq's touch. An exhilarating feeling coursed through Latifa causing her to feel as if she was drifting in the clouds. She widened her legs allowing greater access for him to lap at her essence. Sighing, she turned her head and clutched the blanket beneath her. The heavenly endowment ceased. Latifa lifted her head and looked in protest at Tariq who was looking at her. He smiled and lowered his head. Passion shot through her the moment the sumptuous bounty returned.

Through the haze of delight, she marveled at Tariq's generous skill and ability. She knew she did not want to put an end to his devilish delight. She found she anxiously anticipated what was to come. Nothing else seemed to matter in that moment but Tariq and the new exciting feelings he roused in her.

"Tell me you want me to make love to you," he raised his head and commanded seemingly knowing what she was thinking.

Latifa shook her head negatively. She should not go any further. This was the final time to say no. If she went any further there would be no going back.

"Say it," he commanded gently.

She shook her head negatively again but said, "I want you to make love to me." Surely it was the wine that made her speak the traitor's words.

A smile curled Tariq's lips. "It pleases me to hear you admit what you really want," he rasped then he rose to his feet.

Suddenly, he lowered his *schenti* exposing his magnificent manhood to her view.

Latifa was so enthralled by the long flesh colored tower jutting toward her that she realized she could not take her eyes away from it.

Tariq gingerly stroked his member then reached out, took hold of her hand and placed it on his stiffened tower.

"Oh my God," she murmured at the thick flesh that filled her palm.

"I knew you would call me that." Tariq grinned.

Any response Latifa planned departed her mind when he lay his hand over hers and began to guide her hand up and down his shaft. As he continued to guide her hand along his tower, he whispered, "There's no going back. Now, we shall become one."

Instantly, panic rose in Latifa's throat. Was she really ready to give up her freedom for one night with Tariq? Was she willing to surrender her virtue and honor after only a couple days of foreplay? What of her vow not to forget Kofi? Did she want to give up her dream of becoming a warrior? The man before her was commanded by the Pharaoh. His half brother led an attack on her village. He implied the attack had happened without his consent. Even so, the reality was as Commander of the military at some point he led other acts of aggression against her people.

Surely, a man such as he would regard her as spoils of war and after he used her he would discard her as if she were rubbish. It was not like they loved and cared for each other. He had even said love was not what he was looking for. She never expected love from Kofi but she had known he cared for her. The only thing Tariq truly cared for was her body and he had been sure he could get it. By lying as she was, she was making it easy for him. But, did she really have the strength to pick herself off of the cot and end the titillating tryst between them?

She saw Tariq move closer to her then felt him slide his member along the slit of her essence.

"Dear God!" she called out when she saw liquid on his member catch the light from the lamps and glisten before her eyes. She bit her bottom lip. Yes. She would definitely need God's help to get out of her current predicament. "No!" she called out in a frenzy and scooted back on the cot when his member touched the inside of her thigh.

Tariq let out an agitated sigh. "Amun give me strength! I cannot take much more of your teasing. Are you going to make love to me?" he demanded.

Latifa shook her head negatively. "No... I can't," her voice was a whisper.

Tariq eyed her without speaking.

The tent fell silent except for the muffled sound of the drumbeat in the distance. Latifa heard herself breathing and realized the thumping of her heart matched the feverish beat of the drum.

"You've sent me away before. You shall not send me away tonight. We both need relief from the fire between us. What we have started shall be concluded. We both shall receive satisfaction. The time for persuasion as ended," he stated. Then, reaching out, he clutched her ankles and slid her to the edge of the cot once again. Unrelentingly, he nudged her legs apart. Lowering himself in front of her, he touched his tongue to her feminine treasure once again.

"Oh my God!" Latifa wailed as he began to purposefully lap at her essence.

She inhaled poignantly as shards of pleasure shot through her body. She clutched the blanket under her palm and bent her knees. Lifting her free hand, she ran her fingers over his head and his name escaped her lips. He responded by increasing his pace to match the drumbeat wafting into the tent. Latifa moaned uncontrollably affected by his gentle yet masterful ministrations.

"Oh my! Oh my!" she breathed and closed her eyes as her insides erupted in a rapturous explosion of ecstasy.

For a blissful moment, it seemed she was rising to heaven. In the next instant, she was among the stars. After she drifted back on the cot, she opened her eyes and looked between her limp legs to see Tariq had risen to his feet.

"Listening to you receive pleasure has made me spill my seed," Tariq said lightly before he picked up his discarded tunic and wiped his member. "Once I've rested we shall commence our play. You've received satisfaction. I shall be next. I say unto you, the next time we entertain ourselves, the conclusion shall be more to my satisfaction."

Without further words, he lay on the cot next to her.

"I—"

Tariq put his finger to her lips silencing her. "Let's not speak," he said softly.

෬

Long after Tariq's breathing informed her he was sleep, Latifa lay awake. A multitude of tumultuous emotions swirled inside her preventing her rest. Never had she felt such conflicting feelings before. It was undeniable. Her body heedlessly reacted to Tariq's touch as if he had fashioned her himself. It was as if his very touch brought her slumbering soul alive. The delicious sensations he created within her were delightful. But, how was it possible she could so easily find pleasure with her sworn enemy? How could she be affected by the touch of a man who on the Pharaoh's orders fought against her tribesmen and forced them into bondage? Even now, while she lay beside their captor, her sister and her tribesmen were captives...spoils of war.

82

After all of her big talk about wanting to be a warrior and not wanting to be with a man, she had succumbed to Tariq like a moth to a flame. If she were honest with herself, she knew Tariq was right. The next time they came together, things would not end as before. Things would end as Tariq predicted and wanted. She would wantonly give herself to him and they would make love. No matter how many times she said it would not happen, she knew she would not be able to resist him when he woke and reached for her.

Latifa sat up. Suddenly, being in the tent felt stifling. Quietly, she climbed over Tariq and got out of the cot. Noiselessly, she picked up her discarded kaftan and slipped it over her head then exited the tent.

All was quiet in the camp. A drumbeat no longer sounded and no one moved about. Through the darkness of the moonless night, Latifa walked to where her tribesmen had gathered for the night. She saw that her sister, Aren and a few other people were still awake. As she drew near, all except Tanesha turned their backs to her. Latifa opened her mouth to speak to her sister. However, sound died in her throat when she noted the look of disgust on Tanesha's face.

"Is there a problem?" Latifa asked once she came to stand next to her sibling.

Tanesha responded by turning her back to her as the others had.

A frown creased Latifa's lips.

"What's the trouble? Are you angry with me?" Latifa questioned in confusion.

Tanesha remained silent.

Latifa placed her hand on her sister's shoulder.

Tanesha recoiled from Latifa's touch as if she had been bitten.

"Tanesha, why are you acting in such a manner? Why has everyone turned their backs on me?"

"You have the audacity to ask me that?" Tanesha hissed.

"Why are you speaking to me in such a manner?" Latifa demanded, taken aback by her sister's caustic tone.

Tanesha spun to face Latifa. "Is there another way I should speak to a whore?"

Latifa gasped.

Tanesha put her hand on her hip. "Go back to the Egyptian's tent. Go back to that heathen and be his nightly amusement. Just don't pretend you haven't sold your soul for the pleasure."

Latifa lowered her head in shame. "You now know I share Tariq's tent. That's why you're upset with me."

Aren turned to face her. "You call him by his given name?" he questioned.

Latifa sighed. "He hasn't been that awful to me. Before we met up with all of you, he took me on horseback rides and—"

"I don't want to hear about your exploits!" Tanesha asserted curtly.

"You cavort with him while we are stuck in chains," Aren accused.

Tanesha shook her head. "Go back to the Egyptian's tent. But, this time, don't make us watch you sacrifice your soul to him."

"What are you talking about?" Latifa asked unsettled by the look of contempt radiating from her sister's stare.

Tanesha gazed at Latifa then shifted her gaze to a point beyond her shoulder.

Latifa turned and let her eyes follow her sister's gaze. Her eyes skimmed the rows of dark tents until she spotted a tent glowing brightly against the black night. Latifa realized she was looking at Tariq's tent. Lamplight illuminated the inside of the tent casting shadows onto the tent's off-white canvas. The grey shadow of the cot displayed clearly on the canvas that comprised the wall of the tent. Latifa saw the form of a man lying on the cot and knew it was Tariq.

Suddenly, the significance of what she was viewing dawned on her. Just as she could see the shadows clearly displayed on the tent's canvas, so could Tanesha and the others. She had been lying next to Tariq moments before and they had seen her shadow on the wall along with his. Memory of kissing Tariq and being in his embrace flashed in her mind. She thought about how she had laid nude beneath him while his hands explored her body. She remembered the way he kissed the inside of her thighs then feasted on her womanly treasure. She realized Tanesha and anyone who was still awake had seen it all.

All of the blood drained from her face as shock and embarrassment engulfed her. She could not bring herself to look at her sister.

"I...I..." Words refused to form on her lips.

A chuckle sounded and Latifa turned to see Narmer sneering at her. Behind him stood Jabari who had a disdainful expression on his face. Though there were shadows covering those gathered, the scorn on all of the faces that now stared at her could easily be seen. Suddenly, Latifa felt ill. Her hand flew to her mouth. A sob caught in her throat and she began to run. She ran past her sister, past the others and into the darkness beyond the tents.

Chapter Seven

Wind whipped against Latifa's face. Tears crowded in her eyes obscuring her vision. Her lungs seemed to constrict and her breath burned in her chest. Mindlessly, she ran into the veil of darkness. Racing through the African night, she tread onward until pain stabbed at her side slowing her pace. Determinedly, she forced one foot in front of the other and continued to race into the darkness.

Suddenly, the ground under Latifa's feet crumbled causing her legs to give way beneath her. She was falling. She stretched out her arms an instant before her body slammed against the ground and excruciating pain exploded in her chest. Despite the pain that stung her bosom, she frantically gulped for air. Warily, she raised herself to a sitting position. It was then tears sprang into her eyes and pushed past her lashes to tumble down her face. She closed her eyes as uncontrolled sobs shook her body.

A menacing growl rumbled in Latifa's ears. Her eyes snapped opened then she peered into the black night in time to see a pair of citrine eyes materialize in front of her. A sob caught in her throat when, as if she was seeing an apparition, a second pair of translucent eyes appeared to gaze at her through the dark. Fear pierced her heart. Casting a look over her shoulder, she saw yet another set of eyes. Terror shot through her being as she realized a pack of wild animals surrounded her.

A snarl resounded. Latifa swung her head around to gape at the wild beasts in front of her. As one of the animals crept close, the feeling to flee overwhelmed her and she scrambled to her feet. Instantly, pain shot from her ankle ripping a scream from her throat and caused her to fall back to the ground. A quiver slithered down Latifa's spine when the beast came close enough for her to see its long russet colored legs and the brown tipped hair along its flank. Latifa realized the approaching animal was a jackal when the advancing beast let out a sharp howl. The remaining jackals began to yelp in response. Latifa's heart thumped erratically.

Frenziedly, she looked around for something to use as a weapon. Through the blackness she spied a figure lying on the ground. Her eyes focused on the lump and she realized it was the carcass of a gazelle. Her eyes snapped back to the jackals who began to circle her and she viewed splotches of blood around the animals' mouths and on their paws. She realized the pack must have been feeding on the gazelle when she ran upon them but because she had been so distracted she had not noticed the beasts.

"Get away! Go away!" she shouted and waved her arms about.

The animals responded by moving closer.

Latifa once again tried to stand to her feet. This time, she put her weight on her uninjured foot and managed to stand. The urge to take flight simmered to a boiling point threatening to spill to her feet and send her on an exploration of retreat. Though every instinct in her compelled her to run, she willed herself to remain still. She must keep her wits about her. Even if she was not injured, she knew there was no way she could out run a pack of jackals.

A sting shot through the back of her leg. Latifa shrieked and looked over her shoulder in time to see a jackal slither back into the cover of darkness. Gingerly, she ran a shaky hand down her leg. Blood coated her fingers. She realized the animal had scratched her drawing blood. Stinging pain shot from the front of her leg. A panicked screech tore from her throat. Her head snapped forward and she saw a young jackal expose its teeth as it stared at her. She felt the front of her leg to find her skin lacerated this time because she had been bitten. Terror mushroomed within her as the horror of her predicament illuminated with stunning clarity.

She wailed in anguish but told herself not to let panic and fear doom her. Instead, she reminded herself she had said she wanted to be a warrior. Now was the time to use the cunning and stealth of a warrior and fight for her life. Desperately, she once again looked around for something to use to defend herself. There was nothing to be seen. Images of the pack of jackals feasting on her limbs flashed in her mind. The image ruptured in her thoughts when a jackal suddenly leapt in the air and lunged for her throat. A horrified scream ripped from her lips as she raised her arms and stepped backward. Unable to stand the pressure on her bruised ankle, she fell and landed on her back. She cringed when the jackal landed in a straddle over her then let out a piercing howl. The beast bared its sharp teeth. It lowered its hideous face close to hers and fixed its eerie lutescent eyes on her. The jackal opened its mouth and its fetid breath invaded Latifa's nose.

"Dear God, save me!" she whimpered then closed her eyes to await the excruciating pain of sharp teeth piercing her skin and the agonizing torment of her flesh being ripped from her limbs.

Suddenly, a loud bark exploded through the darkness. In the next instant, there was a gnarl followed by a growl. Latifa's eyes snapped opened and she gasped when she saw Anubis and the jackal that stood over her just moments before rolling on the ground. Stunned, Latifa sat up and watched as the dog and jackal clawed and bit at each other. A bark was followed by a snarl which was followed by a yip. Latifa scanned the faces of the other jackals standing nearby and saw they were watching the rumble with what seemed like stunned amazement.

Latifa screamed when she saw the jackal that was fighting Anubis flash its teeth and attempt to lower them into the dog. In the next moment, Anubis bared her claw and swiped the jackal across the nose slicing the tissue open. The stunned jackal yapped then bolted into the night. The remaining jackals darted after the wounded predator. Anubis barked ferociously at the retreating pack. When all traces of the carnivores were gone, Anubis scuttled over to Latifa and began to lick the unbridled tears that once again streamed down her face. Latifa wrapped her arms around the dog's wide shoulders and buried her face against the canine's neck.

"Anubis! Oh my!" she sobbed.

The dog began to whine when the sound of hooves pounding against the earth reverberated through the night. Latifa raised her head and stared anxiously into the darkness at the dark silhouettes that approached on horseback. When the riders drew near and brought their horses to a stop, she could not help but let out a sigh of relief when she recognized Narmer and Jabari.

"We've found Tariq's concubine. Looks like we should have been here a little sooner," Narmer mused from his place atop his horse.

"Help me!" Latifa called out.

Jabari moved to dismount but Narmer motioned for him to remain as he was.

"Please help me!" Latifa pleaded.

Ignoring Narmer's jester, Jabari jumped from his horse, walked to Latifa and knelt beside her. "You're hurt," he said then carefully inspected the injuries on her leg. "How did you get these wounds?" he asked.

"I was attacked by jackals. I fell and hurt my ankle."

Latifa inhaled sharply when he touched her ankle.

Upon completion of his inspection, Jabari rubbed his chin. "We've got to get you back to camp," he announced.

"You told me this girl was a distraction to your Commander. Did you not say this Nubian wielded far too much influence over your leader? Given such facts, is taking her back to camp wise?" Narmer queried.

"We can't leave her here," Jabari replied casting a glance at Narmer.

"I am not suggesting that we leave a defenseless female alone to be devoured by wild vermin."

"Get to the point."

"Jabari, you are the one who made the point. As we searched for this girl, you said if you could get rid of her you would. You said you wanted things to go back to the way they were before she came to the camp. How can things go back to the way they were if you return her to Tariq? If she's back in his arms before the night is through, nothing shall change. She would be influencing him and he shall once more begin conceding to her whims."

Jabari stood. "I admit I feel the Commander's attention has been divided. I admit I think this girl is not good for him. But, I cannot stop him from being with her."

"Oh but you can," Narmer retorted and climbed from his horse.

"What are you saying?" Jabari inquired.

"I am saying you shall be helping Tariq if you do not return her to him."

"Don't listen to him!" Latifa blurted out.

"Are you going to listen to a woman or are you going to listen to me?" Narmer asked.

"I am not going to leave her out here. It would not be right."

"You are hearing my voice but you are not listening to my words. I have not said anything about leaving her out in the wilderness."

"Be clear about what you are saying."

"For a military man of such rank, you don't seem to be too astute or you would understand my meaning. I am saying you can avail yourself to be of benefit to Tariq."

"You want me to do something that would benefit Tariq? You are not fond of him. Why would you want me to help him?"

"It is not him I want to help. But you. You want Tariq to focus on his military duties. If you do as I suggest, you shall have your wish." Narmer shifted his eyes to Latifa. He strutted to her then knelt beside her. "You are mighty comely," he said to her before touching her braided hair with the back of his hand.

A shudder of repulsion course through Latifa at Narmer's touch and she turned her face from him.

Narmer's eyes darkened with ire. "After what I saw going on between you and Tariq when you were in his tent tonight, you have no cause to shudder at my touch! I shall soon see to it that you despise my touch for a reason!" he pledged then stood to his feet.

Jabari helped Latifa to her feet. "If I do not return with the girl, Tariq shall search for her."

"He would not search if you told him she was dead," Narmer hedged.

"Dead?"

"You would murder me?" Latifa queried anxiously.

Narmer pulled a dagger from its protective sheath.

When he held it up, Latifa recognized it as the dagger she found after the village was attacked and the one Tariq had taken from her. She watched as without speaking another word, Narmer reached out and clutched the top of her kaftan. She winced when he brought the dagger to her throat. With slow deliberation, he forced the knife downward and sliced the garment near the neckline. Using exact precision, he cut the material from the neckline to the hem then yanked the garment from her frame. Latifa let out a screech of relief that she was still alive then grabbed at her clothing.

Narmer snickered and held the garment beyond her reach.

Latifa grimaced and crossed her arms in front of her chest to shield her breasts from the men's view.

Narmer lifted his dagger once more and then decisively sliced through the material of the kaftan. Once the raiment was slashed, he wiped the garment on the blood that oozed down the front of Latifa's leg. When he held up the tattered apparel now stained with blood, he said, "Tell my dear brother she was attacked and killed by spotted hyenas."

"Don't do it! Don't listen to him!" Latifa pleaded.

Jabari fell silent.

"I'll see that the girl lives a life quite different than the one she planned with Tariq. As for you, this is your chance to get what you've been wanting," Narmer coaxed.

Jabari looked at Latifa, a guilty expression showed on his face.

"Don't listen to Narmer! Please!" Latifa cried out when Narmer shoved pieces of her thrashed kaftan into Jabari's hand.

"It is a god forsaken plan but it is what is best for Tariq so it shall be done. He has important work to do. He must regain his focus and remember his destiny and I shall return to mine," Jabari said somberly.

"Don't leave me with this man!" Latifa yelled at Jabari's retreating back.

"You're doing the right thing," Narmer assured Jabari. "I shall take good care of her. Better yet, she shall take care of me." He reached out and slapped her bottom.

Latifa recoiled in outrage then spit on Narmer's face. Without warning, he brought the back of his hand against her cheek in a sharp blow that caused her delicate flesh to sting. Latifa touched her sore cheek and venomously glowered at him.

"Our time together should be very fruitful for I shall enjoy subduing you," Narmer hissed as he wiped her spittle from his face. He pulled off the robe he wore then shoved it as well as several strips of her kaftan that were not stained with blood into her hand. "Put on the robe and bind your wounds. We have a long ride ahead of us," he barked.

Latifa quickly pulled the robe over her body then hastily wrapped the shreds of cloth that had once been her kaftan over her wounds. When she looked up, she saw Jabari had climbed on his horse and was guiding the steed away.

"Anubis!" Latifa called to the dog when the canine began to follow Jabari.

Anubis scampered back to her.

Darkness quickly swallowed Jabari's retreating form causing all hope to flee from Latifa. With all hope gone, she did not protest when Narmer grabbed her arm and dragged her to his awaiting horse. When he lifted her onto his steed, she still did not protest for she was wounded and therefore vulnerable. In such a state, she knew it was useless to fight.

C;

It was around midday when Narmer and Latifa arrived in what looked to Latifa to be a garrison town. Narmer guided his horse to the river's edge and dismounted. After Narmer lifted Latifa to the ground, she gazed at a fort on an island across the Nile and inspected the smooth elephant-shaped boulders that surrounded the large land mass. A familiar bark drew Latifa's eyes from her inspection. She let out a sigh of relief when she realized Anubis had managed to follow them to the town. When the hound ran to her, she pet the canine.

"Peace be unto you," came the greeting from a soldier who approached the new arrivals.

"And you," Narmer responded.

"It appears you have been traveling a great distance. Where are you headed?" the soldier questioned looking inquisitively at Latifa.

Narmer nodded to the island across the river. "It is I, the Grand Chancellor of Egypt. I am headed to the barracks on *Yebu*...Elephantine Island. Send a physician there at once," he ordered before handing the soldier the reins of his horse.

"As you wish, my lord," the soldier replied then led Narmer's horse away.

Narmer grasped Latifa's arm.

"Don't touch me!" she hissed and took a wobbly step away from him then cried out when pain shot through her leg.

Ignoring her protest, Narmer lifted her into his arms. "I don't have all day to listen to you yowl," he remarked icily.

Latifa tightened her hand into a fist and repeatedly punched his chest.

He yanked on her braids causing her head to jerk back and her neck to stretch painfully. "Hit me again and it shall be the last thing you do," he snarled.

Latifa dropped her hands but scowled at her new captor.

"Be sure, I shall wipe the scorn from your comely little face soon enough," Narmer assured. After he removed his hands from her hair, he carried her toward the spot where men who appeared to be slaves loaded burdens on several boats preparing to set sail.

"What are you going to do with me?" Latifa asked desperate to find an answer to her fate.

"I am going to have your wound tended to. After which, I shall have my fill of you. Once I'm done with you, I shall sell you to the men working in the stone quarry so that they can have their fill of you too."

"How could you do such a thing to me?" Latifa demanded.

"You've caught Tariq's eye. That is enough for me. For you see, he's taken everything from me. It is my turn to take from him."

"He's your brother! How could you think about hurting him?"

"Even if I wished to reveal to you the reasons, you couldn't possibly understand. You are but a Nubian. An enemy of Egypt. And you're a woman, which means it's useless to tell you anything important."

Latifa frowned and fell silent.

Once Narmer made it to the bank of the river, he seemed to notice Anubis was still following them. With a surly grunt, he kicked sand at the dog in an effort to discourage the hound from continuing to track them then he strutted to the line of *feluccas*. After boarding a *felucca*, he deposited Latifa on a wooden seat then sat beside her. He bit out an order to the man at the steerage and a few seconds later the boat began to move away from the shore. The vessel glided easily over the water to stop beside the island. Once they made it to the island, Narmer picked Latifa up and exited the boat. As he trekked up the stone steps leading to the fort, Latifa noticed markings on the wall next to the steps.

"Take me to the Lieutenant's quarters," Narmer huffed to a soldier who stood at the top of the steps.

The soldier nodded in recognition of Narmer then he led him through the portal of a massive wall. Several soldiers greeted Narmer when he stepped through the gated entrance. As Narmer returned the greeting, Latifa surveyed the surroundings and realized they were at a military station. The small group headed to what looked to be barracks. After entering the building, the escort led the pair to a room at the base of a flight of stairs. The soldier opened the door then waited for Narmer to step inside before he turned and walked away.

"This is Jabari's room when he's here on The Island. I know he won't mind if we use it for a while," Narmer said before he dropped Latifa on the bed which was in the corner of the room. Latifa scooted toward the middle of the bed and groaned due to the pain that shot through her leg.

"When Jabari's and your deceit is made known to Tariq, he shall make you both pay," she insisted.

"How shall he find out? Shall you tell him?" Narmer snorted.

"Go get the physician," Latifa retorted.

Narmer leered at her for a moment then he exited the room without another word.

Once he was gone, Latifa strained to peer out of an open door on the opposite side of the room and saw it led to a terrace. Unable to see much, she stretched out over the bed and frowned as she ruminated on the sorry shape she was in.

Latifa opened her eyes slowly. She realized she had fallen asleep when she saw a homely looking man standing over her. She sat up.

"I am the physician. I must inspect your wound," the man said gently then began to unwrap the material on her leg.

Latifa clutched the doctor's arm. "You have got to help me. Narmer is a wicked man. He—"

"Enough talk," the doctor cut off her words. "I do not want to hear anymore."

"But it's true."

The doctor shook his head. "I have known Narmer since he was a young man. He is cunning and has guile. But, nothing can be done. Because of his station in life, he has the right to do whatever he wants. There is no use speaking against him."

Latifa shook her head. "You don't understand. He is holding me against my will and—"

"Enough!" the doctor's tone hardened then instantly softened. "I am but a healer. I can do naught about what Narmer or any of his ilk chooses to do. There now." The doctor patted her hand. "Everything shall resolve to your benefit. You shall be fine," he assured after he inspected her injuries.

Falling silent, he pulled out several items from a leather pouch then cleaned her wound and put salve on her lacerations.

"Where am I? What city is that across the water?" Latifa asked when he began to wrap a fresh bandage around her leg.

"You are on Elephantine Island. The city is Swenet better known as Aswan."

After he bandaged her ankle, the doctor handed her a phial. "It's henbane and mandrake. You'll want to take it to ease your pain." He stood to his feet. "You shall be as new in a short time."

"Don't leave!" Latifa called out when the doctor began to collect his things.

The doctor stopped and looked at her.

"I don't want to be alone with Narmer. Please. If you won't hear my plea, at least do this... Tell Narmer I am too ill to share a room with him. Please. I couldn't bear it if..."

The doctor rubbed his chin. "I understand your meaning. You are right of course. No woman should be forced to endure the attentions of a man she does not desire. It shall be as you wish," the doctor acceded. "I shall tell Narmer you are to see no one until you are completely healed."

"Thank you," Latifa whispered and watched the doctor repack the leather pouch he brought with him.

The doctor walked to the door then turned to look at her. "I shall see that food is brought to you so you can eat. I shall also ask that fresh clothes and water be brought to you so you can refresh yourself after your long journey. Peace be unto you," he said before exiting the room.

After the doctor left, as promised, food arrived along with a *jellabiya* and a jug of water. Latifa managed to wash herself. After which, she slipped into the *jellabiya*. Once she was dressed, she ate the lentil soup and walnuts that had been sent to her then relaxed on the bed. As she lay on the bed, she thought about Tariq and wondered what he was doing that very moment. By now, Jabari had told him she was dead. She wondered if he would find he missed her. She was finding she missed him.

Latifa closed her eyes to block thoughts of Tariq. She could not think of him. Her sister would think she was dead too. Poor Tanesha would have no one. Tariq must have released the captives by now which meant her sister was on her way back to Nubia. After her wounds healed, Latifa told herself, she had to find a way to return to Nubia and see her sister. There was no way she would let things turn out as Narmer planned. God would not let Narmer defile her then allow her life be wasted in a stone quarry. Would He? Latifa bowed her head, closed her eyes and prayed she would be spared the fate Narmer intended for her.

Her prayers were interrupted by a sound at the open door that led to the terrace. Latifa opened her eyes and saw Anubis step over the threshold.

"Anubis!" she cried out happily.

The dog scampered to her and began to lick her face. Latifa lay her head against Anubis' neck and her thoughts instantly returned to Tariq. Her feelings for him were so complicated. His unexpected kindness toward her had somehow softened her heart toward him. But, exactly what she felt, she could not put into words. Spending time with him had not been as bad as she first thought it would be, and now that she was separated from him she found she missed a lot of things about him. For instance, she missed the feeling of safety she felt when he was near. She missed the sound of his voice. She missed the feel of his hands on her skin...the touch of his lips against her lips. Such feelings were unexpected and she was not sure it was right to feel as she did. All she knew for sure was that she wanted to see him again...and that was the truth.

�Cঙ

Latifa was not sure what the doctor told Narmer but he did not return to the room. Instead, the next few days crept by for Latifa. Anubis stayed by her side and thoughts of Tariq helped to pass the time. The pain in her ankle began to subside considerably and her wounds started to heal. So, she began to plot an escape.

As she sat in bed one night contemplating ways to get off the island, the bedroom door swung open.

"What are you doing in this room?" Latifa demanded after Narmer staggered into the room.

"You don't loo...look sick to me. You...you look just fine." His words were slurred as he gazed intently at her.

"The physician said I'm to have no visitors. Leave me alone."

"That fool medicine man. I'm... I am beginning to think he misled me as to the seriousness of your condition."

"I am not well," Latifa insisted unnerved by Narmer's perusal.

"You look well enough to avail me of your delights," he smirked.

Upon seeing Narmer advance toward the bed, Latifa swung one leg over the side of the bed and sprang upward. Not prepared for all of her body weight to be placed on her still healing ankle, her knee buckled under her.

Acting quick, Narmer caught her in his arms. His hot breath scratched her cheek and the smell of stale wine assaulted her nose when he lowered his face toward hers.

She turned her face from him. "You're drunk with wine," she accused.

"Let me gaze upon your face, Nubian. Let me behold what draws my brother to you." Narmer's fingers locked in her braids and he turned her head so that she was forced to look at him. "I am the one who should have you. He...he should have nothing. Everything he has by right belongs to me. He took away my birthright. He took away every dream I've ever had. Now, I shall have my revenge."

"Tariq does not care for me. Not like you think."

"That is not what Jabari says."

"Jabari is mistaken. He does not know how it really is between me and Tariq. I am sure Tariq has forgotten all about me."

"From what I saw reflected on the wall of his tent, I know he has not," Narmer assured and leaned in to kiss her.

Latifa slapped his face.

A snarl rumbled from Narmer's lips and his grip tightened on her braids. "I shall take what Tariq desires and place my mark on it. I shall have you whether you like it or not." He pressed his lips against hers.

With a loud grunt, Latifa lifted her leg and kneed Narmer between his legs. He howled and shoved her from him sending her hurling backward to land in a sprawl across the bed.

An instant later, Narmer lunged forward and sank on top of her. In the next moment, his lips touched her neck.

"Leave me alone!" Latifa screeched as she desperately tried to push him away.

Narmer's response was to pin her arms against the bed. A low menacing growl sounded causing Narmer to pause and look around for the source of the sound. A grimace crept over his face when his gaze fell upon Anubis standing beside the bed.

"Damn dog!" Narmer muttered. Turning his attention back to Latifa, he hissed, "I shall have restitution for the losses I have endured." He lowered his lips to her neck once again.

She let out a scream.

Instantly, Anubis lunged at Narmer and nipped his heel which hung over the side of the bed. A surprised yelp left Narmer's lips. He sprang to a sitting position then tumbled off of the bed and onto the floor. From his place on the floor, he reached out to strike Anubis. Anubis scooted backward to avoid being smacked.

Narmer scowled at the dog who growled. With much effort, he rose to his feet.

Anubis began to bark incessantly.

"That damn dog can't protect you forever," he seethed then stumbled to the door.

Latifa let out a sigh of relief after Narmer slammed the door behind him when he made his exit. Anubis jumped on the bed. Latifa smiled happily when the dog settled next to her. Uncontrollably, her smile faded into a frown and tears smarted her eyes. Narmer had been scared off that night. But, surely she had made him angry and left him feeling humiliated. How much longer could she remain safe from him? Was she really destined to be used by Narmer then thrown away like she was trash? Uncertainty and fear crept within her. Despondently, Latifa buried her face in the blanket covering the bed and she began to cry.

CS

When she woke the next morning, Latifa decided to scout out the barracks for a way off of the island. Finding she could put more pressure on her healing ankle, she shuffled out of the room. She walked down the hallway and retraced the steps Narmer had taken when he carried her to the room the day they arrived on the island. As she sidled down the hallway, the sound of two men talking met her ears. She stopped to listen to what they were saying.

"Tariq and his men have entered Aswan," one of the men said.

Latifa's heartbeat quickened.

"He cannot find me or the girl here. I have ordered a boat be made ready for a quick departure. I shall gather the girl and we shall leave within the hour," she heard Narmer reply.

Tariq was in Aswan and Narmer was determined to keep her from him! She had to get off the island and find Tariq before Narmer took her away! If she left the island with Narmer, she might never see Tariq again. Based on what Narmer said a boat was waiting for them. Maybe she could get to the boat and convince the person in charge of the boat to ferry her to the other side of the river.

The sound of footsteps heading in her direction caused Latifa to bolt back to the bedroom. She looked the way she had come. Any second, Narmer would walk into the room. She had to make her escape and she had to do it now. Spinning on her heels, Latifa hastened to the terrace then she made her way from the terrace and around the side of the building. Walking briskly with the hope she did not draw too much attention to herself, she headed toward the gate Narmer had passed through when he brought her to the island.

As she neared the gate, she slowed her pace and looked around for Anubis. She wanted to take the dog with her. However, the hound was nowhere in sight.

"Anubis!" she called out. As she looked around for the hound, she saw her call had caught the attention of a soldier standing nearby.

Lowering her head, she scurried through the portal of the gate then along the wall that led down the steps. At the water's edge, Latifa realized her next task was figuring out which boat to board. She scanned the line of boats and saw a man and a boy busily moving about on a *felucca* docked nearby. Praying she guessed right, she walked to the *felucca* and stepped on the waiting sea craft. The man and boy looked at her.

Recalling Narmer speak his title to the soldier when they arrived in Aswan, Latifa hoped her voice did not sound shaky when she asked, "The Grand Chancellor, Narmer, asked you to prepare to sail, did he not?"

The man nodded.

"He has been detained but has sent me ahead. You are to proceed without him."

"Proceed without him?" the man questioned.

"He does not want the trip postponed. He wants you to set sail with me. He said he'd be along at a later time." Latifa finished speaking and took a seat.

She tapped her foot anxiously as the man and boy returned to their preparation. She looked around one final time in hopes of seeing Anubis but did not see the dog. Latifa breathe a sigh of relief when the man shouted to the boy, "Set sail!"

A few moments later, the boat began to move away from the bank. The wind carried the craft on the water and away from Elephantine Island. Latifa cast one last look at the island to see if she saw Narmer. She did not. The vessel glided past other *feluccas* toward Aswan. Latifa buried her face in her hands and slowly inhaled in hopes of steadying her heartbeat. When she lowered her hands and looked about, she realized the boat was no longer headed toward Aswan but was sailing along the watery corridor.

"I need to get to Aswan!" Latifa announced.

"The Grand Chancellor gave specific instructions on where we are to sail," came the reply.

Latifa fell silent and contemplated her predicament. How could she get the boat redirected to Aswan without raising suspicion? With each passing moment, the boat moved further and further from where she wanted to go.

Where was she headed? How was she going to get to Tariq? As she pondered her plight, she looked over the side of the boat at the teal water lapping against the hull. After a while, the water began to swirl causing the boat to lurch to one side. Latifa noticed the surface of the turbulent water took on a white color. She watched it cascade over a boulder partially submerged in the water.

"We have arrived at a place in the river called The First Cataract," the captain of the boat explained as he directed the boat through the forceful current.

"What causes the water to do that?" Latifa asked as she watched the continuously swirling water.

"Small islets. There are numerous boulders and stones that protrude from the bottom of the riverbed to break the water's surface. We are between a run and a cascade which means we're entering a rapid. This part of the river has a relatively steep gradient so hold on," the sailor explained.

Latifa held on to the side of the boat as it began to heave to one side then the other. When the craft came precariously close to the boulder, water splashed against the rock and into the boat spraying Latifa with a mist of moisture. She closed her eyes against the onslaught. When the midst subsided, she opened them to see a pair of black eyes peering at her from the water. A shriek spewed from her throat and she leapt to her feet.

"What is it?" the man asked.

Too frightened to speak, Latifa pointed over the side of the boat. Suddenly, there was a bump against the boat which caused Latifa to stumble a bit. However, she managed to stay on her feet.

"Something hit the boat. Check starboard side to see what it is," the man instructed the boy.

The young boy looked over the side of the boat.

"It's a hippopotamus!" Latifa yelled informatively.

A second later, the boat was rammed again. A panicked scream wrenched from Latifa's throat the moment she felt her feet leave the bottom of the boat. She sensed she was soaring through the air. In the next instant, frothy cold drenched her causing her to realize she had been knocked into the river and was now buried in a murky cavern of water. Instinctively, she propelled herself upward until she broke the surface then she gulped for air. Water stung her nose and lungs. Frenzied shouts distracted her from the pain and alerted her to the danger of what was no doubt the nearby hippopotamus. Summoning her will to squelch her fear, she worked to clear her mind. Somehow, she found enough lucidness to look around for the river's bank. Locking it in her sight, she focused on the land and swung her arms and kicked her legs about in an effort to swim to dry land.

Despite her efforts, she felt herself slipping under the water. She kicked her feet franticly and felt herself rise but only for a moment. The water seemed like weights around her legs pulling her downward. Persistently, like a malignant growth, the water inched up her neck and over her chin. She splashed about. Water rose to cover her mouth and nose. She inhaled and held her breath as the water kept rising then entombed her. She tried to push herself upward and break the waters' surface again but to no avail.

Her lungs screamed for air. She could not hold her breath much longer. Desperately, she lifted her arms upward and frenziedly flayed them about. Just when she thought she could not hold her breath any longer, she felt fingers curl around her arms. In the next moment, she sensed she was being yanked upward. Higher and higher she was lifted beyond the watery pit. She could breathe again. She felt herself being lowered. Abruptly, the solidness of the boat's deck materialized beneath her feet. Latifa let out a hysterical cry of relief. Unable to find the strength to speak, she collapsed on the deck of the boat.

Chapter Eight

Tariq walked from his room and onto the terrace to look at the city of Aswan across the river. Idly, he stuck his hand in the pocket of his *schenti*. Something cold touched his fingertips. He curled his finger around the object and extracted his hand from his pocket. He lifted his hand to view the item and saw it was Latifa's necklace. Fresh sorrow washed over him as he stared at the golden cobra that hung from a golden chain. He had forgotten he put the necklace in his pocket. Now that he found it and Latifa was gone, a profound sorrow engulfed him.

He had not expected to feel distress ensnare him at the news of Latifa's disappearance. Nor had he expected the sorrow that consumed him when he had been presented with evidence of her death. When she was with him, he had been sure bedding her was all he wanted. Now that she was gone, he found he missed a lot of things about her such as her display of bravado, her courage and her feisty attitude. He even missed the interesting talks they had together. Though their time together had been brief it had been unexpectedly meaningful. If he could have one more moment with Latifa...to see her...to touch her...

He remembered Jabari entering his tent and presenting him with Latifa's bloodied kaftan. He recalled holding the shredded garment in disbelief. Why had she wandered into the night alone and unescorted? Didn't she know of the dangers that lurked on the African plain? Of course she did. He had warned her of the danger. Tariq shook his head. None of it made sense. He had expected to wake and find Latifa lying beside him. He had planned on spending the night planted between her thighs. But, instead, he was brought to his knees by the sudden and unexpected pain that stabbed his heart at the news of her death.

"You have troubled thoughts," Jabari's voice interrupted Tariq's reminiscence.

Tariq slipped the necklace back into his pocket. "My thoughts are troubled indeed."

"You must stop thinking of the girl. You only knew her for a short while. What is there to mourn?"

Tariq inhaled deeply. "I never met anyone like her, Jabari. She was feisty and irreverent. She was courageous…full of fire and life. There is no other like her. Being with her was…refreshing. That is why I mourn."

"You have no time for a woman especially that wildcat. Wipe her memory from your mind. You must show the soldiers you are strong and still in command. Once we return to Thebes, as Pharaoh you shall have much that demands your attention. You must not let our people down."

"I assure you, I shall not neglect my duty to the men who fall under my command nor shall I fail my obligation to those I rule as Pharaoh," Tariq assured.

"After our arrival in Aswan today and our return to the barracks here on Elephantine Island, I find I am famished. I am going to the hall for the noon meal. Would you like to join me?" Jabari asked.

Before Tariq could give an answer, shouts erupted expelling peace from the air. Tariq and Jabari walked to the edge of the terrace and saw a crew of men rushing toward the barracks.

"What is all of the commotion about?" Jabari inquired of a servant who was scurrying by.

"Lieutenant," the servant bowed quickly. "There was a boating accident. They are bringing the victim in now."

Both men watched the advancing pack and saw they carried a female. As the group neared, Tariq blinked unbelievingly when the female's face crystallized and he realized he was looking at Latifa.

"Halt!" he belted out.

The men came to a sluggish stop.

Tariq hastened to the group. "Latifa!" he called out in amazement and touched her cheek.

Upon feeling his touch, Latifa lifted her eyes and looked at him.

Gingerly, Tariq reached out his arms and collected Latifa's soaked body from the men who carried her.

She let out a sigh and buried her face in his chest.

"Someone bring dry clothes for her to my room! The rest of you leave us!" Tariq bellowed when the men started to follow him into the barracks.

Hurriedly, Tariq strode to his room and laid Latifa on his bed.

"Latifa," he murmured and gazed down at her.

"Oh Tariq," she responded in a shaky voice.

"You are alive!" he whispered as he brushed her braids from her face.

"Yes. Yes," Latifa assured.

"You left the camp. I thought you were dead," he explained before he captured her face between his hands.

"I was almost killed when I left the camp. I was attacked by jackals." Latifa lifted the material of the soaked *jellabiya* she wore and gingerly patted the bandage on her leg.

"Oh my god! I can't believe I'm looking at you! I was told you had been attacked and killed."

Jabari cleared his throat before he entered the room holding a fresh *jellabiya* and a new bandage for Latifa's leg. He quickly handed Tariq the items, cast an apprehensive look at Latifa then exited the room closing the door behind him.

Cold and frazzled, Latifa pulled the soaked material from her body and Tariq helped her slip into the dry *jellabiya*.

"What happened that night? Tell me, why did you run away from camp?" Tariq asked when he began to change her bandage.

"I ran away because I could not face what was happening between us. I wanted to be alone. I wasn't thinking clearly. The next thing I knew, I was surrounded by a pack of jackals. Anubis saved me. She is a good guard dog."

"How did you get here on The Island?"

"Narmer brought me here," Latifa blurted out then frowned. She wondered if she should tell Tariq the truth about all Narmer had done. She knew the brothers were at odds with each other. Telling Tariq about Narmer's deception would only cause the feud between the two to ascend to a new level of violence and enmity. On the other

106

hand, Tariq had a right to know what lengths his half brother would go to hurt him. But, did she want to be the cause of a permanent split between the two brothers?

"Where is Narmer?" he questioned.

"I am not sure." Latifa fell silent as she thought about what her next words would be. If she told Tariq about Narmer's actions, she would have to tell him about Jabari's participation also. She knew Tariq trusted and depended upon Jabari. Did she really want to be the one to disappoint him with the truth? She told herself she needed more time to decide if she would expose Narmer's unscrupulous deviousness and reveal Jabari's conspiratorial role in the horrid plot against her.

"Please don't ask me to recount details of that night for I am too exhausted to speak of it now. Just hold me," she whispered and rested her head against his chest.

When Latifa relaxed against him, Tariq wrapped his arms around her. Unexpectedly, an overwhelming feeling of care engulfed him. Unnerved by the power of the unexpected emotion, he thought about extracting his arms from around Latifa but decided against it. Instead, he held her close because he realized he wanted to savor the way it felt to have her in his arms.

ᚣ

"Just as you requested, preparation to leave The Island is underway. Are you sure you feel well enough to travel?" Tariq asked Latifa as they ate a late meal that evening.

Latifa nodded her head. "I am anxious to get out of this place."

"Dusk is upon us. It's customary that sailing ends by nightfall. Are you sure we can't wait until tomorrow to leave?"

"I want to get out of this place today. Please. I cannot stay here another night."

"Anything for you, my little lioness," Tariq soothed.

As mauve and coral colored light from the setting sun shrouded the sky, Latifa followed Tariq onto a spacious *felucca*. Once she was seated on the deck of the boat which was shaded by a small canopy, Tariq nodded to the man at the steerage. The man shouted an order to a second man and the second man adjusted the sails.

The wind caught in the sails and the boat began to drift along the river. Latifa looked at the activity happening on the other side of the waterway. As the vessel floated smoothly over the water, she watched the city grow smaller and smaller until it receded along the horizon.

"Where are we headed?" Latifa asked casting her gaze upon Tariq.

"Thebes."

"I heard Thebes is where your Pharaoh resides. What is he like?"

Tariq smiled. "He is wise, handsome, strong and all of the women in his kingdom swoon at the sight of him."

"I think he's an unscrupulous deceitful snake and one day I shall make him pay for all of the devastation he's caused in my life."

Tariq's smile faded into a frown at her words.

Noting this, Latifa fell silent and looked out over the river. As the light from the sinking sun slowly began to fade, she pointed to a boat following a discrete distance behind them and said, "That boat has been following us since we left The Island. There are guards on that boat."

Abruptly, Tariq snapped his fingers and the man who was not sailing their boat unhooked the sailcloth that hung from the canopy. The man then stretched the material across a thin rope garnering privacy to Tariq and Latifa. Tariq moved to recline on soft rugs strewn over the wooden boards that comprised the deck of the sailboat. He beckoned Latifa to recline next to him. Latifa looked over the river at the boat that held the two soldiers. It seemed to be receding in the distance. She moved to sit next to Tariq. He looked at her for a moment then slid his arm around her. Before he could pull her to him, Latifa placed her hands against him halting the embrace.

Tariq rose on his elbow, placed his hand on her stomach and looked up at her.

"I still can't believe you are real. I truly thought you were dead," his words broke the silence.

"I am very much alive," Latifa assured.

Tariq gingerly took Latifa's hand in his and placed a tender kiss on her fingers. He lowered her hand to her side then brushed the palm of his hand along her waist, over her hip and down her leg. His searching fingers guided the material of the *jellabiya* out of its path. Careful to avoid the bandage, his persistent fingers slid inside her thigh.

Unable to sit motionless as Tariq nudged her legs apart, Latifa ran her hands over his shaved head before she kissed his neck and moaned softly.

"Tell me what you want. Tell me you want to feel me inside of you," he whispered in response to her enticement.

Latifa cast a glance toward the sky to view the remnant of light from the setting sun. "There is still the issue of the wager," she noted.

Tariq's fingers trailed along Latifa's moist folds. "The wager that your maidenhead shall be mine before the next full moon." His finger slipped inside of her womanly treasure. "There's not a chance of me forgetting about that," he rasped then ardently coaxed warm wetness from her essence. "You are so beautiful. You are a vision. I can't believe I possess such desire for you. There is fire between us that only coupling can tame. Ask me to make love to you and it shall be done," he urged and pressed the hardness of his manhood against the side of her leg.

After being kept from Tariq by Narmer and thinking she might never see him again, Latifa found she could not protest. Did not want to protest as she had before. In that moment in time, she wanted to forget the wager and not think about what she would lose by doing so. For a moment, she thought about the fact the two sailors on the other side of the sailcloth could no doubt hear all that transpired between her and Tariq. However, she quickly decided she did not care. "Make love to me," she whispered then reached out and caressed the bulge beneath his *schenti* luring a groan from him.

Tariq straddled her and gently guided her backward so that she lay underneath him. "You shall be mine," he rasped before he hoisted the *jellabiya* around her waist.

She watched him reach his hand under his *schenti* and take hold of his hardened member. After prodding her knees apart, he stretched his body over hers and immersed himself between her legs. She felt his hot flesh at the door of her womanly place. In the next instant, Latifa felt herself expanding to receive his thick shaft. She gasped and frenziedly called out his name in response to the feel of the mass intruding within her tight walls.

He kissed her shoulder then his lips burned a trail of fire from the base of her neck to its top distracting her from the pressure between her legs. Heedlessly, he shoved deeper into her. His mouth covered hers catching the screech that left her lips. He pulled his hips back a bit then drove into her again so that she accepted him to the hilt. Latifa wiggled beneath him in an effort to dislodge his mass and escape the pain that seized her. Unwittingly, her movements fanned Tariq's lust unleashing an inferno of denied desire. He began to drive his hips back and forth and his fingers slithered under the *jellabiya* to claw savagely at her breasts.

"Tariq, what are you doing?" Latifa queried bewildered by the sudden ferociousness of his touch and the nip of pleasure that jabbed her.

His response was to place both his hands on her waist and guide her hips so that her hot warmth moved against his throbbing member to create a friction masterfully designed to coax a sublime surrender from her young body as well as his. Back and forth he guided her hips. Faster and faster. He set a feverish pace. Over and over again, her tight sheath was moved along his pulsating manhood until suddenly a mountain of molten nectar erupted in Latifa sending shards of pleasure catapulting through her entire body and ripping a scream of elation from her lips. Tariq continued to move his hips so that he joined her in creating a masterpiece of delirious ecstasy. As sound faded on her lips, he collapsed on top of her. Both worked to gain control of their pounding hearts. When their breathing slowed, Tariq rolled to lay beside her.

"I did not hurt you, did I? I should have been gentler. I lost control of myself which is something I haven't done since I was a boy," he admitted.

To overwhelmed to speak, Latifa reached out and touched his leg. She looked up at the sky and noticed a full moon now glowed across the darkened heavens.

Noticing her gaze, Tariq looked up at the sky then began to laugh.

"It's a full moon and we both know what that means!" he exclaimed.

"It means I am entitled to my freedom."

"How did you come to that conclusion?" Tariq queried.

"The terms of the wager were you would win if we made love *before* the light of the full moon showed itself."

"And that is what happened so I believe I am the victor."

"While our lips may have met in a kiss as the sun's light graced the sky, I contend it was *after* the light of the full moon showed itself that we consummated things between us. Can you deny it?"

Tariq shook his head. "I was too distracted to notice," he admitted.

"I know it was *after* the full moon showed that we joined as one. So, it is I who has won the wager."

Tariq smiled. "You are a formidable opponent, little lioness. You would make a worthy warrior if you weren't so damn enticing. If I acquiesce to your way of thinking, it would mean you could have your freedom. However, there is one thing you should know."

"What's that?"

"I don't want you to go, dear foe," Tariq whispered and kissed her once again.

CB

It was late when Tariq and Latifa arrived in Thebes. Latifa wondered at the caravan of chariots that awaited them when they exited the *felucca*. Tariq took her hand and helped her into one of the chariots before he climbed in to stand beside her. He then flicked the reins causing the

111

horse to gallop forward. Chariots filled with soldiers fell into position around Tariq's chariot and kept pace with it. As the horses trotted away from the river, rows of wheat along the bank gave way to shops which soon gave way to modest lodgings. Eventually, the worn homes gave way to white washed villas with flat roofs some of which were occupied by sleeping men, women and children intent on catching the night breeze.

When Tariq turned the horse down a wide street lined with date trees, Latifa saw a huge stone palace come into view. Though they were some distance away, enormous columns spaced at intervals around the palace and colossal stone statues guarding the entrance to the palace could be seen. As the chariot drew closer, the grand dwelling seemed to grow in size. Latifa found she could not take her eyes away from the magnificent structure.

Tariq looked at her and chuckled, "I can see you are impressed."

Too awed by what she saw, Latifa was unable to form words of response.

When the procession neared the wall surrounding the palace, two soldiers standing guard at the front gate opened the gate allowing the chariot to enter the palace grounds. The caravan of chariots dispersed at the gate while Tariq's horse sprinted up a pathway. He bought the steed to a smooth stop in front of grand stone steps that led to the stupendous abode.

"Is this your home?" Latifa found her voice.

Tariq nodded.

Latifa's mouth fell open. Tariq's home looked like a palace fit for a king. Surely, he was a great Commander if he pleased the Pharaoh enough to have a home like this.

Tariq jumped to the ground and motioned for Latifa to step down from the chariot. When she did, he said, "Come with me!" before taking her hand and leading her up the steps.

Once the pair made it to the top of the steps, he led her pass a pair of guards and through the massive doors at the entrance of the palace. Tariq paused a moment to let Latifa gaze at the columns, high ceiling etched in gold and the

112

marble floor that made up the foyer. Nudging her arm, he led her down a dark hall lined with nooks dressed with alabaster statues. When the couple came upon a large moonlit room, Latifa stopped to stare at the contents within the space. The room contained richly carved wooden tables paired with chairs that had legs made of gold. A colorful *frescoe* which depicted a king sitting on a throne surrounded by kneeling subjects covered one wall.

"This room is called The Great Room," Tariq remarked before he tugged her hand and steered her to a flight of stairs.

The pair walked up the steps which gave way to a second level where a *bas-relief* of Tariq's face was exhibited in a nook. Following Tariq, Latifa passed several closed doors to a door at the end of the hall. Tariq opened the door and she followed him into a spacious bedroom. Once again, she stopped in mid stride to stare at the opulent sight before her. The bedroom was larger than any she had ever seen. An oil lamp cast a soft glow over a large bed that had an ornately carved wooden frame and tall posts inlaid with ebony and ivory at each corner. An expansive chest lined the wall to the left of the bed. Across the room, a lion's pelt hung on a wall. In front of the pelt stood a three legged table paired with golden fringed chairs with plaited cord seats. Latifa noticed the legs of the chairs and table were finely carved to resemble a lion's paw. A washroom could be seen through an open door and on the far wall there was a door that led to a balcony.

"I have never seen anything this beautiful before," Latifa admitted as she slowly ambled to the center of the room.

"They don't have anything like this in Nubia?" Tariq questioned.

Latifa shook her head negatively.

"The servants did not greet us because I did not send advance word to the palace that I was returning tonight. However, I can summon them if you would like something to eat or if you would like to bathe," he explained.

"No. That shall not be necessary. Let them remain in their beds. I am too tired to eat or bathe. I just want to rest."

"As you wish," Tariq replied then he walked to the large chest and pulled out a woman's robe and a sheer nightdress.

"Tomorrow we shall find clothes your size. Until then, this shall have to do."

Latifa looked at the garments he held up and wondered curiously what woman the clothing belonged to. Too exhausted to discuss the issue, she did not reveal her curiosity. Instead, she quickly put on the gown and climbed into the bed.

When the sun came up the next morning, Latifa was sure she had not slept a wink due to the myriad of emotions that had swirled in her during the night. She was ecstatic to be reunited with Tariq and she marveled at the fact they had finally mated. She recalled the first night she slept in the same bed with him. She had made such a fuss. Never would she have guessed she would willingly lay with him and desire to lay with him for many nights to come. Why had her feelings changed? Was it because he had been kind to her? Was it because she felt safe with him? Was it because she had been separated from him and thought she would never see him again?

It had been during the time she was separated from Tariq after Narmer took her to Elephantine Island that she realized what she felt for him changed. It was then she realized she missed him and wanted to see him again. Never could she have imagined she would care so much for Tariq that her mind would be rattled with questions about the female in his life. He said he spent most of his life on the field of battle but the fact he stored women's clothing in the chest beside his bed declared he was involved with a woman. She found she did not like the fact there was another woman in Tariq's life. Nor did she like the possibility she was one of many who had given themselves to him. Jealousy unexpectedly nipped at her heart at the thought that another woman had lain next to Tariq in the very bed she now lay in.

The sound of Tariq's soft breathing met Latifa's ears. Stealthily, she rolled on her side and looked at him asleep beside her. A feeling resembling affection stirred in her heart. Actually, it seemed to be a feeling deeper than mere affection. What exactly was the feeling that stirred in her?

Befuddled, she sat up and lifted her legs over the side of the bed, stood and walked to the balcony. The city of Thebes could be seen beyond the massive walls that surrounded the palace. She thought about her sister and her tribesmen. At this moment, they were somewhere in Nubia while she remained among the people responsible for the destruction of their homes.

"You look beautiful standing in the morning sun," Tariq's voice sounded behind her.

Latifa turned to look at him. He looked handsome as he reclined in the massive bed. Latifa walked back to the bed and sat on it.

"Did you find our time on the boat as entertaining as I did?" he asked after he placed his hand on her leg.

"I cannot believe we made love on that boat with those sailors so near."

"Things happened as they were meant to happen. Besides, I'm sure those sailors had as good a time listening to you moan with pleasure as I did."

Latifa squealed, swatted Tariq's hands from her leg and rose to her feet.

Tariq stood to his feet chuckling as he did so. Reaching out, he grabbed her waist and dragged her so that her back was against his chest before he placed a warm kiss on her neck.

"I find I want to hear you moan again. If you allow me your favors, I shall not act like a fledgling shepherd boy as I did before. This time, I shall seek to bring you pleasure. Is your longing as mine? Shall we delight ourselves in each other?" he asked.

Latifa relaxed against Tariq. She could feel the hardness of his manhood which had given her pleasure and pain. God help her. Despite the pain she felt before, she wanted to feel him inside of her again. She nodded in response to his question too amazed by her desire to speak a word.

Tariq quickly pulled the sheer nightdress from her body then reaching from behind her cupped her breasts in his hands. Adoringly, he worshipped each chocolate colored mound with his large hands. Tenderly, he moved his hands to her shoulders and turned her so that she faced the bed. He placed his hand on her back and gently nudged her so that she bent at the waist and her bottom was presented to him. A groan left Tariq's lips as the palm of his hand slid over her round bottom before he slipped his fingers into her womanly treasure. His fingers moved masterfully in her until they were coated with her wetness. When they both ached with desire, he extracted the digit from its prize, took hold of his arousal and gently pressed it against her satiny center. He sucked in a sharp breath in response to the pleasure that surged through his body. The following moment, unable to restrain himself, he drove his member in her and he kissed her back. Next, he placed his hands on her waist and began to guide her hips back and forth so that her warm womanhood slid along his aroused ridge. He began to thrust fervently in time to a phantom drumbeat.

Latifa recalled the lesson she learned the night before and began to move her hips on her own. Tariq groaned with delight as she rocked back and forth on him. He reached under her arms and fondled her jiggling breasts. For many moments, her movements captivated him...bewitched him...enraptured him...until a guttural groan wrenched from his throat and he relinquished his tithe into her. He held her hips still in deference to the completion of his surrender. When he loosened his hold, Latifa collapsed on the bed.

"Once again my will power is no match against your delectable body," Tariq acknowledged before he placed a kiss on her shoulder and collapsed on the bed next to her.

ೞ

Selma's sandal covered feet tap lightly against glazed marble as she hastened down the hallway that led to Tariq's bedroom. With an expectant smile, she pushed open the door and burst into the room. Her smile dimmed a bit at the sight of the empty bedroom. Disappointment was short lived when she heard the soft sound of rustling water coming from the other side of a half closed door. Like a panther stalking its prey, Selma advanced on Tariq's washroom and nudged the door open a bit.

Curls of hot white steam scratched her face and a burst of warm air tickled her skin when she stepped inside the bathing quarter. Selma peered through the cloud of steam and spotted Tariq sitting in a pool filled with water. His back was to her. A smile curled her lips once more as she noiselessly crept through the soft mist to the in-ground bathing pool. Kneeling above Tariq, she looked down at him. His eyes were closed. Her smile widened as she looked through the dusky water at his rugged frame and the placated pillar between his legs.

Spontaneously, she placed her hands over his eyes. She felt his body tense. In the next instant, she planted a playful kiss on his neck. With one hand, she untied the sash around her waist. Hastily, she slipped the silk cord over his eyes and tied it before he could turn to look at her. Selma chuckled when Tariq raised his hands to touch the silk. She tapped on his hands indicating he was not to remove the sash from his eyes. Understanding the instruction, he dropped his hands into the water. Hurriedly, she shed herself of her kaftan and slid into the water.

Tariq heard the water rustle and thinking Latifa had gotten into the pool with him, he asked, "Haven't had your fill of me, huh?"

The answer was a pair of hands on his chest. In the next instant, the hands slid around his neck and soft breasts pressed against his chest.

"I am elated to find you respond as you are," he murmured when he felt feminine legs ensnare him in a straddle.

In the next moment, a silken hand touched the placid ridge between his legs. "I need more time to renew my energies," he muttered.

In response to his words, a soft kiss was placed on his lips and the delicate scent of lilacs floated in the air eliciting a flicker of remembrance in Tariq's mind. Baffled by the needle of familiarity that muddled his brain, Tariq reached up and gingerly lifted the satiny barrier that covered his eyes.

"Selma!" he exclaimed when he saw her.

"I crept upon you as if I were an assassin," she giggled.

"What are you doing here?" he asked bewilderedly.

"I heard you arrived home. I knew you would call for me soon. So, I came to see you. How I've missed you, my love."

"Selma, this can't happen! You can't be here!"

"What do you mean?" Selma pouted playfully then rubbed her yearning treasure on his member beckoning an amiable reaction.

Tariq pushed away from her. "Things have changed. We need to talk."

"I did not intend to displease you. I am just so delighted you have returned home. I was sure you would not mind if I was playful with you. I guess I should have known you would be tired from your journey and in no mood for games. You must tell me, how did the meeting with King Rassom conclude?"

"Much has happened since I left the city. This is not the place to speak of it. We shall discuss the matter once we both have clothes on." With that said, Tariq stood to his feet then climbed out of the bathing pool. He picked up his robe as well as Selma's kaftan. Quickly, he wrapped himself in his robe then threw Selma's garment at her when she exited the water. "Put your clothes back on," he commanded sharply.

At that moment, on the other side of the door, Latifa entered Tariq's bedroom. She had eaten and seen the doctor who removed the bandage from her leg. After which, she had taken a brief tour of the palace. Ready to relax, she disrobed and sat on Tariq's bed. She thought about the many servants she had seen going about their chores as well as the beautiful garden she had spotted which she planned to explore very soon. Once again, she marveled at the fact the Pharaoh allowed Tariq to garner such wealth. If Tariq a military man was allowed to live in such luxury, she wondered at the Pharaoh's lavish life. She was sure, if she stayed with Tariq long enough she might see or even meet the Pharaoh. If she met the Pharaoh...

Her thoughts were interrupted by footsteps coming from the washroom.

"Tariq, my love, I want to hear what troubles you," a woman's voice purred.

In the next moment, a pretty woman with honey colored skin, thick black hair that hung about her shoulders and bangs that covered her forehead traipsed into the bedroom. When the maiden saw Latifa, she came to an abrupt stop and her black eyes glittered with surprise.

"Who are you?" the attractive female demanded, a befuddled expression on her face.

A second later, Tariq appeared behind the woman.

Latifa looked curiously at him.

The raven haired beauty shifted her gaze to Tariq. When the woman's eyes landed once again on Latifa, her lips quivered. "What are you doing in my nightdress?" she demanded. Then, without warning, she lunged at Latifa, shoved her onto the bed and pounced on her.

"What the hell!" Tariq gritted his teeth before wrapping his arms around the woman's waist and pulling her off of Latifa. "You're acting like a wild woman!" Tariq hissed as he set the female on the ground.

The woman pointed to Latifa who rose to a sitting position. "What the hell is this Nubian doing in your room?"

"She's my guest!"

"She's in my clothes!" the female fumed.

"You forget your place! I purchased that nightdress. It can be given to who I please!" came Tariq's quick reply.

"As the woman who shall one day be your wife, I am due an explanation!"

"I never consented to marriage," Tariq shot back.

With an irritated huff, the infuriated woman turned to Latifa. "Get out! Get the hell out of this room!"

Latifa stood to her feet.

"The only person leaving this room is you!" Tariq's statement to the angry female stopped Latifa's exit.

"You dare cast me aside for this whore?" the woman questioned belligerently.

119

"I'm not going to repeat my words," Tariq bit out.

The woman flicked her hair over her shoulder. "This isn't right! You can't toss me aside and think that shall be the end of it!"

"Do not tell me what I can and can't do!" Tariq instructed through clinched teeth.

The raven haired beauty inhaled sharply as she resentfully eyed Latifa. Abruptly, she pivoted on her feet, stomped to the door and slammed it shut after she made her exit.

Tariq turned to Latifa.

"Don't!" Latifa snapped when he stepped toward her. "Don't you dare come near me!"

Tariq stopped in his tracks.

"Who is she?"

"Her name is Selma. She has been my companion. She has proven to be a valuable political asset and—"

"I don't need to hear an explanation!" Latifa's voice cracked halting her words.

"You don't need an explanation? Fine. I won't explain. I shall just tell you this, I've spent most of my life leading the military. That was all I wanted. All I needed. Then things changed."

Latifa presented her back to Tariq.

His footsteps advance toward her a few moments before his hand touched her upper arm. She tried to move away from him but he tightened his hold on her.

"I have spent my life commanding people. Whatever order I give... Whatever command I give must be done. However, there is one thing I find I cannot command and that is that you desire me as I desire you."

There was silence between them as Latifa contemplated Tariq's words. She thought of how she felt when she was separated from him. Did she want her feelings of jealousy to add to the issues between them? Tariq had a life before he met her. It was obvious he was betroth to the woman named Selma. Even though that was true, she had no cause to be upset with him about it because she had been betroth to Kofi. Besides, she knew Tariq had not been thinking of Selma when he made love to her. She knew this because she had not been thinking of Kofi. Even if Kofi were still alive, she knew she could never think of him when she was in Tariq's arms. No. She had no room to be upset with Tariq...did not want to be upset with him.

Tariq removed his hand and started to turn from her.

Latifa spun to face him then wrapped her arms around his waist. "Let's not fight. God help me. I don't want to fight you anymore. I want to be with you. I don't know if I should want to be with you but I do," she admitted.

Tariq hugged her and placed a kiss on her forehead. Looking intently at her, he said, "Before whatever this is between us goes any further, there is something about me that you need to know. Once you know it, I hope you feel you still want to be with me."

"What do you mean?"

"The Pharaoh has returned to the city."

"The Pharaoh?"

Tariq nodded. "Today a parade is to be held on his behalf."

"I don't understand."

"When we were on the trail and when we were sailing to Thebes, you made your ill feelings for the Pharaoh known."

"I despised the man. But, what does that have to do with you? How shall I find out what it is about you I need to know?"

"Share my chariot during the parade and all shall be revealed," Tariq replied cryptically.

Chapter Nine

Excited voices and joyful shouts filled the air as Tariq's chariot rolled along the sand packed street. From her place in the chariot, Latifa looked at the horde of people that lined both sides of the street jockeying for a glimpse of the majestic procession. Tariq's chariot rolled near the market place and Latifa saw vendors their stands emptied of customers meld into the jubilant crowd.

"Our great Pharaoh has returned with his mighty Egyptian army! They have conquered the Nubians of Kush and have returned victorious!" a man exclaimed loudly from a rooftop.

"Amun-Ra be praised. The Pharaoh is back in Waset!" a female voice called out.

Tariq stretched out his hand in a commanding sweep. Instantly, vivacious cheers erupted from the multitude as dark blue irises with ruffled petals and crisp white lilies littered the air.

Elated voices called out, "Long live the Pharaoh!" and "The King brings peace to Egypt!"

Latifa clutched the top of the chariot then turned and looked behind her to see if she could glimpse the Pharaoh…the man who was the cause of so much of her grief. Instead, she saw rows of soldiers uniformed in coats of wadded leather wearing bronze helmets that gleamed in the sun.

"The Pharaoh!" someone shouted noting the Pharaoh was near.

Certain the Pharaoh was nearby, Latifa once again looked around for the Egyptian King. From her vantage point, she saw *Medjay* standing along the street performing their policing duties by pressing the excited multitude to maintain their distance from the procession.

"Tariq!" another voice called out.

Latifa scanned the crowd to see who had called Tariq's name. Unfortunately, with such a sea of faces, it was impossible to tell who had spoken. She turned her eyes upon Tariq. The sight of him took her breath away. He was no longer dressed in military attire. However, he still looked dominant and powerful dressed in a bronzed helmet and gold collared white pleated tunic that hung to his ankles. Masterfully, he held the reins of the horse in one hand and waved to the crowd with the other. Latifa shifted her gaze ahead of the chariot and saw the procession was approaching a massive wall. As the chariot neared the wall, two pylons seemed to grow out of it.

"Where are we headed?" she asked Tariq.

"We are approaching Karnak Temple. Some call it *Ipet-isut* which is The Most Sacred of Places. Today, invited guests are being allowed in the interior of the temple. For you see, a festival is being held there in the Pharaoh's honor."

"The temple is very grand," Latifa remarked as they neared the sprawling complex.

"Yes, it is grand. It has been added to over many years by Pharaohs eager to leave behind testaments of their rein."

As Tariq finished speaking, the formation of soldiers at the front of the procession came to a halt near a quay preceding the pylons and an avenue lined with statues. Tariq pulled sharply on the reins and his stallion came to a stop. He reached out and caught one of the lilies that was thrown at him. Slowly, he turned and placed the fragrant flower in Latifa's hair. At the jester, a feeling of serenity trickled through Latifa.

Once again, she reflected on the time she and Tariq spent together. At one point, she had denied the possibility that she could ever want him. Now, however, she could admit to herself that she did indeed have feelings of care for him. She wondered if he could possibly have the same sentiment for her or if her body was all he would ever desire. But what did it matter? Latifa told herself it was fruitless to examine her feelings for Tariq because it was not like she could ever love him. If by some miracle she could find love in her heart for him, Tariq once told her that a man in his position had no use for love...that love made a man weak. Not to mention, another woman was a part of his life. Since this was the case, it was not useful to wonder what feelings could develop between the two of them.

Instead, she should think about returning to Nubia before he tired of her and cast her aside as he had done Selma.

Latifa looked at Tariq. "This morning you said there was something about you I needed to know. What is it?" she asked anxious to be distracted from her thoughts and find out what it was Tariq wanted to reveal to her.

"Can you not see what is in front of you? Once you allow yourself to see it, all shall be revealed," Tariq replied mysteriously then waved to the people in the crowd who called his name.

The soldiers near the quay began to march again. This time, they filed down the avenue. Tariq flicked the reins and the horse pranced forward.

"Great Pharaoh! Great Pharaoh!" the mass of people chanted as they waved their hands in the air.

Latifa surveyed the crowd. Seeing the delight on the people's faces, she knew with absolute certainty the Pharaoh was near. Once again, she turned and looked behind the chariot expecting to see the Pharaoh and his men traipsing up the street. However, as before, all she saw were rows and rows of soldiers. She turned to again survey the crowd.

"You are the greatest!" she heard someone shout.

Latifa sought out the spectator and spotted a man standing on the street. She followed the man's gaze and realized the man was not looking down the street for the Pharaoh but he was looking at Tariq.

"Tariq the greatest!" someone else shouted.

"Ruler of the world!" another man exclaimed.

Latifa's brow wrinkled when she realized everyone who spoke was also looking at Tariq.

"They love you just as much as they love the Pharaoh," she commented on the joyous calls.

Tariq looked at her but remained silent as he brought the chariot to a halt near the avenue.

A man wearing a leopard print robe appeared and when Tariq stepped from the chariot the man bowed in deference to him.

"Greetings Great One. Karnak Temple is blessed with thine presence this glorious day. As High Priest I, Moswen,

124

am at your service," the man proclaimed after he straightened himself.

Latifa noticed a sardonic expression coat the man's face when Tariq turned to help her from the chariot. The man's expression became placid and he fell in step behind Tariq when Tariq began to walk down the avenue. Latifa followed the men along the path which was flanked by massive statues. She stopped to examine one of the statues and saw it was made of stone and was meticulously carved to reveal the body of a lion and the head of a ram.

"You are viewing a sphinx."

Latifa looked up and saw the holy man now stood beside her. She cleared her throat and hastened to catch up with Tariq who was nearing the pylons, one of which had a mud brick construction ramp in front of it and appeared to be under construction. Latifa followed Tariq inside the ostentatious complex. Ignoring a building with sloping walls on her left, she followed Tariq to a courtyard with towering columns.

As they passed between the huge columns, the priest appeared beside her and said, "We are passing through the Colonnades of Taharqa."

When the trio advanced upon two colossal statues near a second set of pylons, the priest looked at Latifa and pointed to the massive statues. "Those are of Ramesses the Second. Do you know much about Egyptian history and the gods we worship?"

Latifa shook her head. "I do not," she admitted.

The priest frowned but remained silent until they came upon an imposing building. Informatively, he said, "We have arrived at the magnificent Hypostyle Hall. This Hall was built by Seti the First and his son Ramesses the Second. You see the etchings on the exterior walls? They depict the Pharaoh's military campaigns in Palestine, Syria and also the Qadesh battle which was a fight against the Hittites." The Priest finished speaking in time to enter the building behind Tariq.

Following the men's lead, Latifa strolled into The Hall. Immediately, her senses were assailed by the sunlight that

125

streamed through the clerestoried windows. The glowing light illuminated a forest of lambent columns and gleamed on the alabaster stone that covered the floor. Gluttonously, she drank in the sights around her. When the trio finally exited The Hall, the silent parade came upon another set of pylons. Stepping near the pylons, a bright light stung Latifa's eyes. She squinted and leaned away from the light. Blinking slowly, she looked for the origins of the luminous shine. A quick inspection revealed the shiny light was caused by the sun's rays reflecting off a garden of four-sided *obelisks* varnished in gold and topped with pointed *pyramidions*.

A soft breeze brushed Latifa's cheek summoning the smell of burnt embers to her nose. Trailing the poignant aroma to rest in her ears was the spectral sound of an incantation chant. As she followed Tariq and the priest past the portal of a temple, she strained to glimpse those reciting the intonations and spied men with bowed heads and outstretched arms.

Pulling her eyes from the pious looking worshippers, she scurried to keep up with Tariq and the High Priest. Her mouth fell opened when a bed of glistening blue water came into view. A short distance from the water, stakes crowned with red and gold pennants fluttering in the wind lined steps leading to the top of a large platform. The expansive platform was shaded by a canvas and filled with men dressed in pleated robes with leather sandals on their feet along with Jabari who was dressed in military garb. Two guards stood at attention behind a golden throne.

At the sight of the throne, Latifa slowed her pace. Her heart began to thump in her chest. She was sure that throne was meant for the Pharaoh and they were headed straight for it. When she made it to the bottom of the platform, she came to a stop and watched Tariq stride to the top of the platform.

Jabari and the guards saluted Tariq while the men arrayed in fine garments bowed low. Tariq nodded his acknowledgment then turned from the men and motioned for Latifa to come to him. Latifa was not sure her feet would move. If she walked upon the platform, she would be stuck there when the Pharaoh arrived. She looked at Tariq. He was looking expectantly at her. She looked at the other men on the platform. All eyes were on her. She forced one foot in front of the other and ascended the steps. Once she was at the top of the platform, Tariq pointed to an empty seat next to the golden throne.

"Where is the Pharaoh?" she asked in a shaky voice.

Wearily, Tariq cocked his head to one side. "Can you really not see what is right in front of you? You are looking at the Pharaoh."

"What? Where?" she asked and quickly shifted her gaze to the men on the platform. Anxiously, she scanned each of the men's faces.

Suddenly, she realized all their gazes were trained on Tariq. Her mouth fell open and she turned to gawk at Tariq. "You are the Pharaoh of Egypt?"

Tariq nodded. "Yes! I am Pharaoh of Egypt!" he proclaimed.

◌ঽ

At Tariq's words, sound faded and Latifa's vision blurred. Her head began to pound. She could not breathe. Tariq was Pharaoh? It could not be! The Pharaoh killed her father. He was a brute who destroyed her life. She hated the Pharaoh for all of the destruction and pain he wrought. Was it indeed possible Tariq was that man? Latifa collapsed into the seat next to the throne as her mind raced to the day she met Tariq. She recalled a soldier calling him 'Sire'. She thought of how guards were ever present wherever he went. Soldiers had trailed him when they had taken a walk by the river, gone horseback riding and sailed from Aswan. At the time, she thought the extra security was because he was the Commander of the military. But, the truth was, it was also due to the fact he was the ruler of Egypt.

Slowly, sound returned. Her vision cleared. She was breathing again. She watched Tariq sit in the gold encrusted chair. Following Tariq's lead, the men on the platform including the High Priest who had made his way to the top of the platform took their seats behind Tariq's throne.

"You are Pharaoh? Why didn't you tell me? Why did you have me believe you were Commander of the Army?" she demanded of Tariq.

"I am Commander of the Army. But, I am also Pharaoh," he replied.

The bold sonorous bravado of a *hasosra* filled the air drowning out any other sound. A formation of soldiers appeared. Their leather sandals crunched against the earth as they marched at a steady disciplined pace and began to form a line around the perimeter of the commodious lake. Latifa scanned the perimeter of the lake then blinked unbelievingly when she spotted a group of her tribesmen being prodded to stand a short distance from the platform. Latifa gasped in shock when her gaze fell upon her sister.

"Tanesha!" Latifa exclaimed noting her sister's torn clothes, bloodied arms, legs and bruised ankles.

Tariq looked at her.

"What are they doing here?" she questioned nodding to her tribesmen.

"They are prisoners," Tariq revealed.

"Prisoners? I thought you were going to release them."

"I considered releasing them but decided against it."

"What do you mean you decided against it?"

"The night you went missing was the night some of them committed a horrendous crime then tried to escape. Most of the escapees were tracked down and recaptured. Two were never recovered."

"Oh no!" Latifa groaned.

"They are all to be punished for their crimes," Tariq revealed.

"What do you mean punished for their crimes?" Latifa queried.

"Today those you see before you are to be executed."

"Executed!" Latifa shrieked.

"They cracked the skull of one of my soldiers and killed him. Their execution is part of the ceremony you are about to witness."

"*What?* But that can't be! My sister is with them!"

"Which one is your sister?"

"There." Latifa pointed to Tanesha. Leaning toward Tariq, she said, "Since you are the Pharaoh, you can help her."

"What would you have me do?"

"Release her!"

"A soldier is dead. She cannot be released."

"She didn't kill anyone!"

"How do you know?"

"I know my sister. She would not harm a scarab beetle let alone a human."

"If it were possible I would do as you request. But, it is not possible. Further discussion is futile."

Latifa's heart began to pound in her chest. Her sister was about to be murdered in front of her eyes. She had to rescue her sibling from such a fate. She had already lost her father and her mother. She could not lose her sister too. Somehow, she had to get Tariq to discuss releasing her sister and get him to change his mind. Her sister's life depended on her ability to do so.

"Please consider a pardon. You are the Pharaoh. You could command it."

"You don't concede easily do you?"

Latifa licked her lips nervously. "No. Not when it's something as important as this."

"I told you, your request is not possible."

"Just tell me why! Why won't you even consider a pardon? I guess I know the reason! It is because you are as cold hearted and unscrupulous as I knew the Pharaoh of Egypt would be. I'm not sure there is a shred of kindness in you. If there were, you would heed my request. But, I should know it's useless to expect compassion and decency from an Egyptian!" Latifa spat even as she wished she had maintained her composure.

Tariq was silent for many moments. He finally grunted, "Take your sharp tongue and go get your sister. She is the only one I shall pardon."

கூ

129

Latifa rose from her seat and despite the faint ache in her leg scurried down the steps and to the area where the condemned captives stood. Quickly, Latifa examined those in the group and frowned at their sorry appearance. Up close, her tribesmen looked very disheveled. Guilt washed over her as she thought about how she had eaten and slept in luxury while her sister and her tribesmen had been beaten and held as prisoners. Latifa pushed back the tears that crowded in her eyes and told herself to remain strong for her sibling. Feeling all eyes on her, she walked past Aren and the other captives and traipsed to where her sister stood.

"Tanesha!" she called out and grabbed her sister's hand.

"Latifa! You're alive!" Tanesha squeezed her hand in return.

"Yes. I am. Are you all right?" Latifa asked.

"I am frightened. They are going to kill us."

"No! No!"

"It's true. They are going to kill all of us because of the death of that soldier. But, none of us who are going to die killed that man. Mateo did it."

"Mateo? How?"

"After news came you had been mauled to death, no one thought we would be freed. It was decided to escape. That soldier caught us. Mateo fought back. There was so much blood..." Tanesha's voice faltered and tears began to stream from her fear filled eyes. "I don't want to die. I just want things to go back to the way they were before our village was attacked. Now, we are going to be killed for something we did not do." Tanesha lowered her head.

"No! No! Don't cry. I shall not let you die," Latifa vowed.

Tanesha lifted her head to look at Latifa. "What can you do? What can anyone do?"

"I talked to Tariq. The man we knew as the Commander is the Pharaoh."

"That man you're with is Pharaoh? Then he is treacherous and depraved."

"No. He is not like that. He says you can be released."

"How did you get him to say that? Was it while you were lying on your back?" Tanesha inquired frostily.

"Hold your tongue!" Latifa exclaimed surprised by the unexpected viciousness of Tanesha's words.

"That man betrayed our father! If you think I want one thing from him, you've forgotten your mind! If you want to be his whore, don't use me as an excuse!"

"How can you say such things to me? I am trying to help you! Come with me! You have been freed!"

Tanesha yanked her hand from Latifa's grasp. "Do you think I am going to walk away and leave Aren behind? There is no way I am going anywhere without Aren!"

"Tanesha, please—!"

"Aren is the man I love. I am not going to abandon him. My life is meaningless without him."

"Please come with me!" Latifa pleaded.

Tanesha shook her head to ward off Latifa's protest. With a mixture of distain and sorrow in her eyes, she said, "I am staying with Aren. As for you, go to your Pharaoh. His touch has defiled you. You are no longer a sister of mine."

With that said, Tanesha took a step back and folded her arms defiantly.

Latifa stared dumbfounded at her sister.

The *hasosra* blared again turning everyone's attention back to the platform in time to see Moswen rise to his feet and stretch out his arms.

"I, the High Priest of Karnak, stand before you. It is a great day. Our Pharaoh has returned from his journey. Yet today is a sad day. One of our sons was murdered in the service of this great nation. He proudly served our Pharaoh and our country. There must be reparation for such a life. Just as he did his duty we must do ours. In service of the great Amun-Ra, we honor this fallen soldier. Let our homage begin."

A drumbeat rumbled then faded quickly.

"Let the prisoners be brought forth so that they may be viewed before the festivities begin."

The thump of the drum started again.

The captive women began to sob and the men began to tremble as a few of the soldiers advanced upon them.

131

Latifa followed the soldiers as they led their wards to the foot of the platform and lined them in front of it. The drumbeat continued steady and sure. One of the soldiers stepped behind the row of prisoners and withdrew his sword from its sheath. He lifted the sword above his head. A loud grunt erupted from the soldiers when the long steel blade caught the sunlight and glistened lustrously. The swordsman swiped the sword widely as if he were practicing cutting through the necks of the captives. Anguish filled Latifa as once again the assembled military men grunted their approval.

The soldier raised his sword again and the drumbeat quickened. Latifa knew the next time the man brought the sword down it would be to exact retribution for his fallen military companion. Her feet found speed and with a cry she raced to the platform. Acting quick, a soldier stepped to block her path. Ducking under the man's outstretched arms, Latifa ran up the steps of the platform.

Tariq rose to his feet, an astonished expression plastered on his face.

The guard near Tariq flew into action and rushed toward Latifa.

"Halt soldier!" Tariq commanded tersely.

Instantly, the guard straightened his stance.

The drumbeat stopped and a shocked gasp rippled through the assembled crowd when Latifa fell to her knees and touched Tariq's feet.

"Pharaoh! Please don't kill them! Don't kill my sister!" she whimpered.

Tariq reached down, slapped his hand on Latifa's arm and yanked her to her feet.

Latifa looked at Tariq and was taken aback by the outrage simmering in his eyes. Nervously, she glanced around the platform at the men on it and noted their contemptuous stares. Silence permeated the air only to be broken by the snap of the flags as they flapped in the wind.

Tariq's voice finally broke the silence. "Return to the palace!" he ordered through clenched teeth.

"But—"

"Return to the palace!" His bark interrupted Latifa's protest.

"I shall see that your request is carried out." Jabari stepped forward.

"We shall have words upon my return to the palace. Go with Jabari," Tariq commanded Latifa and pushed her toward the Lieutenant.

The *hasosra* began to blare as Latifa blindly followed Jabari from the platform. She ignored Jabari's outstretched hand when he turned to assist her down the steps.

"I don't need you to help me! The last time you helped me, you left me in Narmer's clutches!" she snapped.

Jabari lowered his head without uttering a word of response.

Latifa stomped ahead of him.

When they were a short distance from the portal along the back wall, Jabari appeared beside her and said, "Tariq has not confronted me so I know you haven't told him of my involvement with Narmer. I salute you for that. But, I say, I left you with Narmer because I knew this would happen. I knew if you were taken back to Tariq there would be trouble. I thought the problem would be Tariq giving into your whims. Little did I know you would also bring such chaos.

"Tariq needed this day to go seamlessly. It was imperative that the Priests and Councilmen see his father made the right decision in naming him Pharaoh. This should be a day of triumph for him. This day should have been a day when his detractors saw him as a victorious leader. It should have been a day when their grumbling ceased. But, now, that cannot be because you have served to hurt his standing and his leadership."

"How have I hurt his leadership?" Latifa wanted to know.

"Tariq shall stop the punishment of the Nubians. Everyone shall see your ability to sway his thoughts and conclude he is weak for being influenced by a woman. A Nubian."

"How do you know he shall stop the punishment of the Nubians?"

"He shall do it because it is what you want done."

"Those people who you want murdered are innocent! They are my people and they do not deserve to die!"

"Egyptians are my people! They deserve a leader who is strong! They deserve a leader whose first allegiance is Egypt! As men of war, we learn to ignore our hearts. But, you...you have made Tariq's heart stir which means trouble...nothing but trouble! You give his enemies a foot hold to attack him! You are no good for him!"

With the words spoken, Jabari stormed out of the temple gates and stomped to a man standing by several horses. After he said a few words to the man, Jabari strutted back to Latifa who had stopped by the gate. He pointed to the man. "Go with him. He shall take you to the palace. I shall return to the celebration to speak with Tariq and try to undo the damage you've done."

☙

"You do not look pleased," Jabari said to Tariq after he returned to the platform.

"I am not pleased," Tariq admitted.

"Is the sentence imposed on the Nubians going to be carried out?"

"Latifa says some of the Nubians are innocent."

"And you believe her?"

Silence followed.

"The men wait impatiently for the ceremony to commence." Jabari nodded toward the Councilmen and Priests gathered at the far side of the lake.

Tariq folded his arms in front of him.

"From the very beginning of our friendship, you told me I could speak my mind freely. Is that still true?" Jabari questioned.

Tariq nodded.

"I do not believe it's good the way you concede to that girl. I contend she is nothing but a distraction to you. Even while we were on the trail, she had too much sway over your thoughts and actions. At this moment, it seems you are being coerced by her."

134

"No one controls me. I do as I please," Tariq snapped.

"And what do you please? You parade her in front of us all. Are you going to marry the girl and officially give her a place among our people?"

"I never said it pleased me to make Latifa my Queen. I never said I would marry her."

"Then what are your plans for her? Is she to be your concubine?"

"My mother was a concubine to my father. I do not see why Latifa can't be my concubine."

"And what does your fiery companion have to say about it? Did she say she would settle for the role of harlot?"

"Hold your tongue! You know nothing of Latifa!"

"You're extremely defensive of the girl for no cause. Since the day that girl was brought to you, she has meant unrest for you. You returned to Egypt in triumph and victory. But, in one day's time of her being in our city, the unrest continues. There is no chance you can have a proper future with that girl. It is folly for you to parade her before your subjects. Surely you know there can be no place for her in your life as Pharaoh."

Tariq did not answer. Instead, he stomped down the steps of the platform.

Jabari traversed after him. "You and I have been through much, my friend. It is not my intent to anger you. As always, my concern is for you and this nation. The people of this nation were adjusting to the fact you were crowned ruler instead of Narmer. It pleased you to bring that girl to the ceremony. Now, all have seen her in a place of honor...standing beside you as if she were your Queen. There is no way this nation can accept someone like her sitting beside you on the throne. The Council was resigned to respect your father's decision. Now, they are discontented." He nodded once again to the group of men conversing in hushed tones. "Moswen has influence over The Council. Hence, he shall be harder to mold since you have vexed his daughter, Selma, by consorting with the girl. As for the men of the military, they want to see the Nubians' lives forfeited for what happened to their brother. If you do not proceed with the execution of the Nubians, discord shall fester. You shall be seen as being coerced by a woman. As Pharaoh that is something you cannot let happen."

೫

Latifa wrung her hands nervously as she tread over the plush rug beneath her feet. Walking to the threshold of The Great Room, she looked into the hallway and fervently prayed Tariq would walk through the doors of the palace. Inhaling deeply, she turned and retraced her steps. Her sister's face flashed in her mind. The look of fear that had been etched on her sibling's face caused her stomach to feel as if it were tied in knots.

Latifa walked to one of the gold encrusted chairs and slumped in it. She stared at the *frescoe* of a king sitting before kneeling subjects and watched as shadows caused by the waning sun crept through the window to alight on the stoic scene. As Pharaoh, Tariq's declaration that he was going to have her sister killed had brought her to her knees before him. Had her actions of falling at his feet obtained a reprieve for her sister or was her sister already dead?

She felt disgusted that she had given herself to Tariq. If she had known he was Pharaoh and would one day order the execution of her sister... How could she have let the man touch her? The nights they spent together in his tent should not have happened. How she loathed the way her body responded to him!

Despite her claims of regret, she had to admit to herself the way she currently felt was in sharp contrast to the way she felt when Narmer held her against her will and she thought she might not see Tariq again. At the time, she had not been able to name her changing feelings for him. Now, she was sure of her feelings. She hated Tariq. Completely and irrevocably.

Slowly, the darkness that obscured the *frescoe* began to fade foretelling the rise of the sun. Latifa realized she had sat awake all night. She closed her eyes and breathe in the smell of food being prepared for the morning meal. Though her stomach rumbled, she knew she was too upset

136

to eat. She could not eat a bite until she found out her sister's fate.

"Were you trying to discredit me?" Tariq's voice bellowed sharply as he strode into The Great Room.

Startled, Latifa sat up then heedlessly leapt to her feet, flew at him and slapped his face. "I hate you! I hate you! How could you? How could you, you brute!"

She slapped his face again.

Tariq captured Latifa's wrist in a tight grasp when she moved to slap his face once more.

"Why didn't you tell me the truth? Why did you not tell me you are Pharaoh?" she demanded.

"It would have changed nothing."

"It changes everything!" Latifa yelled and unsuccessfully tried to jerk her arm from Tariq's grasp.

"Tell me, how would it have changed anything?"

"How can you ask me that?"

"Now that you know I am Pharaoh and you admit knowing I'm Pharaoh changes things, you should change the way you speak and act around me. Your hysterics in front of everyone yesterday were not amusing!" he bit out.

"Any hysterics you saw were because I love my sister. She is the reason I acted as I did!" Latifa asserted as she shoved from Tariq and stomped to the far corner of the room so she would not be near him.

"I told you your sister could be released!"

"She wouldn't go without Aren her intended."

"If your sister chose to refuse my generous pardon, I can hardly be blamed for her choice," Tariq barked.

"You condemned innocent people!"

"A soldier was murdered! The men of the military want justice for their brother. The people want justice for their countryman. I am their leader. As Pharaoh, I am responsible for getting that justice," Tariq explained.

"The Nubians you captured did not kill that soldier."

"*That* soldier has a name! His name was Kwame!"

"All of the slaves you've captured for your glorious Egyptian empire have names too!" Latifa shot back sharply.

"From the day I met you, your tongue was bold and needed to be tamed. Now that you know I am Pharaoh, you

137

best reconsider the way you speak to me," came the steely reply.

"I use my bold tongue to speak words of condemnation for what you've done!" Latifa persisted.

"I no longer wish to discuss this subject so this subject shall no longer be discussed!" Tariq thundered angrily.

"You may have command over Egyptians but I am not an Egyptian! You don't have command over me and I say I want to discuss it! I want to know why it's so easy for you to murder innocent people!" Latifa shouted and stomped her feet.

"Those captives took a life! The lives of those Nubians aren't worth that of an Egyptian let alone an Egyptian soldier!"

"So that's it! You think a Nubian is not as important as an Egyptian! That is why you've dedicated your life to the business of murdering them!" Latifa accused venomously.

Tariq looked at her with an expression that revealed her sharp tongue had rendered him speechless. Turning his back to her, he took several steps. Silence permeated the room for many moments. Finally, he said, "Your sister was not slain. Yesterday, I postponed carrying out the sentence on the captives for a day. I did it for you and your sister. Now, I, the Pharaoh of Egypt, remind you, I pardoned your sister. It is up to you to persuade her to save herself. If she does not accept the pardon, that is her choice. The executions shall proceed at sundown tonight."

Chapter Ten

A shiver went through Latifa as she stared at the baleful building beyond the iron gate in front of her. The gate creaked when a prison guard opened it. Latifa stepped past the man and into the dusty courtyard. She looked at Jabari who stood beside the guard. Suddenly, she hoped he would accompany her on her mission. As if reading her thoughts, Jabari shook his head. Without speaking a word, Latifa turned from the men. As she began to walk across the courtyard toward the prison, she thought about what had brought her here. Her sister along with so many of her tribesmen were set to pay the ultimate price for the soldier Kwame's death. It was unfortunate he was dead. The last time she had seen him was on the trail when he led her through camp before she had finally been reunited with her sister. Then he had been full of life. It was hard to believe he was gone.

Her thoughts were interrupted when the front door of the prison swung wide as she neared it and a portly man filled the threshold.

"The Lieutenant said you want to free one of the Nubians who was sent here by the Pharaoh," the man said as he took a moment to examine Latifa. After she nodded, he motioned for her to follow him inside the building.

A fetid smell assaulted Latifa's nose the moment she stepped over the threshold and into the prison. She watched the worker lift a torch from its holder on a nearby wall then walk to a stairway. Careful not to touch the malodorous grime covering the mortar filled walls, she followed the man down the wooden steps.

Dark shadows receded under the light of the torch to reveal a narrow hallway lined with cells. Behind the iron bars of the cells were unkempt prisoners with morose expressions on their faces. The worker stopped in front of a crowded cell. Latifa stared into the aphotic enclosure. Not seeing her sister right away, she called out, "Tanesha?"

A dark form moved at the back of the pen.

"Latifa?" a shaky voice answered.

Latifa watched as the dark form rose then advanced toward her. Gold light from the torch spilled onto Tanesha's face when she walked to the front of the cell. A moment later, the worker moved to stand at the foot of the stairs taking the light of the fire with him. Latifa grimaced as shadows cloaked her sister's mirthless face. Latifa reached her hand through the opening between the bars. Tanesha lifted her hand and touched Latifa's fingers.

"I can't stand to see you like this," Latifa confessed.

"What have they done with Aren? I haven't seen him since they put me in here. Do you know where he is?"

Latifa shook her head negatively. "I haven't seen him."

"Latifa, I am going to die. I am so frightened."

"No...No... Don't say that. Just come with me and this shall all be over."

"It shall be over for you but there is no life for me without Aren."

"You have more to live for than Aren!" Latifa hedged.

"After I heard you were dead, I was the one who insisted we try to escape. The others felt sorry for me and agreed to go along with my plan. I can't let the others die for that. I can't walk away from the man I love knowing I am the one who put him in such peril."

"It wasn't you. It was Mateo who caused this."

"He didn't want to do it but the soldier caught me as we were escaping. Aren stopped to help me. That soldier started to beat Aren. Mateo hit him with his drum. The soldier fell and hit his head. There was so much blood. Mateo was just defending me and Aren." Tanesha's voice faltered. Tears began to stream from her eyes. "I just want to spend my life with Aren. That's all. That's why I wanted to escape after I was told you were dead. I couldn't imagine being apart from him. With you dead, I knew the Commander would not release us. I knew we would be sold once we reached Egypt. If that happened...with mother gone and father and you dead...I would truly be alone. Now we are going to be killed because I dared to escape so I could be with the man I love." Tanesha hung her head low.

"No...No...Tanesha. I promised you I wouldn't let you die and I meant it."

140

"You can do nothing. You can't drag me out of this cell. This is my fault. If Aren or anyone else dies, I should meet the same fate."

"Don't talk like that. You have to change your mind and return to the palace with me."

Tanesha removed her hand so that it no longer touched Latifa's hand. With a mixture of anguish and despair in her eyes, she murmured, "You cannot save me. So, go back to him. To your Pharaoh. Don't let the loss of my life stop you from feeling his touch. After all, his touch is what you want." With that said, Tanesha turned from the bars and retreated into the sooty shadows leaving Latifa staring stupefied after her.

Somehow, Latifa managed to gather herself enough to turn from the cell. She walked to the worker who still remained standing at the foot of the steps.

"Where are the Nubian men who were brought in yesterday?" she asked.

The worker led her to another cell. Aren spotted her and walked to the front of the cell.

"How is Tanesha?" he questioned, a somber expression on his face.

"I wish I could say she was doing well."

"I can't forgive myself for letting her get entangled in this mess. She shouldn't have to go through any of this," he lamented despondently.

"The Pharaoh has given her a pardon but she refuses to accept it."

"She's got to accept it! Make her accept the pardon!"

"I've tried. She won't listen. She is the only one the Pharaoh shall release. But, she shall not accept the pardon unless you are freed as well."

Aren gripped the bars that separated them. "She's got to forget about me and save herself!" he proclaimed desperately.

"She won't!"

Aren shook his head. "There is not much time. The executions are set to take place in a few hours. You've got to save her. Save your sister!" he insisted.

By the time Latifa walked out of the prison, she was near tears. Anxiety mushroomed in her as she made her way back across the courtyard toward the prison's gate. Her eyebrow arched when she realized the male standing by the gate talking to the guard was not Jabari. Though his back was to her, she recognized the male as Narmer. She looked back the way she had come for a way to escape. Seeing none, she picked up her pace and decided to pass him by without speaking a word to him. However, as she neared where the men stood, Narmer turned to look at her.

"I have words which must be spoken to you," he stated.

"Stay away from me!" Latifa snapped when he stepped to block her path.

"My dealing with you is of importance."

"Where is Jabari? Is he involved in this?"

"I suggest you hear what it is I have to say."

"How did you find me? What are you doing here?"

"I know your sister and all those with her are to be executed at sundown."

"Get out of my way!" Latifa marched past him.

"I can save your sister and all of those with her!" Narmer called out.

Latifa stopped and turned to look at him. Eyeing him sharply, she said, "You can do no such thing!"

He nodded. "I can help you."

"What do you mean you can help?"

"I know a way to save your sister."

"You attack my village, murder my people, assault and hold me against my will. Now, am I to believe you care about whether my sister lives or dies? Surely, you take me for a fool."

Narmer splayed his fingers apart then bringing his hands inward pressed the tips of his fingers together. "You and your people have suffered at my hands. I have the ability to free them all and I shall do it. This is my pledge to you."

"What can you do? If you try and challenge Tariq, you shall fail."

"How can I challenge my brother when he has the military behind him? He knows he took a foolish risk

142

yesterday when he held off punishing the Nubians. Now, he has seen the error of his ways and he is anxious to carry out the sentence so that the soldiers garner retribution for their cohort. You must see, it is to my advantage that the Nubians not be killed. If the Nubians are not killed, the soldiers' admiration for Tariq shall lessen. It is only then that I can get what I want…what I deserve!"

"Why do you think you deserve to be Pharaoh?"

"Because I am firstborn. By all rights, I should be the one ruling this kingdom."

"If the crown should go to the firstborn, why was it passed to Tariq instead of you?"

"We were both conceived very near the same time. I was born here in Egypt by our father's wife. Tariq's mother was my father's concubine. I was born before him. But, Tariq's mother was traveling with my father when Tariq was born. Tariq was the son my father saw. As a result, not knowing I was born, he declared Tariq the oldest son.

"When he returned to Egypt, the dates of our births were compared and it was determined I was actually the eldest. My father acknowledged I was the firstborn. Everyone came to an accord. Since I was firstborn and the legitimate son born of my father's wife, being Pharaoh is my birthright. Everyone believed I would become the next Pharaoh. Even Tariq's mother conceded. I remained in Egypt and was groomed to be the next King. Tariq had our father's thirst for war and chose the life of a soldier, living most of his life away from this city. He was committed to garnering the gold and human treasure of other nations."

"I don't see what any of that has to do with me."

"Oh? You are very important indeed. Your assistance is vital," Narmer assured.

"You are a cunning treacherous snake. If you think I am going to help you, your delusion knows no bounds."

"You help me and I shall help you," Narmer continued undeterred.

"I want nothing to do with you," Latifa insisted.

"If I can stop the executions, what then? I know your sister is one of those condemned and I know how much you care for her. That is why I came here today when I heard you were here."

"How do you know about my sister?"

"I am more than just the Pharaoh's brother. I am the rightful Pharaoh. I find a way to know what goes on in my kingdom. I say unto you, with your help, I can free your sister and your kinsmen within the hour."

Latifa was silent a moment as she contemplated Narmer's words. "What would you have me do?" she finally asked.

"Invite Tariq to visit with you at midday." Narmer reached into the pocket of his cloak and pulled out a phial filled with clear liquid. "Before he arrives, put this in his drink."

"What is it? You want to harm Tariq! I shall not do it!"

Narmer's expression hardened then relaxed. His voice was light when he spoke. "No...No... Nothing like that. If I wanted to harm my dear brother, don't you think I would have done it before now? No. All this shall do is cause him to fall into a deep sleep. When he does not appear to oversee the executions at dusk, the military men shall be outraged.

"The effects of the drug shall last long enough for me to be declared Pharaoh. When he comes to, sure he shall dispute my right to rule. The military may even put aside their anger at him but it shall not matter. For you see, the dispute shall have to be put before The Council. I've been told by the High Priest, The Council shall side with me. It seems my dear brother insulted the High Priest's daughter, Selma, by bringing you to the palace, bedding you and flaunting you before the people."

"I won't do as you suggest!"

"Do as I say. If you don't, your sister shall be dead by nightfall."

Narmer placed the phial in Latifa's hand. "Once Tariq has succumbed to sleep, meet me here at the prison and everyone you desire shall be freed. Don't forsake your sister," he prodded then thrust her past the gate and out onto the street.

144

Latifa clutched the phial tightly and looked around for Jabari. He was nowhere to be seen so she began to walk down the street. Nervously, she glanced over her shoulder and looked for Narmer but did not see him. Why was she nervous? Could she trust Narmer when he said Tariq would not be harmed? She had said if she had the chance she would make the Pharaoh pay for the misery he had caused in her life. She had once wanted to end the Pharaoh's life. Now that she knew Tariq was the Pharaoh, did she really want to harm him? Now that she had the chance to have revenge, could she go through with it? Not going along with Narmer's plan meant certain death for her sister. She had promised Tanesha she would save her life. Could she live with herself if she did not try to do all she could for her sibling? Latifa lowered her head as she thought about the answers to her questions. As she continued her trek back to the palace, she began to contemplate her next course of action.

☙

"You go too far." Jabari appeared beside Narmer after Narmer exited the prison grounds and began to walk along the street.

Narmer's brow crinkled in surprise. "Why do you speak such words?"

"You lied about the reason you wanted to speak to the girl. You told me you wanted to talk to her alone so you could apologize for what happened in the past. But that was a lie. You did not apologize. I was waiting near the gate and heard what you told her. Is that really a sleeping potion in the phial you gave her? I know you have no real concern for releasing the Nubians."

Narmer stopped walking and looked at Jabari. "I am in a battle for the future of this nation. You have never been one to shy from battle. Do you now lead with your emotions as Tariq does?"

"Tariq is a good man who honors the promise he made to your father. He shall let no harm come to you. You

145

should not harm him. You should see him as what he is, a great Commander and brother."

"He is no brother of mine and I shall never accept him as such! His very existence was an insult to my mother. He is the bastard son who has no right to claim the throne! Once he is out of the way, I shall ascend to my rightful place," Narmer snarled.

"You speak treason! Your father gave Tariq the right to the throne when he appointed him Pharaoh!" Jabari countered.

"My father's brain had been poisoned by his concubine!"

"Hatred has poisoned you! You are a fool if you think you can oust your brother and ascend to the throne. For years, you have tried to undermine your brother at every turn. I paid little heed because you are Tariq's brother. I could see you were jealous but I thought you were harmless. Now I see, you have grown too bold and too cunning.

"I went along with you and misled Tariq into thinking the girl was dead because you spoke of making Tariq focus on leading. But, now that I see your true motive, I shall not be a conspirator to his destruction. Tariq and I have faced many foes together. If you go through with your plan, you shall have me against you," Jabari growled.

Narmer folded his arms as his lips clamped into a frown. Obstinately, he stretched out his arms, placed his hand around the back of Jabari's neck and pulled the Lieutenant close. Staring the military man in the eyes, he snarled, "Jabari, you can let memories of fighting battles with Tariq sway you and bring you to ruin. Or you can side with me and when I'm on the throne, all of the riches you desire can be yours. Now is the time for you to decide whose side you're on for Latifa heads to the palace as we speak."

146

Chapter Eleven

Latifa ran her hand over the front of her kaftan in hopes of steadying it. When she splayed her fingers in front of her, she noted her hand continued to shake violently. Squaring her shoulders, she managed to open the phial. As she held the phial over two goblets, she thought about how her hand started trembling the moment she took the phial of liquid from Narmer. Could she really tamper with Tariq's drink? What was in the phial? Was it really something that would render him unconscious or was Narmer more sinister than he claimed? Could she trust that putting the liquid in Tariq's drink would not kill him? And even if it did, did she care? She had vowed to make the Pharaoh pay for all the destruction he caused. So, why was it such a dilemma for her to decide what to do? After all, he had betrayed and killed her father. It was because he insisted on executing her people that her sister was condemned to die in a few short hours.

What was she thinking? She couldn't go through with tampering with Tariq's drink. Narmer said the liquid in the phial would not harm Tariq. But, in truth, she knew Narmer was devious and could not be trusted. What if the liquid in the phial was poison? She was not the type of person to kill someone in cold blood. On the other hand, she said she wanted to be a warrior. A warrior would not hesitate to defeat an enemy any way possible. She had vowed to make the Pharaoh pay for his treachery. Now was her chance. She couldn't think about it anymore. She just had to do it. If she did not, it meant certain death for her people. If she thought about it anymore, she might lose her nerve. Latifa tipped the phial over one of the goblets causing the liquid to stream into the cup.

"Pardon," a voice sounded.

Latifa inhaled sharply and almost dropped the phial she held in her hand. Moving her hands behind her back, she turned and saw a servant standing by the entrance. "What is your purpose for being here?" she asked testily.

"The Pharaoh is on his way," the man announced.

"Oh. Thank you." Latifa softened her voice willing herself to sound as normal as possible.

"Are you feeling ill?" the servant inquired.

"No. I am fine. Please, just leave," Latifa requested.

Latifa exhaled when the man left the room. She put the phial into the potted celosia on the table and stared at the cup that now held the deleterious liquid.

"After our conversation this morning, I did not think you would want to see me today," Tariq's voice sounded.

Latifa spun around to face him. "I wasn't certain you'd come." She was sure her voice sounded shaky.

"I wasn't certain I'd come either. But I'm here. I am anxious to see how things unfold," he said cryptically and slowly walked to her. "Why did you send word that you wanted to see me? Is it you've come to understand what must be done?"

Before she could answer, he took her hand and led her to the balcony. She removed her hand from his, walked to the edge of the balcony and looked at the city beyond the wall that surrounded the palace. An arid breeze blew against her cheeks as the noon sun warmed her skin. She felt Tariq's presence behind her a moment before she heard him speak.

"Thebes is a great city with an unlimited future. It is a future which I shall lead. Those who would undermine me and my authority do so at their own peril."

Tariq's tone was cold in Latifa's ear and caused a shiver to slither up her spine.

"You once swore you would make the Pharaoh pay for all of the sorrow you believe he brought into your life. Now that you know I am Pharaoh, tell me, do you still have the same goal and feel as you once felt?"

Latifa cleared her throat as she contemplated Tariq's inquiry. The truth was her feelings for him were so complex. Every time she was in his arms she felt safe and desired. When she had been separated from him, all she wanted to do was see him again. Now that she knew he was Pharaoh, she told herself she hated him. But, when she did not know he was Pharaoh, she had begun to feel tender feelings for him. Had all that changed the moment he told

148

her his true identity? Even if she still cared for him, she was right to think it useless to examine her feelings because it was not as if she could forgive him for betraying her father and ending his life and her sister's life. She looked in the direction of the prison. Even as she shared this conversation with Tariq, her sister was a moment closer to death. Any feelings of care she may have felt for Tariq must be forgotten.

Realizing Tariq was no longer behind her, Latifa turned to look at him. She gasped when she saw he stood by the table holding one of the goblets. She looked at the remaining goblet on the table. From her vantage point, she could not tell if he had picked up the cup she had poured the liquid into.

He lifted the cup and put it to his lips.

Horror filled her and spilled from her lips in the form of a scream when he drained the contents of the cup in two gulps.

"No! What have I done?" she shrieked and ran to him.

"What *have* you done?"

"I think I poisoned you!" The words rolled out of her mouth as tears stung her eyes. Latifa wrapped her arms around him. "I am so sorry! He told me the liquid would not harm you! But, I should not have done it!"

"No. Latifa, you should not have done it."

"I…I…should not have—"

"Listened to Narmer," Tariq finished the sentence in an eerily calm voice.

Latifa's mouth fell open and she took a step from Tariq. "You know about Narmer?"

Tariq nodded his head affirmatively.

"But how?"

"While Jabari was waiting for you at the prison, he overheard the conversation between you and Narmer. He told me Narmer ask you to pour something into my drink. It doesn't take much to conclude Narmer is using you. Though I did not want to think on it, I knew the day would come in which I must take a stand against him. At this moment, he is being sought because he must answer for his treason. I can no longer abide his traitorous ways in his attempt to become Pharaoh."

"I am such a fool to have gone along with Narmer's plan."

"It was foolish that is true," Tariq murmured as he pulled a thin strip of leather from his pocket. Without warning, he grabbed her hands and pressed her wrists together. Quickly, he looped one end of the leather around her wrists before tying the leather tight.

"What the... What are you doing?" Latifa screeched.

Ignoring her inquiry, Tariq dragged her to the bed and jerked her arms over her head. Swiftly, he looped the loose end of the leather over the top of the bed post and yanked it causing her wrists to be pulled upward so that her feet were lifted from the floor and the tips of her toes barely touched the ground.

Looking directly into her eyes, he said, "You made an attempt on the Pharaoh's life. You must be punished."

"You don't have time to do this now. You could have drank poison. You need to go see a physician!" Latifa blurted out.

"You're worried about my health? How gracious of you," Tariq remarked as he walked to the large chest and began to rummage through it.

"Please send for a physician!" Latifa begged.

"A physician shall do me no good."

"Please. There may still be time," Latifa persisted.

Tariq turned to her and Latifa saw he now held a long leather whip. "Just tell me why you did it," he ordered mirthlessly.

"I...I did it to help my sister. She refused to leave unless the others were released too. Narmer said he would free her and all of the other captives if I poured that liquid in your drink."

"So you did it for your sister? She means that much to you?"

"She's my sister. I can't let her die."

"Now I am to die?"

"No. Not if you get to a physician. Maybe there is something that can be done."

150

"I was wondering how you would react upon seeing me drink the tainted wine. If you had shown no regard for my life, punishing you would be easy. Your reaction complicates things."

Tariq advanced toward her tapping the whip against the palm of his hand as he did so.

Latifa gulped back the apprehension that rose in her. "My deepest apology. I didn't mean to poison you," she murmured.

"I didn't drink any poison," Tariq revealed.

"What?" Shifting her gaze, Latifa looked at the table that held the goblets. "How can you be sure?"

"Jabari escorted you to the prison as I asked him to. He overheard you speaking with Narmer and told me of your plans. While we were on the balcony, he came and replaced both cups. The reason I led you on the balcony was to let Jabari make the switch."

"You really trust Jabari."

Tariq shook his head. "We've been in many battles together. He has saved my life many times and I his."

Latifa sighed with relief. However, her relief was short lived when Tariq reached out and clutched the top of her kaftan. Determinedly, he yanked the material causing it to rip down the front. Latifa gasped as the kaftan fell from her shoulders exposing her breasts to his view before cascading to the ground to pool at her feet.

"What are you doing?" she questioned.

Ignoring her words, Tariq took a moment to gaze at her breasts then he reached in his pocket and brought out a strip of cloth. A second later, Latifa was cast into darkness when he placed the cloth over her eyes. The smell of leather filled her nose a moment before she felt leather from the handle of the whip between her breasts.

"You seem remorseful enough for your actions. Even so, you must be punished for trying to kill the Pharaoh. Let me think. What is a good punishment for a beautiful assassin like you?"

Latifa felt the handle of the whip slide up the side of her right breast then glide over its horizon. She felt the leather glide along the edge of the soft mound then underneath it.

151

The knob drifted to her left breast only to repeat its exploits. The course leather was dragged down her stomach then made to circle her belly button. Suddenly, the handle was removed from her skin.

"Apologies, Tariq. Please understand."

Her plea was met with silence. Latifa's heart began to pick up speed.

"What are you going to do to me?" she asked into the silence.

"I am going to do what I should have done the first time you tried to kill me. I am going to give you the punishment you deserve." Tariq's breath tickled her ear causing a shiver of nervous anticipation to slink down her spine.

"No, please!" Latifa screamed when she heard Tariq uncoiled the whip by cracking it through the air. Her whole body tensed as she awaited the first blow of the leather against her soft skin. The first blow fell but to her astoundment it was not the scratch of the whip but a tickle of a feather across her shoulders.

Did Tariq plan on torturing her by alternating beating her with a whip and a feather? She was sure since she was blind folded and unable to see what was coming next, her torture would be intensified.

"What do you want from me?" she asked her unseen tormentor.

"I want what I've always wanted from you," Tariq replied as the feather flittered over her shoulder then down her arm.

The softness made its way to the side of her right breast then circled the mass causing the nipple that topped it to become taut. The delicate fluff moved to repeatedly circle the tender mound. Each circle, smaller than the one before, moved closer to the expectant nipple but never touched it.

To Latifa's horror and delight the feather traveled to her left breast to mimic the endowment given to its twin. Just like the handle of the whip, the feather slid down her stomach and was made to circle her belly button.

The feather was removed only to be replaced by Tariq's fingers between her breasts. His fingers circled both

152

breasts. First the right then the left, just as the two instruments before. The digits brushed down her stomach then came to a stop at her belly button.

His fingers left her skin.

Brazenly, Tariq pressed his body provocatively against hers. With his skin flushed against her, Latifa felt his nude form. Her body reacted to the feel of his flesh. As always, desire shot through her being. Her knees felt weak. She jerked against the strip of leather that bound her wrists. His lips found hers. Hungrily, he drank from them. His manhood hardened against her leg revealing his need and ripping a moan from her lips.

Tariq peeled his lips from hers then kissed her left shoulder before his lips moved to trace the path of the whip, feather and his fingers. Each breast was seared as it was circled and teased. His lips came near but never touched her yearning nipples. She knew he had knelt to his knees when his lips touched her stomach and then the patch of hair between her thighs. To her mitigated delight, his hands moved to cup her bottom.

"Tariq..." his name melted on her lips when one of his hands was removed from her bottom and placed on her inner thigh. Acting quick, she squeezed her legs together in an attempt to discourage his inquisitive fingers.

Persistent fingers grazed the bed of black hair in the valley between her thighs and drifted to her soft center. His fingers stroked the nub of her maidenhead then they were hastily removed.

"Tariq!" Latifa called out uncertain if the call was for him to return his fingers to her flesh.

She felt Tariq rise to his feet. Seductively, he slid his arm around her waist and he drew her body against his once again.

"Tariq," she whispered.

"Yes, Latifa." His lips were close to hers.

"Release me, please."

"After what you've done, I do want you to beg. But not for me to release you."

"For what then?"

"Let's see if you can figure it out," he said softly.

The touch of his lips returned to once again trace the mounds of her breasts and tease the skin around her nipples.

"Please!" she cried out in delirious torment when he refused to claim her ravenous nipples.

"Now you're getting it," Tariq uttered and rewarded her plea by flicking each nipple with his tongue.

Unable to contain herself, Latifa moaned euphorically as pleasure rippled through her. "How can you think of making love at a time such as this?" she questioned bewilderedly.

"How can you deny you want it?" he taunted. Then, to prove his point, he again flicked each nipple with his tongue coaxing another moan from her lips before his mouth once again attended each breast. Kneeling once more, his lips glided down her belly, over her belly button and as before over the triangle of hair between her thighs. This time, as if on their own, her legs widened giving him access to her most sacred jewel.

Tenderly, at first, his tongue teased her maidenhead sending chills of delight coursing through her. The movement of his tongue accelerated and the frequency of his efforts intensified ripping a wanton groan from her. Just when she felt her pleasure about to crest, he stilled his tongue. Desperately, she pitched her body to him in an effort to regain the pleasure deprived her.

"You'll do anything to get what you want," Latifa accused addled by her unchecked desire.

"I did not get where I am by not taking advantage of every opportunity," he acknowledged then commenced his effort.

Working feverishly, he brought her once again to the brink of ecstasy. Defiantly, he stilled his tongue before gluttonously recommencing his brand of punishment.

Knowing she could not take another round of Tariq's titillating torment, Latifa strained against her bonds and blurted out, "I can't take this anymore."

"Let me hear you beg."

Latifa licked her lips and breathing deeply cried, "Please!"

"Please, what?"

"Please make love to me!"

Tariq's response was a gentle chuckle. "I thought you'd never ask," he replied then in the next instant removed the blindfold from her eyes.

Immediately, Latifa noted that light the color of apricots had spilled through the open door leading from the balcony and into the room to announce the sun had continued its trek across the sky. Her observation was interrupted when Tariq unbound her wrists. After her arms dropped to her side, he scooped her into his strong arms then deposited her in the middle of the giant bed before climbing in after her.

He straddled her, his body taut with devouring lust. "You're a goddess. You embody the goddess Bastet to be sure. There has been a war of wills between us since the day we met. It must end today, Latifa," he rasped then ground his lips in to hers.

Latifa's answer to his statement was to passionately return his kiss. Hungrily, she drank from his lips and widened her legs beckoning him between them. Eagerly, he accepted her invitation and settled against her. Locking his eyes with hers, he guided his hardness into her treasure engulfing her as he did so. The desire between them fueled their passion binding them together. Tariq began to move in her. Over and over again, she accepted him until she finally cried out in ecstasy as Tariq spewed his essence into her. When his member finally grew limp, he pulled out of her. Without speaking a word, he gathered her close and lay back on the bed.

As Latifa relaxed in Tariq's arms, she willed herself not to think of anything beyond the moment. She had enjoyed Tariq's command of her body. Truth be told, the tender feelings she felt for him were returning. Unfortunately, guilt accompanied her feelings due to the fact her sister was set to die.

As if reading her thoughts, Tariq spoke. "I want to remove the animus between us. I shall do what I can for your sister and your people."

"You shall release them?"

"It is not as simple as that. What happens next is a delicate balance. The men of the military want justice for their brother. I told you, as their leader it is my responsibility to obtain that justice."

"Jabari says because you waited to execute my people, your people shall say you were swayed by a woman which means trouble for you."

"Those people are mistaken and you would be mistaken too if you think because I desire your body you have power over me. I am not so weak I can be swayed by any woman."

"So, what are you going to do?"

"I've been thinking about what you said and in this instance I am of one accord with you. Innocent people should not be put to death for a crime they did not commit. No one thinks all of the captives killed Kwame. Yet all of them stand condemned. The sentences shall be postponed again. I shall demand evidence be given against those in custody proving which one committed the offense. If no evidence is given, the Nubians shall be freed. That way no innocent blood shall be shed."

"Oh Tariq! Do you think it shall work?" Latifa asked.

Tariq placed his hand over hers. "The acrimony between us must end. I like to see you happy," came his reply.

Latifa snuggled close to Tariq extremely happy he had said he did not want innocent blood to be shed. Without warning, a revelation hit her. She did have the power to sway Tariq's thoughts. It dawned on her that her power did not come from might or cunning. Nor did it come from her size, physical strength or ability to outsmart her opponent. It came from somehow turning her opponent into her lover and her lover into someone who listened to her. Jabari had claimed she persuaded Tariq's thoughts and he was right. If Tariq did not recognize her power to influence him, that was fine. What was important was that her sister be freed.

03

Latifa could barely contain her excitement once Tariq left the palace to see to postponing the execution of her tribesmen. She quickly ate, bathe and put on the fresh linen kaftan a servant brought to her. Once she was redressed, time seemed to crawl by. Unable to contain her anxiety, she paced the halls of the palace ignoring the inquisitive looks of the servants. When she felt she could not endure the confines of the palace one more moment, she decided to explore the garden.

The instant Latifa walked into the garden, a delicate floral fragrance met her nose and splashes of bright color assailed her eyes. Drawn by the lush landscape, she strolled along the stone pathway to view beds of blue cornflowers and spires of plum, crimson and gold celosias. She stopped in front of a planter that cradled jasmine and inspected the flowers' delicate white lobes.

Lifting her head, she spied a pomegranate tree deluged with reddened fruit near the wall to her right. A jujube tree laden with purple fruit was near the gate to her left. She noted a willow tree shaded a pavilion at the rear of the garden.

She headed to the pavilion and passed through a pergola woven with a cluster of vines laden with grapes. Once she made it to the pavilion, she sat on the stone bench within the structure and looked at a two tiered fountain beside the pavilion. As she gazed at the lotus flowers floating in the tranquil water of the fountain, her thoughts began to wander to the events taking place regarding her imprisoned tribesmen. She closed her eyes and prayed that everything would turn out all right.

"I should have known you wouldn't have the courage to taint Tariq's drink."

Startled, Latifa opened her eyes and saw Narmer leaning against the willow tree.

Latifa stood to her feet. "How did you get in the garden?" she questioned.

"This use to be my home. I was to be Pharaoh, remember?" Narmer queried as he walked into the pavilion.

"Tariq knows you asked me to taint his drink. He has given orders to have you brought before him."

"On what charge? It shall be my word against yours since you did not do as I requested."

"To my shame, I did as you requested."

Narmer shook his head. "No, you did not. If you had, Tariq would not have showed up at the military station at the edge of the city a short while ago."

"Jabari switched the drinks."

"Jabari spoiled my plan!"

Latifa nodded. "He refused to harm Tariq just as I should have refused to harm Tariq!"

"You speak of harm? What about the harm done to me?" Narmer's eyes became slits as he peered at her.

"Why do you hate your brother so? He has been nothing but kind to you."

"He has taken everything from me! He has taken my crown, my home, my birthright, my dream and as I already said I shall have my revenge. I thought you could be of assistance but you are like him. You think you can ignore me. Soon he like you shall learn I will not be ignored.

"You are unaccustomed to our ways and because of you he has contrived a strange notion to protect the innocent. If he thinks for one moment his soldiers are going to have a positive reaction to him releasing any of those captives or the Egyptian people are going to accept him with a Nubian whore, he is mistaken."

"You can be very vicious! You told me you were going to release my people if I gave Tariq that liquid. Now, your words indicate you had no intension of releasing them."

"Why would I be lenient on a bunch of Nubians who have defiled my homeland?"

"You would murder innocent people?"

"Innocent blood should be sacrificed to Amun."

"Was it poison you asked me to give to your brother or a sleeping potion like you claimed?" Latifa wanted to know.

"By not going through with your part of the bargain, you undermined me. You played me falsely. I shall find a way to make sure you're given the potion you were to give Tariq. Then, you'll find out first hand if it was poison."

"You are a very wicked man, Narmer! I am ashamed I listened to you! Stay away from me! I want nothing to do

158

with you ever again!" Latifa shouted before running from the pavilion, through the garden and back into the palace.

Chapter Twelve

From her place in the litter, Latifa peered out at the multitude of people along the street all of whom parted to make way for the royal transport and its armed escort. As she scanned the crowd, she watched men in fine robes, slaves with burdens on their backs and women with babies on their hips all bow low to the ground in deference to the regal transport.

Latifa cast her gaze on Tariq who sat beside her, smiled then spoke. "I am glad you suggested we get out of the palace. I don't think I could have taken another moment worrying about everything. Now, it seems it's only a matter of time before my sister and my people are released. That makes me feel I can relax a bit. So tell me, where are we headed?"

"As I said when we left the palace, it shall be made known to you soon."

"The last time you didn't tell me something, I found out you were Pharaoh."

"This time, I know you shall like what you are about to see."

"Are we headed back to Karnak Temple?"

"Not today. We can return there on a day when we have more time for you to see more of the temple."

"How many gods do you Egyptians have?" Latifa inquired.

"Nearly two thousand."

"Two thousand!"

Tariq nodded. "There are gods aplenty. Some deal with daily matters while others oversee state matters. Still others govern the realm of the dead. Many statues can be found within tombs. A great selection can be found in the Valley of the Kings and the Valley of the Queens."

"The Valley of the Kings and Queens?"

"The Valley of the Kings is the principal burial place for Kings while the Valley of the Queens is the principal burial place for royalty and privileged nobles. The Valleys are located in the necropolis on the west bank of the Nile."

"Are there temples there?"

"There are mortuary temples built at the foot of the hills and tombs dug into the mountains."

"Religion seems to be very important to you Egyptians."

"It's extremely important to most people for it touches every aspect of their lives."

"And what of you?"

"A soldier on the battlefield has to face death just once before he begins to pray to at least one of the gods."

"What are the names of some of the gods?" Latifa inquired.

"Ra is the god of the sun and universe. Amun is widely revered in these parts. Amun united with Ra to become Amun-Ra. He is known as the King of Gods. His consort is Mut and his child is the moon god Khonsu. Geb and the Goddess Nut are credited with giving birth to the earth and the sky. Their four children are also revered. Osiris is the god of the Underworld, Isis is the Goddess of love, healing and fertility and there is Seth and Nephthys.

"Egyptians believe the Sun God Ra, Lord of Creation, rose from Nun to a four sided mound of earth that pointed toward the sun called the *benben*. The rays of the sun fell on Ra marking the way to heaven. For Egyptians, structures like pyramids represent the rays of the sun and *obelisks* point the way. *Obelisks*, pyramids and the sun all work together to assist a dead King's ascension to heaven."

As Tariq finished speaking, the litter moved along the market square and Latifa turned her attention to the activity on the street. The air was filled with the sound of vendors haggling with prospective patrons over the price of blankets, sandals and rugs. She watched shoppers rifle through stands cluttered with baskets, brightly colored mats and clay pots etched with depictions of people, boats and animals. Scattered among all of the wares were statutes of cats, hawks, lions and jackals.

"There seems to be many statues of animals. The one of a jackal makes me think of Anubis. I haven't seen her in far too long. Where is she?" Latifa asked.

"Animals are revered and worshipped because it is believed a god's spirit resides in certain animals. As far as Anubis, she is at the military station at the edge of the city.

161

She was taken there because the military station is her home. It used to be my home before I was crowned Pharaoh."

"That dog saved my life. I find I miss seeing her."

"You shall see her again."

Suddenly, the litter came to a stop due to a herd of sheep crossing the pathway. Latifa could not help but giggle when the apologetic shepherd offered his entire herd to Tariq to compensate for the delay. Once the litter was moving again, Latifa watched the bustling city give way to farm land. In one field, an ox drawn plow raised earth. In another, cattle rested in the shade of palm trees. When they passed children running through a grove of date trees, Tariq loosened the sash near his shoulder and a cream colored shroud fell to cover half of the litter. He motioned for Latifa to do the same. In compliance to his request, she lifted her hand and untied the sash near her shoulder. When she withdrew her fingers, cream colored material closed like a rippling curtain over the second half of the litter shutting out the activity outside of the transport.

"So tell me, what god do you believe in?" Tariq asked when she settled back in her seat.

Latifa looked at Tariq and saw he was looking intently at her. She reclined slightly then answered, "The people of Nubia, Kush, Aksum, Abyssinia and Sheba once believed in the power of the sun, moon and stars and worshipped them. Now, many people of these lands worship the God of the Hebrews."

"How did this conversion come about?" Tariq wanted to know.

Latifa clasped her hands together. "Of course you know my people had a history of being ruled by virgin Queens. One such Queen was named Makeda. She was known as the Queen of Sheba and is highly revered throughout all of Abyssinia. She is credited with changing the tradition of virgin Queens ruling over our nation to males of the Solomonic line ruling as Kings over our land. It was she who introduced the religion of the Hebrews to our land."

"Queen Makeda sounds very influential. Your account of her is interesting. Tell me more."

162

"During Makeda's rule, Sheba was wealthy with resources and prominence just like Egypt. Makeda's date with destiny began when she traveled to Jerusalem to meet a Hebrew King renowned for his wealth and wisdom. His name was Solomon. On her journey to Jerusalem, Makeda traveled over the Sahara Desert with extravagant gifts for Solomon. It is said nearly eight hundred camels carried satchels brimming with precious stones, pouches full of exotic spices and packs loaded with a treasure of one hundred and twenty talents of gold."

"The treaty I signed with King Rassom called for Nubia to trade gold with Egypt," Tariq noted.

At the mention of her father's name, Latifa lowered her head. Recalling Tariq's efforts to make amends by freeing her sister, she continued, "When King Solomon met Queen Makeda, he must have been impressed with her for he allowed her to observe him as he performed his stately duties. The royal pair spent a lot of time together and began to develop feelings for each other. However, Makeda refused to give into her feelings because she was a virgin Queen and she knew she must remain chaste. But, despite her vow of chastity, the shrewd King managed to seduce her."

"I wonder if she was as hard to bed as you were," Tariq mumbled.

Latifa playfully swatted his arm.

He smiled. "So tell me, how did the wise King manage to seduce the Queen?"

"Queen Makeda spent many months among the Hebrews. She learned their ways and also learned about their God. She learned of one God who spoke the world into being. An all knowing God who reads men's hearts. Makeda began to believe in this God.

"When she was ready to return to her home, Solomon suggested they have one last meal together at his palace. The meal was sumptuous with heaping helpings of spicy foods being served well into the night. Because it was very late when the meal finally ended, the King suggested Makeda spend the night in his palace. She was hesitant to agree because she feared staying the night in the King's home might result in her compromising her principles. The King assured her he would leave her untouched on one condition...the condition that she pledge an oath not to take anything from his palace for the rest of the night. Thinking it was an easy request to abide by, Makeda agreed not to take anything from the palace before the sun rose the next morning. Content with their agreement, she retired for the night.

"Hours later, the Queen woke very thirsty from the spicy foods she had eaten. She saw a cup of water by her bed and drank it to quench her thirst. King Solomon appeared and declared that by drinking the water she had broken her oath to take nothing from his palace. Makeda protested saying surely the agreement did not include something as trivial as water. However, Solomon contended that water was not trivial but very significant since it gives life to all that lives. He pointed out water is very important for without it nothing can live. Realizing the truth in the King's words, the Queen conceded she had been outsmarted. The King happily declared her actions released him from his promise. By the time the sun rose the next morning, Queen Makeda was no longer a virgin."

"King Solomon was indeed a very shrewd man," Tariq grinned.

"Makeda's life was transformed by what she'd learned from Solomon. She discovered what was believed about the sun and moon was wrong. According to the Hebrew Scriptures, the reality is the sun, moon and stars have no special powers. The truth is they were placed in the heavens to divide the day from night. Upon returning to the land of Sheba, Makeda stopped worshipping the sun and moon and no longer looked to the stars for answers. Makeda's subjects followed her lead and learned about the God of the Hebrews by studying the Hebrew Scriptures for themselves."

"The story is an interesting one. Is there more?"

Latifa nodded. "A little more, for you see as it turned out Makeda conceived a son the night she was with Solomon. The child born from their union was named Menelik. He became known as 'Son of the Wise Man'. Beginning with

Menelik's reign, it was decreed that going forward only males descending from Solomon and Makeda's royal lineage would be eligible to rule the land of Sheba."

"That was a very interesting story. It means King Rassom descended from the lineage of Menelik."

Latifa nodded then looked at her hands in hopes Tariq did not see the mask of sorrow that captured her expression at the mention of her father's name.

"We are passing a Hebrew temple now," Tariq announced.

Latifa lifted her hand, nudged the curtain aside and peered at a large complex surrounded by white washed stone.

"It's beautiful!" Latifa exclaimed of the building with the massive alabaster columns. "I thought Hebrews in Egypt were slaves. How were they able to build such a beautiful temple?"

"There was a Hebrew named Joseph who was instrumental in the building of such temples throughout our land. Sold into slavery by brothers who hated him, he was brought to Egypt. Here he excelled and became so powerful his authority was surpassed only by the Pharaoh. He was wise...a Vizier of sorts who prepared Egypt for a famine which struck our land."

"I have been told of Joseph. His father was Isaac who was the son of Abraham. Abraham is the father of the Hebrew faith," Latifa revealed.

"I can get you a statute of your Hebrew God if you'd like."

"Those of us who believe in God do not make statues of Him. We are commanded not to make graven images to worship. Besides, it's not like we know what He looks like since God is not of Hebrew origin but He's invisible."

"An invisible God? That is strange and such a peculiar concept. The Hebrews must make an idol of Abraham to worship."

"They do not worship Abraham. You see, they worship only one God."

"One God?"

"Yes one God who views everyone the same. No matter slave or nobleman."

"A single God who makes no difference between a slave or a nobleman? That religion shall not survive."

Latifa frowned at Tariq's words. His religious beliefs were yet another obstacle of difference between them.

"Egyptians don't know much about the Hebrews and their God," Tariq remarked seemingly noting her change in demeanor.

"Well they should. After all, Egyptians have played important roles in the history of the Hebrews. Take Abraham for instance. The mother of his firstborn son was an Egyptian handmaid named Hagar," Latifa stated informatively.

"You've told me Makeda's story. Now tell me the story of Hagar," Tariq requested.

"Some people think Hagar was given to Abraham by an Egyptian Pharaoh. According to the Hebrew Holy Scriptures, Abraham was in Egypt to escape a severe famine in the land he was living in. When Abraham and his wife Sarah left Egypt, Hagar had to go with them and be a servant to Sarah.

"After leaving Egypt, Abraham and his household dwelt in the land of Canaan. While there, God spoke to Abraham and told him he would be the father of a nation so great there would be too many of his descendants to count.

"Sarah heard this and believing she could not have children insisted Hagar bear Abraham's child. Once Hagar conceived Abraham's child, the relationship between mistress and slave became untenable. Unable to bear it, Hagar headed back to Egypt. She made it as far as Shur."

"A woman who was with child made it unaided to Shur? That is incredible considering the desert conditions of that area and the fearsome winds."

Latifa nodded in agreement. "While getting water at a spring in the wilderness of Shur, an angel spoke to her and advised her to return to Abraham's household. Hagar did as she was told and bore a son who was named Ishmael.

"Eventually, Sarah had a son of her own. He was called Isaac. By that time, Sarah could no longer stand the sight

166

of Hagar and Ishmael. She had Abraham banished them so Ishmael could not claim his inheritance. Mother and son lived in the wilderness of Paran until Ishmael reached manhood. After Ishmael became a man, Hagar made sure he found a wife from her native country, the land of Egypt."

"It sounds like Egyptians do indeed have a lot in common with Hebrews," Tariq noted as the litter came to a stop near a landing that overlooked the Nile River. "The Hebrew Holy Scriptures are compelling. Do you really believe in the God of the Scriptures?" Tariq asked after they descended from the litter and began to walk toward the river.

"When those jackals were about to devour me, I cried out and asked God for help. The next thing I knew, Anubis appeared and fought the pack back."

Tariq looked sympathetically at Latifa. "That had to be a horrible time for you."

"Unimaginably horrible."

"I am grateful you're alive and not dead as was thought."

"I debated whether to tell you this or not. But, I shall tell you, it was Narmer's idea to lie to you and tell you I had been killed."

"What?" Tariq stopped in his tracks.

Latifa nodded. "He said you had taken from him. He wanted to take from you. He took me to Elephantine Island and held me there against my will. He thought to use me then send me to a stone quarry."

"That bastard!" Tariq slammed his fist into the palm of his hand. "He shall pay for his treachery!" he growled. Suddenly, he pulled her against his chest. "I don't ever want to lose you again," he whispered and wrapped his arms around her.

Latifa lay her head on Tariq's chest and listened to the sound of his heartbeat. She loved how safe she felt in his arms. She never thought she would be content to be with him. But she was. Not too long ago it was incomprehensible that she would feel as she now felt. When she first met Tariq, she viewed him as a cunning warrior with no regard for kindness. On the trail, he said he

167

wanted to show her she had an incorrect assumption of who he was. He had accomplished that goal because now she knew him as an affectionate lover and compassionate leader and her heart was filled with care for him. No. It was something more than care. What was the feeling she felt? Was it possible her heart was opening to him and she was developing feelings of love for him?

But, if she were to admit love for Tariq, could she hope he would someday love her in return? If by some miracle he could look beyond his desire for her body and find love in his heart for her, the facts were there were too many obstacles between them. Now that she knew he was Pharaoh, it was just not possible for the two of them to have a future together. She had to just ignore whatever feelings she felt for Tariq.

She stepped away from him ending their embrace.

Tariq reached into the pocket of his cloak. When he pulled out his hand, a gold chain dangled from his fingers. Instantly, Latifa recognized it as her necklace with the pendant in the shape of a cobra. Her eyes widened.

"It's time I gave this back to you," he said.

Latifa smiled.

"If you remember, the day we met, I broke this chain when I plucked it off of your neck. I had it repaired." Tariq secured it around her neck.

Latifa touched the pendant. "This pendant is shaped to resemble the figure of the cobra that is inlaid on my father's crown. Thank you for returning it to me," she breathed.

"To show my contrition, I have a peace offering to give you."

"A peace offering?"

Tariq reached in his pocket once again. This time he pulled out a small box and handed it to her. "Open it," he ordered softly.

Latifa lifted the lid of the box and saw a bracelet made of gold laying in it. She picked up the bracelet and saw several small pendants all shaped like a cobra dangling at intervals around the chain.

"It's made to compliment your necklace. Now, you have a matching set."

"I…I don't know what…what to say," Latifa stammered.

"Say you like it." Tariq took the bracelet from her and fixed it around her wrist.

"I love it," Latifa admitted.

"It's the least I could do. But, there is something else I think you shall like even more."

Latifa's brow wrinkled.

"It's the reason I brought you here. Walk with me down by the river," Tariq prodded then led her to a long flight of stairs that led to the bank of the Nile.

As they headed down the stone steps, Latifa pointed to lines etched in the walls. "There are markings just like these along the steps leading to the barracks on Elephantine Island."

"Those markings are called *nilometers*. They help measure water levels. The *nilometers* in Aswan are particularly important. For you see, Elephantine marks Egypt's most southern border and it is the place where the onset of the annual flood is detected."

"The river flows so peaceful in its banks. It's hard to imagine it ever floods," Latifa remarked when they made it to the river's edge.

"Every year the river overruns its banks. When the water recedes, a fertile silt covers croplands."

"If I were to stand in this spot and see the river when it floods, I am sure I wouldn't recognize it."

"I hope this is someone you recognize." Tariq turned his eyes to look upstream.

Latifa let her gaze follow his. She was surprised to see a woman and a soldier walking toward them. A flicker of recognition prodded Latifa at the sight of the woman's shapely form and she strained to see the approaching female's face. A second later, the woman seemed to notice Latifa for she began to run toward her. When the approaching woman's face crystallized, Latifa's eyes became as big as saucers and her breath caught in her throat. She blinked unbelievingly at the sight before her.

"Do you recognize that person?" Tariq asked.

Latifa nodded her head unable to speak.

Chapter Thirteen

"Latifa? Is that you? Are you all right?" the woman's voice quivered as she hastened up the steps and to Latifa's side.

Latifa nodded her head as tears made their way down her face. "Yes, Mother. I'm all right and it is me."

In the next instant, Latifa reached out and hugged her mother. Both women began to cry as they held each other tightly.

"My dear child, it really is you. I didn't believe I would ever see you again."

"I've missed you so much!" Latifa cried before turning to look at Tariq. "You found my mother. How is that possible?"

"I listened when you told me your mother was captured and brought here to Egypt. You also told me her name was Aleka. Once we made it to Thebes, I instructed Jabari to start a search for her. She was being brought to the palace. But, when it seemed you were restless and needed time away from the palace, I thought it prudent to bring you to see if we could intercept her here."

Latifa wiped tears from her mother's cheek. "I am so grateful. How can I ever repay you?"

Before Tariq could answer, a shout sounded causing the trio to look up and see a soldier running down the steps. The soldier approached Tariq and nodded.

"Speak," Tariq commanded.

"The reports have been confirmed. King Rassom has been spotted near Aswan. An army of Nubians is with him. It appears he aims to start a war."

Latifa and her mother gasped in unison.

Tariq looked inquisitively at the women.

"My father is alive? I thought... I was sure you had him killed before Narmer attacked our village."

"Your father? Is King Rassom really your father?" Tariq questioned.

Latifa nodded. "I told you I was of royalty," she reminded him.

"I did not believe it when I heard you say it. Looks like we are both getting a surprise today." Tariq turned his attention to the soldier. "Send a messenger to Rassom and inform him his village was attacked without my knowledge. Tell the King I have no grievance against him. He is invited to be an honored guest at my palace and his people are invited as honored guests in our city."

Latifa's heart began to pound in her chest. What if her father did not believe the message? What if he refused to come to the palace? What if he and his men began a war of vengeance? Acting quick, Latifa took off her golden necklace then reached out and touched Tariq's arm. When he looked at her, she said, "If my father sees this, he shall know what you say is true."

Tariq took the necklace from Latifa. He handed the necklace to the soldier. "Have this piece of jewelry presented to the King. Tell the King his daughter and his wife, Akela, await him in my palace."

"I shall see that it is done." The soldier nodded then turned and traipsed up the steps.

"We must return to the palace at once," Tariq stated then he snapped his fingers.

As if from thin air, four guards stepped from behind a nearby wall.

"We are ready to return to the litter," Tariq announced.

The soldiers nodded curtly then flanked the trio and walked with them up the stairs.

When they made it to the litter, Tariq mounted the horse of one of the soldiers and let Akela take his place in the litter in order that mother and daughter could reunite. So much were mother and daughter caught up in their reunion that the ride back to the palace seemed to pass quickly. Once they arrived at the palace, Tariq dismounted and led Latifa and her mother to a bedroom on the ground level.

"This shall be your room," he said to Akela.

Akela smiled, amazement showing in her eyes.

"I shall leave the two of you to reunite," Tariq said before he exited the room.

Latifa followed him into the hallway. "Tariq," she called his name.

He turned to her.

171

"I am truly touched by all you have done. I am so grateful that you went to such lengths to find my mother," Latifa admitted.

"I was leading raids into Nubia around the time your mother was taken. I believe I am the reason you and your family were separated. That time can never be given back to you. But, I want to do what I can to make things right."

"This day has been so special. Almost overwhelming. My mother and I have reunited and now my father who I thought was dead shall be here soon."

"Your father must be furious since he thinks after the treaty was signed I burned down his village."

"Once he finds out the truth, he shall understand you are not to blame."

"From what I've seen of your father, he is a very reasonable man. We both became of one accord regarding lucrative trading deals between our nations. It would be good for both sides to put aside the idea of war and live in prosperity with each other."

"You are right of course. I just wish I let you explain exactly what happened between you and my father. If I had not been so quick to assume the worst, I would have known my father is still alive."

Tariq patted her hand. "I shall be sure to notify you and your mother as soon as your father arrives."

When Tariq turned to walk away, Latifa watched until he was gone from the hall. Smiling, she reentered the room her mother was staying in. During the next hours, the two women rotated between crying and speaking. As they ate the food that was brought into them, Aleka inquired about Tanesha and Latifa filled her in on everything that had transpired regarding her sister. When the hour was late, Latifa departed for Tariq's room where she changed into comfortable clothing.

After she returned to her mother's room, the pair talked most of the night. When mother and daughter grew tired, Latifa lay beside her mother on the bed. Both women vowed not to fall asleep until they heard of word from her father.

However, when the first light of dawn touched the sky and awakened Latifa, she realized both she and her mother had fallen asleep. Quietly, so she did not disturb her mother, Latifa got out of the bed and scurried up the stairs to Tariq's room.

"My father has not come has he?" she questioned when she entered his room.

Tariq's brow wrinkled and he shook his head. "I wonder if he's hesitant to meet because he thinks my offer is a trap."

"Was it explained to him that the village was raided without your consent? That Narmer was acting on his own?"

"There is no way to know since the messenger has not returned."

"Is he still near Aswan?"

Tariq nodded. "Your father has set up camp at the edge of the city. I am considering gathering some of my men and going out to meet him."

Latifa shifted nervously on her feet. "If you show up with a horde of soldiers, it could be interpreted as an act of aggression. Maybe something happened to the messenger before he could make it to my father. Maybe you should let me go. I can make my father see that you did not betray him as he thinks."

Tariq shook his head. "It is said I let you sway my thoughts. I don't need it said I let you speak for me as well."

"If my father doesn't believe what he is told, whatever can be done to prevent bloodshed should be done. I can't stand by and let something horrible happen between you and my father. Please let me go to him."

"I no longer wish to discuss the issue with you."

Tariq lifted his hand to silence Latifa when she opened her mouth to speak. "Need I remind you, when the Pharaoh says he does not wish to discuss an issue the issue is not discussed," he said then walked from the room.

ᙍ

When her father's camp came into view, Latifa pressed her legs into the flanks of the horse she rode. Leaning forward, she strained to catch a glimpse of her parent among the line of men who stood at the edge of the Nubian encampment. She knew Tariq would be furious with her when he found out in flagrant disregard of his command she had caught a *felucca* to Aswan. After exchanging goods she garnered from the palace for a horse, she had travelled to meet her father. As she neared the camp, two horsemen came out to meet her. Upon recognizing who she was, they escorted her to her father who stood with outstretched arms.

"Latifa!" Rassom called out excitedly.

She jumped from the horse and ran into his embrace.

"Father!" she exclaimed. "I thought you were dead."

"I am alive. Very much alive. Let me look at you. You look well. I thought you were imprisoned."

"Tanesha is in prison. I was never in prison."

"Were you made a slave?"

"No, Father. I was not."

"And your mother?"

"She is alive and well and waiting to see you."

"Where are they holding her?"

"We are staying in the palace with the Pharaoh as his guests. Didn't the messenger tell you?"

Rassom nodded. "I was told that by the messenger sent from the Pharaoh but I think it's a trap. I do not believe it."

"I didn't think you would believe it that is why I sent my necklace to you. The Pharaoh is a good man. He has a good heart."

A look of confusion crossed Rassom's face. "You defend the man?"

"I care for him, Father." The words rolled from Latifa's tongue before she could stop them.

Rassom removed his arms from Latifa's shoulders. "Come to my tent where we may speak in private," he said and led her to a nearby tent.

After they both entered the structure, he looked at her. "You say you care for the Pharaoh?"

174

Latifa nodded her head.

"How can that be? He promised peace between our nations yet he destroyed our village! He enslaves our people! He cannot be trusted!"

"Didn't the messenger tell you? It was his half brother, Narmer, who destroyed and burned down our home. You've got to believe it. Tariq wants peace between our nations. He is a good man."

"Are you so taken with him that you speak his given name? I can't believe my own daughter has turned against her people!" Rassom barked.

"Father! That is not true! I do care about our people. That is why there can be no bloodshed between the Nubians and the Egyptians."

"Even now that man holds your sister—"

"He is willing to let her go. He is willing to let them all go."

"But he has not! Until my Tanesha is safe there can be no peace!"

"Just talk to him. Please. After he explains everything, you shall see Tariq is a kind man."

Rassom gritted his teeth. "I never thought I would live to see the day when my own daughter would defend an enemy."

"If you won't believe the messenger then believe me, your daughter, when I say just speak with him to know he is not our enemy. He did not attack our village and it was Narmer who killed Kofi."

"Kofi is not dead."

"Kofi isn't dead?"

"No. He was injured...too injured to make the journey here. He told me of the Egyptians' deception and that they are the ones who sacked our village."

Latifa shook her head. "It happened without Tariq's knowledge. The offer to go to the palace is no trap. It's a miracle. I have the Pharaoh's ear. No harm shall befall us. You all must trust me. Tariq just wants to speak with you."

"He has my wife. I shall speak with him," her father conceded.

C8

When the palace came into view, Latifa cast a quick glance ahead at the messenger who had been sent by Tariq then at her father who was beside her. "We're almost there," she said to her parent.

Upon reaching the palace gates, the messenger spoke to one of the soldiers standing watch and said, "The Pharaoh asked to see King Rassom. This is he."

"The Pharaoh welcomes you," the soldier called a greeting to Rassom then let the father and daughter duo pass between the palace gates.

Once they made it to the stone steps, Latifa took her father's hand and led him to the front door of the palace. The guards standing by the door opened it and let the pair enter into the palace. Latifa led her father inside. Once they made it to the room where her mother was staying, she opened the door then stepped aside and let her father walk into the bedroom.

"Rassom?" her mother's voice quivered.

"Aleka?" her father's voice faltered.

A moment later, she spied the couple in each other's arms.

An arm reached in front of her and closed the door that led to the bedroom.

"They deserve a moment alone," Tariq whispered.

"Are you unhappy with me for going to my father and speaking with him?"

Tariq was silent a moment then he shook his head negatively.

Latifa smiled and wrapped her arms around him. "My parents are reunited. I am forever thankful."

"Let us wait in The Great Room," Tariq suggested and led her to the spacious room near the entrance of the palace.

Latifa was surprised to see Jabari in the room. She sat in a seat when Tariq and Jabari began to talk together. Sooner than expected, her father and mother walked into the room.

Tariq strode to meet his guests. "King Rassom, welcome to Thebes. You have my gratitude for coming. The last time we met, we became of one accord regarding a treaty that would benefit both our peoples. I am committed to the agreement that was made to trade gold and ivory between our countries. Jabari, I appoint you acting Vizier for this task. Make sure the agreement is written in the Book of Covenants and presented to The Council as approved."

Jabari nodded.

Tariq continued speaking. "King Rassom, I know after we parted your village was pillaged. Your people were killed or captured. It is to my regret this happened. It happened without my knowledge."

King Rassom nodded. "I was unaware of the truth that is why I came to seek justice for the destruction."

"Egypt has been shamed by the unprovoked attack on your people. The person responsible for the attack is my half brother. He has constantly sought to undermine my authority. Now, he has gone too far. I recently learned that he held your daughter against her will. I made my father, may he rest in peace, a promise that no harm would befall my brother. However, he must be punished. It pains me to think of what must be done. But, I promise you, something shall be done."

Rassom nodded again. "To that I am agreeable."

Tariq clasped his hands together. "While I cannot bring the people who were killed back, I can stop a travesty from happening again. Some of your people including your youngest daughter, Tanesha, are jailed for the murder of one of my soldiers during an escape attempt. In recognition of your good faith in coming to see me at the palace, I order the prisoners released at once."

Latifa gasped and her mother sighed with relief.

Jabari cleared his throat. "Sire, with all due respect, it is necessary the release of the prisoners be given more consideration."

"I have considered it."

"I must protest. The release of the prisoners shall be taken as an offence by many," Jabari protested.

177

"I asked that proof be provided to me to show which of the prisoners killed Kwame. No one witnessed the killing so there is no evidence proving which of those recaptured delivered the fatal blow. I said if no evidence was presented, the prisoners could go free."

"Your generosity is unmatched," Rassom stated and wrapped his arm around his wife.

"Sire," Jabari tried again. "There are many who want retribution—"

"Your protest is noted," Tariq assured.

"But—"

Tariq put up his hand halting Jabari's protest.

"The discussion on the issue shall cease at this time. Preparation for tonight's feast shall commence. King Rassom you are welcomed to stay in the palace for as long as you like. The people in your camp are invited to come to the city. They are invited to enjoy the hospitality of the city for as long as you desire."

Rassom held out an arm to Latifa. Latifa gladly walked into her father's embrace. Rassom looked at his wife wrapped in one arm and Latifa wrapped in the other. He smiled as he looked at Tariq. "You have given me back my life and for that I am truly grateful. So, yes, my family shall stay. We look forward to joining you for the evening meal."

☙

Tanesha and Aren arrived at the palace a short time later. The pair looked disheveled and exhausted but seemed very happy to be free. Tanesha was shocked yet overjoyed to see her mother. Hugs were given all around and many tears shed. After the joyous reunion, everyone decided to retire to the rooms that had been prepared for them in order to rest and ready themselves for the evening meal. As Latifa made her way to Tariq's room, she realized now that her family was reunited she felt she could truly relax. With a sigh, she lay on Tariq's bed and fell into an exhausted sleep.

Sometime later, Latifa was awakened by a servant.

"You must prepare for the banquet," the woman said and pointed to a white linen kaftan and a gold *usekh* lain out on the table.

The servant helped Latifa dress then slid the large *usekh* over Latifa's shoulders. After inspecting Latifa's appearance, the servant directed Latifa to sit at the table. The woman then secured her braided hair so that it no longer touched her shoulders. Next, she applied green eye shadow to Latifa's eyelids and lined her eyes with kohl. When her work was completed, she inspected Latifa from head to toe.

"You look very Egyptian," the kind woman stated.

Latifa smiled and straightened her stance. "Take me to the Pharaoh," she instructed.

The woman bowed briefly before leading Latifa to a room down the hall from Tariq's room and knocked on the door. The door was opened by a male servant.

"Let her enter," Tariq's voice sounded from within the room after the servant announced it was Latifa who wanted to see him.

The male servant stepped aside and Latifa walked into the large bedroom.

When she entered the room, she saw Tariq dressed in an ankle length pleated tunic with elaborate red fringing along the hem. A servant stood before him balancing a large tray on which lay a red and white crown with a golden cobra carved on it. A *nemes* that had red and white stripes also lay on the tray. Latifa watched Tariq place the *nemes* on his head and saw the headdress fit behind his ears, hung down his back and had two large flaps which hung in front of his shoulders. He then donned the crown. She could not help but note how regal he looked.

"You look very authoritative. I've never seen you in a crown," Latifa remarked.

"I am dining with a King. So, I wear the crown which symbolizes the unification of Upper and Lower Egypt."

Tariq looked at the servant, snapped his fingers and motioned toward the door. The man understanding his meaning exited the room. Once the servant was gone, Latifa walked to him.

"You look breathtaking," he said to her.

"Why are you dressing in this room?" she inquired.

"Out of respect for your father, I thought it best that I let you have my room all to yourself."

"You are very considerate," Latifa noted.

Tariq smiled then touching her arm led her from the room to the stairs. Tanesha and Aren could be seen standing near the foot of the stairs. Latifa saw Tanesha had been cleaned from head to toe and was now dressed in a brightly colored *boubous* while Aren wore a brightly colored *dashiki* with a black *kofia* on his head.

After Tariq and Latifa made it to the foot of the stairs, Tanesha walked to Latifa, hugged her and said, "Thank you for releasing us."

"I am not to be thanked. It is because of the kindness of the Pharaoh that you were released," Latifa explained.

Tanesha looked at Tariq then lowered her head before she whispered, "Thank you."

"Yes, thank you. Words cannot express our gratitude for sparing our lives," Aren explained.

Tariq's response was to smile and nod his head. When he turned and began walking down the hall, Aren followed his lead.

Tanesha touched Latifa's arm. "I am very repentant for the things I said to you and the way I treated you," she revealed.

"Let's not think of it for it is already forgotten," Latifa replied as the sisters walked arm in arm behind Tariq and Aren.

As the group neared the banquet hall, music floated to their ears. When they entered the room, Latifa saw it was filled with all of her tribesmen who had once been imprisoned. She spotted her mother conversing with a group of women on one side of the room. She watched Tariq walked to the front of the room and sit down beside her father before the pair began talking intently to one another.

Latifa, Tanesha and Aren found a place to sit near the musicians in the far corner of the room. As she listened to the music, Latifa noted how the soft hum of voices consorted with the undercurrent of a lyre, a *kithara* and a *kinnor* to create a festive atmosphere.

A few minutes later, servants dressed in white ankle-length linen kilts with blue *klafts* on their heads appeared holding platters laden with melons, grapes, figs and dates. Once the fruit was passed out and consumed, the servants appeared again. This time their platters were piled with beef, chicken and grilled lamb stuffed among lettuce and cucumbers in pita bread. To make sure everyone had their fill, carp and perch were offered to the diners as well.

Once all of the food was dispersed, a musician began to strum on an *oud*. Acrobats in costumes adorned with green and blue feathers appeared and performed feats that were met with many oohs and aahs from the onlookers. After the performers departed, dancers appeared to the clang of tambourines and cymbals. When their first set ended a drumbeat began. As the steady beat of the drum filled the room, Latifa watched the dancers' movements. She thought back to the night on the trail when Tariq let her tribesmen dance around the fire. She remembered the events that followed and thought of how she had lain in Tariq's arms. She shifted her gaze to Tariq and saw he was looking at her. The glint in his eyes told her he was remembering that night as well.

After the dancers departed, Rassom stood to his feet. As he brushed his hand across his *kanzu*, the individual conversations ended and the room fell silent.

"Nubians, we all have been through much," he began. "Our homes were destroyed and I came to this city on the brink of war. But, fate had different plans. As you can see, the Pharaoh is generous and kind. Though he is a man of war, he is also a man of peace who does not desire unrest with our people. He has released you all from prison and..." Rassom pointed to his wife. "He has restored our *Kandake* to us. His actions bring peace to us all!"

The crowd began to clap at his words.

Rassom motioned for quiet in the room. When silence returned, he continued, "The Pharaoh has kindly offered us respite in Thebes for as long as we like. We shall refresh ourselves in this land then return to our home."

The crowd clapped excitedly and her father sat. Servants reappeared. This time their trays contained sweet pastries.

As Latifa bit into the sweetened *halva* she had selected from a tray, she noticed Jabari enter the room. She watched Jabari trek to Tariq and whisper something in his ear.

Slowly, Tariq stood to his feet and waved his hand causing the room to fall silent once more before he said, "Honored guests, it seems the noblemen of The Council are here and would like an audience with me. With your indulgence, I bid them entry."

A low hum commenced in the room when the High Priest, Moswen, wearing a leopard's pelt secured by a strap over one shoulder and men Latifa recalled seeing on the platform by the lake at Karnak Temple walked into the room. Latifa lifted her brow in shock when she saw that Narmer was among the group. Her mouth fell open when Selma trailed the men into the room. Latifa studied Selma. The female looked breathtaking dressed in an amber colored *kalasiris* with a turquoise and amethyst *pectoral* covering the hollow between her breasts. She let her eyes follow Selma's gaze and saw the female had Tariq in her sights.

Tariq was looking at Moswen who stood at the front of the silent group. "You may speak," he permitted.

"My lord, as High Priest, greetings and tidings I bring you. We, your humble noblemen and priests, interrupt this banquet to speak on an issue of great importance for it is in regards to the Nubians within our midst. May I speak freely?"

Tariq nodded.

"Your loyal subjects and I have come to humbly protest the Nubians in our midst. Having the Nubians here has brought nothing but division to our land. The execution of the prisoners who killed a favored son of Egypt failed to happen. This is an affront that has opened wounds among the people. That is why it is asked that you spare our people such a slight and consider reversing your decision."

"To protect the innocent, the Nubians were released because no evidence was presented verifying the identity of the guilty culprit in the allotted time frame," Tariq said.

Narmer stepped forward. "There was no way to get evidence to you yesterday due to the fact you were away..." his gaze slid past Tariq and those in the room to settle on Latifa before he added, "...with your dalliance."

"Those accused are here tonight. Point them out and present the evidence against them now," Tariq ordered.

There was silence.

"Kwame served under my command. He was a young man who would not want anyone to be put to death for a crime they did not commit. Let it be noted, in honor of Kwame, the soldier killed, I order a military funeral held at his final burial place which shall be in the shadow of the Valley of the Queens." Tariq focused his gaze on Narmer then continued speaking. "A crime was committed and there is a perpetrator who should be punished. Narmer, you led an unprovoked attack against the Nubian village. It is because of you the Nubians are here. There must be reparations for the lives you took and the damage you caused."

"The lives of Nubians are of no consequence to an Egyptian," Narmer responded loudly.

"Is that why you abducted King Rassom's daughter?" Tariq questioned.

Narmer fell silent.

"It is to Egypt's everlasting shame that their favored son has acted in such an unscrupulous way. Egypt was demeaned by the unprovoked attack on the Nubian people. You have sought to undermine my authority at every turn. Your actions toward King Rassom's daughter and in your attempt to harm me, you have gone too far. You acted in the knowledge that I promised our father no harm would befall you. However, you have broken that sacred trust and must be punished. So, no harm shall be done to your person. But, it is my command that you be banished from Egypt."

A collective gasp rose from the group of men surrounding Narmer.

"Let it be noted, in honor of my father, Narmer shall be allowed to keep his possessions." Tariq looked at the men before him. "However, starting at sundown tomorrow, he is banished from all of the provinces under my rule."

"Sire," the High Priest began. "Narmer is of royal blood. He has a seat among The Council. Banishing him shall cause continued unrest with The Council. I must protest."

Tariq waved his hand to silence Moswen. Turning to look at Rassom, he said, "While I cannot bring back the people from King Rassom's tribe who were killed, I can help rebuild. Let it be known, all Nubians, whether slave or free, who want to return to Nubia with King Rassom when the King returns to his home can do so. This is my decree. The crown shall pay a fair price for any enslaved Nubians who choose to leave with King Rassom. The payments are to be made and dispensed so that their owners are made whole. The Nubians who return with the King can be the labor force that helps to rebuild King Rassom's village."

At his words, it seemed everyone in the room began to talk among themselves about the unexpected declaration.

"Your generosity is unmatched," Rassom said rising to his feet.

Jabari clenched his fist. "Sire, with all due respect, the release of all Nubians from enslavement should be given more consideration."

"I have considered it."

"You release the prisoners and now you release the slaves. I must protest," Jabari persisted.

Selma glided in front of the group of men to stand beside her father. She placed her hand on her father's arm. Moswen patted his daughter's hand, cleared his throat then looking at Tariq spoke again. "There shall be much discord at what has unfolded this night. As High Priest, I must say to you before all, it would go a long way if you were to take a wife. It would show there is stability to come."

"And I suppose you have someone in mind," Tariq remarked.

The High Priest nodded. "The Council would be satisfied if you were to take my daughter, Selma, as your wife."

Latifa's heart began to pound in her chest. She watched Moswen rub Selma's arm as he continued to speak.

"Once you are joined with my daughter, I shall speak to the people and help them understand the changes. My support for your decision shall aid in bringing calm back to our land."

"Your words are intriguing," Tariq replied. He fell quiet for many moments. Finally, he spoke, "I suppose you are right. I should take a wife. An alliance is just what is needed. A marriage of royals is commonly done to unify nations. I think it should be done in this circumstance, if the maiden is willing."

"I am willing," Selma spoke up.

Tariq looked at Selma then shook his head. "You misunderstand me." He turned and scanned the crowd of faces. His search ended when his gaze landed upon Latifa.

Latifa inhaled deeply as every pair of eyes followed Tariq's gaze to stare upon her as well.

"Come to me," he commanded of her.

Her heartbeat quickened. Slowly, she rose to her feet. With everyone watching her, she walked to Tariq.

"Is the maiden willing?" he asked her when she stood before him.

Latifa gulped as she looked into Tariq's eyes. "You want to get married?"

"I do."

"You want to marry me?" she questioned in amazement.

Tariq nodded. "I want to marry you. A Pharaoh is expected to marry a royal. Selma is not a royal. King Rassom's daughter is a royal," Tariq commented keeping his eyes locked with Latifa's.

"No Tariq! You can't do this! It is written in the stars you are to marry me," Selma's shriek echoed through the room.

Acting quick, Moswen grabbed Selma's arm when she stepped to advance upon the couple.

"Well, Latifa, will you marry me?" Tariq asked as if Selma had not spoken.

Latifa nodded. "I shall marry you."

Purposefully, Tariq swept Latifa into his arms. Unified gasps filled the room when with everyone watching Tariq captured Latifa's lips with his.

When Tariq's lips touched Latifa's lips, it was as if their hearts touched and began to beat as one. In that moment, time stood still. Like a wave hitting the shore, a ferociously delightful feeling cascaded over Latifa's entire being. When their lips parted, unable to move from his arms, Latifa clung to Tariq. It took several moments for sound to return to her ears.

Sound returned with Selma's scream. "You can't marry that Nubian harlot!"

"You shall not speak ill of your future Queen!" Tariq growled casting Selma a caustic glower.

"That Nubian shall never be my Queen!" Selma screeched and lurched against her father's unyielding grasp.

Tariq shifted his stance to address those seated. "Nubians enjoy this feast for it is to celebrate the engagement of the soon to be Queen of Egypt. As for all of you," he turned to Selma and the group of men behind her. "The Pharaoh no longer desires your presence."

Looks of shocked outrage covered the faces of the group assembled in the center of the room. Dejected, they began to make their exit.

"This isn't over yet!" Narmer shouted just before he disappeared from the room.

"No! This is definitely not over!" Selma warned as her father hastily dragged her from the banquet hall.

186

Chapter Fourteen

From her place on the balcony off of Tariq's bedroom, Latifa gazed at the argent moon that glowed in the sky. Many moons had shined in the sky since the first time she shared a bed with Tariq. At first it had been unwillingly. Now, just as he intended, she desired to be with him. There was no way she could have foreseen this day would come. She never dreamed Tariq would ask her to marry him. Now, she was set to be the wife of the Pharaoh of Egypt...the man she swore she hated and wanted to bring harm. She had sworn vengeance because she thought her father was dead. But, her father was not dead. In fact, everything she thought she lost to the Egyptians had been restored to her. Her mother was back in her life and her sister was safe. The people who were once condemned to death were now free. Miraculously, it was all because of Tariq. He was indeed a different man than she first supposed. He was no doubt fast asleep in the room down the hall. She wished he would be lying beside her that night because at the moment it seemed there were no longer any obstacles between them.

Something slick touched Latifa's hand interrupting her thoughts. She looked down and saw Anubis standing beside her. It was then she realized the dog had touched its nose against her hand to get her attention.

"Anubis!" she exclaimed and knelt to pet the dog. "Where did you come from?"

"I sent for her," Tariq's voice strong yet gentle responded.

Latifa looked up to see Tariq standing beside the bed. She stood to her feet and smiled as she thought the sight of him was what she wanted to see every day for the rest of her life. She walked to him and tenderly touched his hand before beckoning him to follow her onto the bed.

"I wasn't sure you would still be awake but I could not stay away," he said when she settled in his arms.

"I am glad you did not stay away for I am too excited to find sleep. I can't believe you want to get married let alone marry me. Selma can't believe it either. She wants to be your Queen," Latifa responded recalling Selma's outbursts.

"I could have married Selma a long time ago. It was what she wanted. My mindset was not to turn the relationship into an official union, because the truth is, my feelings for her never equaled those she had for me."

"But the High Priest is her father. He and those men of The Council can make things difficult for you, can they not?"

"I have half a mind to banish them all."

"As your Queen, shall I be left in Thebes while you are away on a military campaign?"

"Now that I am Pharaoh, there shall be no more military campaigns for me. I shall leave that to Jabari. As for me and you, we shall found a house together. After all, Pharaohs marry to seal alliances and establish dynasties. I choose to establish a dynasty with you. The sooner the better. Let's marry in one week's time."

"That soon!"

"Is that not agreeable to you? After all, the sooner we're married, the sooner I can sleep in my bed with you next to me even when your father is near."

"It shall be as you wish," Latifa affirmed.

Tariq pressed his lips against hers. She moved her lips over his. Her arms slithered around his neck and his hands moved under the thin material of her nightdress to find her breasts. He flicked away the material that covered her nipple and replaced it by placing his hands over her breasts.

"Take off your clothing," Tariq ordered.

Latifa complied without a word.

He followed her lead and shed himself of his clothing.

"I took you as my prisoner. But, it's you who has captured me. You are my Delilah. Yes. I read the Hebrew story. I am as Sampson and it's you who has managed to subdue me. You managed to provoke me to near madness with longing and desire yet enchant me so that now I say I am yours. My kingdom is yours if you so desire for I hunger for you as I've hungered for nothing else."

"You touch me with your words," Latifa murmured.

188

"Words are not the only thing I want to touch you with," he assured.

Latifa smiled and lay back on the bed. Tariq stretched over her length. She widened her legs. Placing his hand on his member, he began to guide it into her. Latifa's groan mingled with the sound of his moan as he pushed himself into the tightness of her sheath. When he was immersed in her sheath, he stilled himself. After several seconds, he began to move slowly inside of her. In that moment, Latifa was sure of how she felt about Tariq. Her affectionate feeling of care could be defined in one word and that word was love.

Latifa realized she could finally admit to herself that she loved Tariq and she wanted to blurt out her new found revelation. But, she held back. She would not be the first to speak of love. If Tariq loved her, he would have to declare his feelings first. He did love her. She was sure of it. The way he looked at her made her sure he loved her...or at least felt something close to love. Latifa looked into Tariq's eyes. Yes. She could definitely see it in the way he gazed at her. Surely, he would confess his love soon.

"What are you feeling? You can tell me," she could not help but prod.

"I am not sure there are words that can describe how I feel," he replied.

Just as she opened her mouth to question him further, he increased his pace.

Enthralled by Tariq's masterful movements, Latifa let her question die on her lips and she wrapped her legs around him. She thought how fortunate it was that she was going to be his wife. After all, whether he truly loved her or not, being a wife had its privileges. One privilege would be she could have him make love to her this way every day for the rest of her life.

అ

The following days were ones filled with joyous chaos for Latifa as preparation for her wedding commenced. Akela and Tanesha fretted over every detail of the upcoming nuptials. The women constantly coaxed Latifa to agree with their choices on everything from the flowers to the music that was to be played at the ceremony. When the trio discussed the menu, Akela insisted the meal contain Nubian fare of *kisrah* and lamb *kofte*. The desire to find the perfect wedding garment drove mother and daughters to the market.

"Daughter, you shall have a great life as Queen of Egypt," Akela assured and nodded toward the slaves carrying the trio in the litter.

"Look how the people stare enviously at us," Tanesha smirked as she eyed the onlookers.

"It's beyond amazing that I shall be the Queen of all of Egypt," Latifa replied.

When the women arrived at the market, the guards who were with them cleared a path so that they could browse the sundry wares in peace. Despite Aleka's prodding to purchase a *boubous* for her wedding dress, Latifa selected a white *kalasiris* similar to the one she had seen Selma wear.

The ride back to the palace seemed to fly by for Latifa, Aleka and Tanesha who chatted about their eventful day. When the women returned to the palace, Akela and Tanesha said they wanted to take a nap. After her mother and sister departed to their rooms, Latifa contemplated taking a nap as well. However, due to all of the excitement of the day, she knew she would not be able to rest. So, she decided to find Tariq and tell him about her day.

Eagerly, she searched the palace. When she neared the open door that led to the garden, the sound of Tariq's voice met her ears. She smiled and headed to the garden. Her brow wrinkled when a woman's sultry voice responded to Tariq's voice. Picking up her pace, Latifa hastened to the door that led to the garden. She came to an abrupt halt when she spied Selma standing close to Tariq. Remaining unobserved, she watched the pair.

"I have loved you since the day we met at The Temple and I shall love you until my last breath drains from my body. Yet you choose to repay my love for you with betrayal. You dismissed me as if I were a common slave without regard for my feelings." Selma's dark eyes held a captious glitter.

"I did not consider your feelings and that was unfair to you."

"You admitted we were good together. I thought we would one day make our relationship official by joining in marriage."

"The time we had together was good...very good...for we had many enjoyable encounters with me enjoying your body and you mine. Nevertheless, the truth is, no promises were made. Our relationship didn't need to be defined by a marriage ceremony," came Tariq's reply.

Latifa watched Selma turn her back to Tariq.

Tariq placed his hand on her shoulder then said, "I would not send you away empty handed. I shall see that you are well compensated for your many efforts on my behalf."

"You think coins are what I want?" Selma sulked and spun on her heels to face Tariq once again. "You chose that black over me! Do you think paying me off shall ease my embarrassment? There is no way I can be compensated for the humiliation you have caused me! You have spurned me before the entire nation!"

"That was not my intention," Tariq answered.

"You want to rid yourself of my presence just as you rid yourself of Narmer. You should know I won't go easily and neither shall Narmer. Don't you see, I am still needed by you. My father told me there are many unhappy with your actions. The Councilmen, the people of this nation, even many of those in the military are outraged that you released the Nubians set to be executed for Kwame's death," Selma stated.

"I have been Pharaoh for a brief time. However, I have been in the military for many many years. The men under my command have seen my dedication to them."

"You no longer have their total support. They see you as a traitor."

"I am no traitor!"

"The Council also sees you as a traitor. Even now, they remember Narmer's words that he deserves to be King.

191

Don't you see? I was a great asset to you in the past. You know I have sway over my father. You know I can convince him to have members of The Council do anything you want done."

"I shall fight my own battles."

Beseechingly, Selma circled her arms around Tariq's broad shoulders and pressed her lips to his neck. "My Tariq, come back to me. Don't abandon me. Let my love be enough for the both of us. I know our union was ordained by the Goddess Isis. You should be mine."

Latifa watched as Tariq wrapped his arms around Selma. Determinedly, Selma rose to the tips of her toes and pressed her lips against Tariq's lips. For a moment, Tariq seemed to relinquish to her kiss. Abruptly, he broke the kiss by stepping away from Selma.

Selma looked at him inquisitively then her eyes lit with ire. "You humiliated me when you asked for *her* hand in marriage! After all I've done for you! How could you wound me so? You dare discard me for that Nubian whore!"

"I told you before, you shall not speak ill of your future Queen!" Tariq shot back.

"That harlot shall never be my Queen! I shall never bow before her that would be even more humiliating since she is the one who turned you against me! Everything was good between us until she stole your affections! I was to be your Queen but she's taken my place!"

"Latifa has taken nothing from you."

"Then kiss me. Hold me in your arms and tell me you made a mistake...That what we had meant something to you. Tell me you shall toss her aside and return to me," Selma pleaded earnestly and looked expectantly at Tariq.

Tariq gritted his teeth and remained silent.

"Does what we shared really mean so little to you?" she demanded.

"Apologies that I hurt you. But, Latifa is the one I desire," Tariq confirmed.

Selma let out a frustrated growl. Angrily, she flicked her black hair over her shoulder and stomped away from Tariq.

Latifa scurried down the hallway and stepped behind a column. Remaining unobserved, she glimpsed Selma's entry into the palace. Anger rose in Latifa as she watched Tariq's former lover glide brazenly down the hallway. Selma had come to the palace to try and seduce Tariq. Now, the dark haired beauty walked brashly through the palace while she, Latifa, hid behind a column. Well, there was no way she was going to stay in hiding. After all, Tariq had made it very clear what he once shared with Selma was his past not his future.

Squaring her shoulders, Latifa stepped from behind the pillar. "This is now my home. You are no longer welcomed here," she stated crisply.

Selma stopped abruptly and spun around to look at Latifa. "If you know what's good for you, you'll leave and return to your real home. This palace is no place for a Nubian."

"Tariq wants me here. But, you already know that. I just heard him tell you so," Latifa replied curtly.

Selma's lips twisted. "Tariq and I are destined to rule this nation together. You shall not be his wife! You are a thief who stole the life that should be mine! I shall see to it that you are parted from Tariq!" Selma spat and advanced toward Latifa.

Latifa put her hand on her hip. "I stole nothing! Anything I've received from Tariq, he freely gave to me and there is naught you can do about it! You need to face the fact you had your chance with Tariq and now he's done with you!" Latifa reached in the pocket of the robe she wore and pulled out a coin left over from her shopping trip. "Tariq offered to compensate you for your services. I don't know what a suitable endowment is for someone who has been discarded like you, but this should do," she jeered and tossed the coin at Selma's feet.

Selma inhaled sharply and clenched her teeth. In an eerily confident tone, she swore, "I pledge this oath before the gods, I shall not rest until all you have…everything is taken away from you." With those words spoken, she turned, stomped down the hallway and out of the palace.

ॐ

193

Latifa woke early the next morning excited about her wedding which was to take place in a few days time. Just as she was about to dress for the day, Tanesha burst into the room and told her their father wanted to see the wedding dress she had chosen. Happily, she let Tanesha help her into the beautiful white *kalasiris* and don her freshly braided hair with a lotus blossom.

"Now you are ready to show father your beautiful look," Tanesha proclaimed with a smile before turning to lead Latifa out of the room.

Latifa returned the smile then picked up the bracelet Tariq had given her from the table. Quickly, she slid it over her wrist before following Tanesha out of the room and down the stairs.

Latifa was greeted warmly when she walked into the room where Tariq dressed in military garb, her mother, father and Aren sat eating their morning meal.

After everyone commented they loved her wedding dress, her father stood and motioned for Latifa to walk to him. When she stood beside him, he said, "Life has brought us unexpected change. Nevertheless, through it all, we have come together as a family and for that I am truly grateful. I want to say to my wife I love you and to my daughters I love you both. Latifa, as your special day approaches, I would like to tell you that you're a beautiful person inside as well as out."

Murmurs of agreement went up from everyone around the table at Rassom's words.

"The messenger Tariq sent gave this to me. You should have this back so you can wear it with your wedding dress." Rassom held up her necklace that contained the cobra pendant.

"Thank you father. I shall not take it off again," Latifa promised as her father placed the gold chain around her neck.

"I remember when your father gave you that necklace," Akela commented softly. "I am glad you still have it."

Latifa smiled. "I shall never part from it just as I shall never part from this." She raised her arm and showed her family the bracelet she wore. "Tariq gave this bracelet to me," she announced proudly.

Everyone eyed the bracelet admiringly then all eyes turned upon Tariq.

He cleared his throat then stood and said, "It delights me to see Latifa likes her gift as much as she does."

"I shall never part from it," she proclaimed again as a servant walked in.

"Apologies for the interruption." The servant bowed low.

"Speak," Tariq instructed.

"A visitor is here to see the mistress." The servant nodded toward Latifa.

"I have a visitor? Who is it?" Latifa inquired.

"She said you'd know her when you saw her. She waits for you in the garden," the servant disclosed.

Overcome by curiosity, Latifa said, "I shall speak with her."

Tariq looked at everyone sitting around the table. "I must be on my way. A chariot waits to take me to the military station. I go to join my soldiers to bid Kwame, the soldier who was killed, a final farewell and peace in the afterlife."

Everyone present bid Tariq farewell before Latifa followed him from the room. After he secured his sword in the sheath that hung from the strap around his waist, he left the palace and she headed for the garden. When she entered the botanical grounds, her eyes scanned the enclosure until they landed on her adversary who stood before a vine of grapes.

Latifa gritted her teeth as a wave of apprehension rolled through her. Why was Selma here to see her? Did she really need a confrontation with Selma to spoil her day? Deciding to put an end to Selma's uninvited trips to the palace, Latifa headed to where her adversary stood.

"I behaved badly." Selma spoke without turning to look at Latifa. "I behaved badly and I am ashamed of my actions. I know I do not deserve it but I'd like your forgiveness and to call a truce." The black haired beauty popped a grape in her mouth then slowly turned to face Latifa.

As Latifa approached Selma, she eyed the woman cautiously not sure what to make of her opponent.

"I am not as bad as I have acted. Though I must admit, finding you in Tariq's bed the first time I saw you was a bit of a shock. You see, I love him and it wounded me to find him with another woman."

"Especially a Nubian?" Latifa questioned.

A slight smile creased Selma's lips as she fingered the sash tied around her small waist. "My feelings are laid bare. I have acted horrendously," she admitted after a moment.

Latifa stopped a short distance from Selma. "Why the sudden change of attitude?"

"I confess my first reaction was to make trouble. But, the truth is, whether I've liked to hear it or not, Tariq has always been honest about what it is he desires. He's continuing to be honest now. So, I have decided I am going to be happy with his choices." Selma eyed Latifa poignantly then lowering her lashes she purred softly, "I know it is too much to ask that you and I be friends. Though that is so, I want you to know, I apologize. I shall never again do anything to undermine Tariq or belittle you."

Latifa took an uncertain step closer to Selma.

"Well, aren't you going to say anything? Won't you say you accept my apology?" Selma pried.

Latifa inhaled deeply as she pondered the validity of Selma's words. It was hard to believe such a change could take place in Selma so suddenly. Selma had vowed to part her from Tariq. On the other hand, if Selma truly meant what she said about being happy Tariq found love, things would be peaceful.

"You told me I should go home. You said you would never accept me. You said you would see to it that I was parted from Tariq," Latifa reminded her.

Selma nodded. "What you say is true. However, I want to make things right. There's something I want to share with you." Turning gracefully, she glided to the pavilion.

The soothing sound of water trickling in the fountain reached out invitingly to calm Latifa as she followed Selma to the pavilion. She watched Selma pick up two silver goblets from a tray that was on the stone bench.

196

"I asked one of the servants from the palace to bring this wine. I want to show you I meant what I said. Let us drink the wine in celebration of your upcoming wedding." Selma smiled sweetly and held out a goblet to Latifa.

Latifa looked at the silver cup then looked back at Selma whose smile softened still. She took the goblet from Selma's hand.

Selma raised the goblet she still held in her hand. "To new beginnings," she said then drained the liquid from her cup in two swallows.

Latifa tipped the goblet she held to her lips and mimicking Selma drank the liquid from the cup. The fruity taste of the wine dissolved into a tangy balm as it slithered over her tongue and down her throat.

Reaching out, Selma touched the lotus tucked amongst the braids in Latifa's hair. She lowered her hand and strummed her fingers along Latifa's shoulder. "For the life of me, I can't figure out why he chose you. He let you ride beside him in his chariot then sit beside him for all to see. He never asked me to do that. He even kissed you in front of everyone." Brazenly, Selma brushed her fingers across Latifa's lips.

Latifa pushed away from Selma and stumbled backward. Suddenly, she felt dizzy and it seemed a haze was quickly crowding her mind. She closed her eyes then opened them to find her vision blurred. "I don't feel so well," she moaned.

Selma looked at the goblet Latifa held in her hand. "The potion is working."

Latifa dropped the cup as if it burned her hand. "You viper! You've poisoned me!" she screeched even as the pavilion seemed to begin to spin.

"That's the problem with you Nubians. You want peace so bad you'll believe anything," Selma said dryly and advanced toward Latifa.

Latifa lifted her feet in an effort to retreat but stumbled backward again.

Selma chuckled and took another step toward Latifa. "You didn't think I'd let you have him, did you? You didn't think I'd just give him to you and walk away?"

The sound of the gate opening gave Latifa hope that one of the servants had entered the garden and would come to her aid. Horror gripped her when she looked at the gate and saw Narmer step through the portal and into the garden. Willing herself to remain strong, she staggered toward the palace.

Narmer stepped on the walkway blocking her path.

Latifa stopped in mid stride.

"I told you, you would rue the day you failed me," Narmer stated and tread toward her.

Latifa tried to move her feet but found she could not lift them. She looked over her shoulder and saw her foe watching with a ghoulish glint in her eye. Latifa turned her attention back to Narmer and watched with apprehension as he advanced toward her. When he was upon her, she tried to lift her arms and push him away. But, her limbs felt as if they were weighted with heavy stones. Suddenly, her legs seemingly unable to support her weight buckled beneath her. She felt herself slither downward. Acting quick, Narmer caught her in his arms before she hit the ground.

"You have partaken of the serum you were told to put in Tariq's drink. Unlike you, Selma had no problem following my orders. Ssshh. Don't try to speak. I have kept my word to make you pay for undermining me. You should have never crossed me. Now, you must sleep," he whispered.

Latifa wanted to scream in horrified protest at Narmer's words and touch. However, she found she could not move a muscle. Maybe if she focused on something she could fight the drowsiness that beckoned her and threatened to consume her. The sound of a bird chirping met her ears only to be replaced by the sound of Selma's chortle. Latifa tried to focus on something besides Selma's laugh but Selma's cackle echoed in her ears and refused to fade as darkness emerged to claim her.

Chapter Fifteen

"There now. Open your eyes."

A gruff voice rumbled through the darkness of Latifa's mind. She managed to open her eyes slightly to find a shadowy figure hovering over her. Heaviness saturated her eye lids and they slammed closed again.

"Time to awaken," the voice sounded again.

Fighting the fog that clogged her brain, Latifa managed to pry her eye lids apart once more. She held her eyes opened and her vision crystallized to reveal Narmer staring down at her.

"The comely one awakens," he muttered then moved from her view.

Latifa became aware of the fact she was lying on her back. Mustering her strength, she lifted herself onto her elbow and found Narmer standing beside her. Dismissing the grogginess that cradled her, she looked around and saw she was in a room that was dark except for the glowing light of a torch. Latifa frowned when she realized it was Selma who held the torch. "Where am I?" she asked.

"You are not in the afterlife if that's what you're asking. Sending you there so quickly would compromise justice. Though you shall soon wish you had drunk poison and not a sleeping potion," Narmer tilted his head to point to a place behind her.

Latifa turned and looked in the direction Narmer indicated. She gasped when she saw the form of a human body swaddled in white burial cloth laying on an alter.

"There lies Kwame's body. He was a good soldier. He knew the value of fighting one's enemy. Someone must pay for his death. Tariq did not want your sister to pay for it. So, you shall pay."

"What?" Latifa gaped at Narmer.

"You have served Tariq enough. Now, you shall serve Kwame on his journey in the afterlife."

"No!" Latifa lifted herself to a sitting position. "I have to get back to the palace. There are things that need to be done in preparation for my wedding."

"There shall be no wedding. You shall not be leaving this place. This is not only Kwame's tomb this is your tomb too," Narmer revealed.

Latifa scanned the tenebrous space once more as the meaning of Narmer's words sank in.

Narmer continued to speak. "You are in a tomb near the Valley of the Queens. It is a cave of sorts carved into the foot of a stone mountain. You are below ground in a burial chamber. Today, Kwame's military funeral is set to take place. Soldiers shall gather just beyond these walls of stone. Tariq shall be among the mourners. No one, not even Tariq shall know you're in this tomb. Not even that dog can save you."

"You mean to bury me alive!" Latifa exclaimed.

"Consider it an honor to die beside an Egyptian. After all, Egyptians are your betters," Selma spoke.

"You can't leave me with a dead body!"

Narmer nodded. "Once the door to this chamber is closed, you shall be locked in this room. A stone shall be rolled in front of the cave confining you in this underground grave forever. No one shall know what happened to you. Tariq shall never see your face again."

In a flash, Latifa leapt to her feet and ran for the only door in the chamber. Reacting quick, Narmer reached out and grabbed her around the waist stopping her in her tracks.

Latifa let out a horrified scream. "Let me go! Let me go, you demon!" she hollered as she clawed at Narmer's face and kicked her legs wildly.

Narmer raised his arms and lifted her off of her feet. He shook her savagely then flung her so that she was propelled through the air. An instant later, she landed on her hands and knees in front of the alter that held Kwame's remains.

"Tariq has forced my hand. I refuse to leave this land and the two of us cannot coexist in it. I now see to obtain what is mine, I must be unyielding. No more restraint shall be shown. No mercy shall I give. I shall take everything from Tariq including his crown. But first, I shall do away with you which is what I should have done the first time I had the chance. If I had, I wouldn't have to deal with you now," Narmer wrenched out fiendishly.

"No! Please! Don't do this!" Latifa implored frantically. Turning to gape at Selma, she challenged, "How can you let him do this? How can you be a party to such an evil deed?"

"I meant it when I told you I'd make you pay for everything you took from me. If I can't be Tariq's Queen, you won't be his Queen. If I can't have Tariq's love or the title of Tariq's wife, no black girl shall have it either." Selma smirked as she sauntered across the chamber to the door.

"How can the two of you do this? How can you?" Latifa shouted as panic lumped in her throat and tears began to seep uncontrolled from her eyes.

"Save your breath. You're going to need all of it," Selma taunted as she opened the door of the chamber. Moments later, she exited the chamber taking the torch with her and inviting darkness to saturate the room.

"Don't leave me in here!" Latifa screeched above the rhythmic click of Selma's retreating sandals.

Finding strength to fight for her life, Latifa leapt to her feet then raced to follow in Selma's wake. Brutally, she shoved past Narmer. Ignoring his shout, she dashed out of the burial chamber to the foot of a wooden ramp. She peered up the ramp and eyed Selma at the top of it. In a flash, Latifa sprinted up the ramp toward the fading torch light. As Selma stepped out of the cave and into the sunlight, Latifa was upon her. Ruthlessly, she elbowed Selma causing her to stumble and drop the torch. Instinctively, Selma reached out and grabbed Latifa's arm to steady herself. Latifa yanked her arm from Selma's grip.

In the next instant, Narmer rammed Latifa from behind sending her hurling to the earth. She hit the ground with a thud. Instantly, her eyes, nose and mouth filled with sand. She opened her mouth to spit out the sand and more sand filled her throat causing her to succumb to a fit of coughs.

"You can't escape your fate! I won't let you take my victory from me!" Narmer growled. Clinching his fist in her braids, he lifted her to her feet. Turning her to face him, he smashed his hand across her cheek ripping a piercing cry from Latifa's throat.

Instantly, Narmer covered her mouth with his hand then he dragged her back into the underground cave and down the ramp that led beneath the earth.

With all of her might, Latifa twisted against Narmer's iron grasp but to no avail. Callously, he thrust her back into the burial chamber. She fell to the floor. Narmer kicked her extracting a yelp from her lips. Determinedly, he stomped from the chamber. Refusing to be defeated, Latifa leapt to her feet once more and ran toward the door. Just as she reached the door, Narmer slammed the door in her face casting her into complete darkness.

"Please! Don't do this!" Latifa hollered and feverishly pounded on the door.

The answer to her plea came several minutes later in the form of the sound of something being rolled in front of the entrance of the cave...presumably a massive stone.

Franticly, Latifa screamed and continued to pound on the door until she was hoarse and the tenebrous gloom depleted her strength. Defeated, she slid to the ground and stared into the darkness.

ဢ

The moment Tariq stepped from the building at the military station Anubis scampered to him. He petted the dog's head. The hound licked his hand and followed him as he walked to the transport. During the transport to the banks of the Nile, Tariq thought of how beautiful Latifa looked in the dress she was to wear at their wedding. He remembered how happy she had been earlier that morning chatting with her family until it was announced someone was in the garden waiting to see her. He wondered who the person was who stopped by the palace to see Latifa. On the trip across the river, his speculation continued. When he joined the funeral procession, he was so engrossed in thought that he barely felt the heat of the sun as it rose in the sky. By the time members of the procession stopped to rest themselves from the heat, Tariq decided he would return to the palace as soon as he could to find out who had stopped by to see Latifa and what had been discussed.

Finally, the procession arrived at the edge of the Valley of the Queens. They walked through the canyon where large stone mountains rose toward the sky. The host of soldiers gathered at the foot of the rocky hill where Kwame was entombed.

"Kwame was a good soldier," Jabari reflected as he and Tariq headed toward the somber scene before them.

Tariq opened his mouth to respond but words died on his tongue when he saw Selma materialize out of the cluster of men. With a glint in her eye, she gazed demurely at him then bowed in deference to him when he passed her by. His brow wrinkled. What was Selma doing here?

Turning his attention back to Jabari, Tariq said, "He was a good soldier indeed."

Suddenly, Anubis darted from Tariq's side and scampered to the massive stone that covered Kwame's burial place. As Tariq and Jabari approached the tomb, Anubis let out a whine and began to scratch at the base of the stone.

After casting a quick glance at Anubis, Jabari said, "No one's life has been forfeited for Kwame's death. As you know, that does not sit well with many of the men gathered here. They are trained to respect your decisions and do not grumble aloud unlike Narmer who attempted to use the unrest to his advantage. The fact Narmer appeared at the banquet with Moswen and members of The Council lays bare the fact his vitriol has taken hold of some of the people. His attempt to have your drink tampered with was an unforgivable grievance. It is good he was banished.

"Do not forget, there's still Moswen. The Priest is upset for many reasons. He is not pleased that you chose another over his daughter. He let it be known he spoke with Latifa when she was at Karnak Temple. He said she knows nothing of our gods. He and other priests are angry because you allow her to pay homage to the Hebrew God instead of Amun or Isis. Moswen says Latifa has asked that Hebrew Scripture be read at your wedding ceremony."

Abruptly, Anubis stopped scratching at the stone and let out a piercing wail.

"Enough!" Tariq snapped tartly at the dog as he and Jabari came to a stop near the stone.

Anubis quieted, walked back to Tariq and sat near him.

Tariq turned his attention to Jabari once again. "Regarding the issue of the Hebrew God, I do not see the problem with accepting diverse thoughts and ideas. As far as the others, disloyalty shall not be tolerated from anyone. Just as all of the soldiers under my command must respect my decisions, so must every citizen of Egypt."

A bark charged the air. Both men turned to look at Anubis and saw she had returned to the rock that covered the underground cave and once again scratched at the ground. The dog placed her nose low to the ground before another bark emanated from the animal followed by several consecutive barks.

Piqued by the dog's insistence, Tariq walked to the canine. "What is it, girl? What is it?" he questioned and reached down to pet the dog.

A sparkle of gold light caught his eye.

"What is...?" His voice trailed off as he eyed a gold-colored object partially covered by sand. He knelt and brushed away the sand that covered the object. Reaching out, he picked up the object and saw it was a small gold pendant in the shape of a cobra. Instantly, he recognized it as one of the pendants from the bracelet he had given Latifa. He recalled seeing the bracelet earlier in the palace on Latifa's arm when she held out her arm so her family could see the bracelet he had given her. *"Tariq gave this bracelet to me. I shall never part from it,"* she had said. So, what was Latifa's pendant doing off of her wrist outside Kwame's grave site in the Valley of the Queens?

"What do you behold?" Jabari inquired a moment before he spotted the pendant in Tariq's hand.

From his place on his knees, Tariq looked up at Jabari. Shifting his gaze, he let his eyes scan the mass of men then still when they fell on Selma. She was many miles away from the city at a place she had no cause to be. Something was not right and whatever it was involved

Selma. Intently, he inspected his former lover noting that her eyes glimmered with deviance. His gaze left her face and traveled down the white robe she wore then stopped on the sash around her waist. His eyes locked on what looked like gold thread dangling between the sash and the robe. Tariq rose to his feet and beckoned Selma over. She glided forward and came to a stop before him.

"Tariq?" her voice was laced with uncertainty when she said his name.

Reaching out, Tariq clinched the unknown thread with his fingers and plucked it from her garment. He held it up and it unraveled to reveal several pendants shaped like a cobra dangling from a gold chain. Instantaneously, Tariq recognized the bracelet as the one he had given Latifa. There was an empty space on the bracelet indicating one of the pendants was missing from the chain.

Suddenly, Tariq realized the missing pendant was the one he had picked out of the sand. His eyes locked with Selma's. "How did you get Latifa's bracelet on your robe?" he inquired as he dangled the bracelet and the pendant in front of her face.

Selma lifted her chin and displayed a smug expression.

He clamped his hand over her wrist. "Tell me!" he hissed.

"I...I..." she stuttered.

He tightened his grasp.

Her smug expression evaporated. "I have no idea what you're talking about," she hedged.

Anubis began to bark in earnest while the soldiers stared inquisitively at the scene unfolding before them.

"It was you who visited the palace and asked to see Latifa."

Selma shook her head negatively.

"I can confirm it when I return to the palace so do not lie to me. What happened between you and Latifa?" Tariq growled over the noise of the dog's bark.

"Release me!" Selma shot back and with her free hand tugged on his arm.

"Tell me what happened!"

"You're hurting me!"

"Tell me!" Tariq bellowed.

"I...I told you, I don't know what you mean!" Selma insisted.

Tariq clinched his hand around Selma's neck. "What have you done? Answer my questions or so help me you shall breathe your last breath!" he snarled.

"There's naught to tell!" Selma spat.

Mercilessly, Tariq compressed his fingers against Selma's delicate flesh. "You have one more chance to tell me or so help me, I shall snap your delicate little neck!" He tightened his fingers.

Selma gasped for air and she placed her hands over his hand in an attempt to loosen his iron grip. Her face darkened as blood pooled in her cheeks.

"Sire!" Jabari cautioned.

A wheezing sound rattled Selma's throat as she stretched out her arm and pointed to the stone that covered Kwame's grave.

Tariq's grip loosened and he looked where she indicated.

Gasping for air, Selma shoved away from him and stumbled backward into Jabari's arms.

"It was Nar...Narmer's idea to leave the Nubian in there with that soldier. I went along with...with it because I love...love you," she sputtered.

As the gravity of Selma's revelation sank in, Tariq pivoted on his heels and placed his hand on the massive stone that covered the entrance. "Get this tomb open! Now!" he bellowed as he shoved the bracelet and pendant into the pocket of his *schenti*.

Jabari motioned for several soldiers to advance. "You heard the Pharaoh! Find a way to get this stone moved!"

"No one is moving that stone!" a caustic voice blustered a second before Narmer stepped from around a boulder near the tomb with a sword in his hand.

Several soldiers pulled their swords and advanced to stand beside Tariq.

Jabari waved them back. "It's time this issue is settled. It has to be settled between the brothers with no interference," he announced.

The soldiers moved to stand in their previous places.

"Surprised to see me?" Narmer questioned Tariq once the soldiers put their swords away.

"I banished you from Egypt," Tariq countered.

"You can't banish me for it is I who is the true Pharaoh of Egypt. This is my land and my army!" Narmer shouted.

"Yet again, you dare undermine me! Today is the day you shall answer for it!" Tariq reached for the sword at his waist and pulled it from its sheath.

Narmer advanced toward Tariq. "I shall not be banished and we cannot coexist in this land. Only one of us shall survive this fight," he uttered then lunged at Tariq.

Reacting quick, Tariq swung his sword forward. The clink of blades hitting each other echoed through the stony canyon. The men backed away from each other slightly then lurched forward. Their swords clanked again.

When the men moved apart, they circled one another.

"Father was manipulated into giving you the title of Pharaoh," Narmer quibbled.

"Don't speak such falsehood. Father was not manipulated into appointing me Pharaoh. He had his reasons for appointing me Pharaoh. Whether you like it or not, his decision must be honored."

"If Father was not manipulated then he would not have appointed you successor. I am his legitimate son. My bloodline is pure. You...you are naught but a bastard!" Narmer charged Tariq and thrust his sword forward.

Tariq parried Narmer's attack then took several steps back in deference to Narmer's onslaught.

"It no longer matters what Father's reasons were. You are no longer a creditable ruler. You have forsaken the people and the men of the military for your Nubian whore! You have betrayed your people! Now, I shall be placed on the throne and I shall rule—" Narmer's words were cut off as he raised his arm to ward off Tariq's jab.

The brothers trampled over rocks as they sparred at the foot of the mountainous hill. They battled for dominance as one's offensive move was thwarted by the other's defensive block. The soldiers present stalked the men's erratic course around jagged boulders. Shouts rose from

207

the onlookers as the seemingly equally matched opponents battled in front of one stone covered tomb after another.

Tariq was the first to make contact. His sword split the material of the tunic that covered Narmer's chest.

Narmer jumped backward onto a plank lying over a fresh whole being dug for an underground tomb. The thin wood wobbled precariously under the burden of his weight. Glancing down, he looked into the darkened pit. Catapulting off of the plank, his sword made contact with Tariq's shoulder and sliced through Tariq's tunic and across his upper arm. Tariq inhaled sharply as a red stain marred his tunic and blood began to ooze against the torn material. With a grunt, Tariq advanced on Narmer. Narmer held his ground. After many moments, Tariq's relentless assault propelled him backward.

Narmer backed toward the plank again. Unexpectedly, sand slid from under his feet into the hole causing his foot to slide beneath him. Acting quick, Narmer managed to remain upright. He thrust his arms outward and the tip of his blade struck Tariq's torso.

Tariq leaned backward.

Narmer leapt back onto the plank which once again shook under his weight. He raised his arms to balance himself on the flimsy wood and teetered for a moment. Suddenly, the wood snapped. Narmer let out a screech then dropped his sword. Selma screamed and a collective gasp sounded from the soldiers as Narmer began to descend into the black pit. In a flash, Tariq dropped his sword and growling reached for Narmer. His hand grazed Narmer's shoulder. He managed to clutch Narmer's retreating arm. Unable to grip it tightly, Narmer's arm slid through his grasp. Tariq closed his fingers around Narmer's retreating wrist stopping his half brother's descent. He looked down at Narmer then into the atramentous hole.

Narmer gaped at Tariq in horror then following Tariq's gaze bent his head to peer into the endless darkness beneath his dangling feet. He turned his eyes back to Tariq. "Don't let me go!" he pleaded fervidly.

"I won't!" Tariq promised his half brother as soldiers crowded around the side of the hole.

Tariq let out a grunt and pulled on Narmer's wrist until Narmer's body began to ascend the chasm. Narmer lifted his free hand so that it breached the pit. Once Narmer's hand showed beyond the pit, a few soldiers grabbed him and quickly hoisted him out of the hole. They laid him on the sandy ground next to the pit then the soldiers backed away. Breathing deeply, Tariq collapsed in an exhausted heap beside his sibling.

"You saved my life," Narmer wheezed.

"You're my brother. I promised Father no harm would befall you," Tariq panted.

Narmer rose to his knees and eyed Tariq for a second. "You are a fool to have saved me. I told you the day would come when you would regret making that promise." In a flash, Narmer withdrew his dagger from its sheath at his waist and pointed it at Tariq.

Jabari with several soldiers at his heels withdrew their swords and rushed toward the brothers.

Acting quick, Narmer lifted the dagger high in preparation for a fatal thrust into Tariq. All of a sudden, the sand beneath him began to cascade into the open hole behind him. As the earth rapidly disappeared beneath him, Narmer dropped his dagger. Terrified of his rapidly approaching fate, he let out a screech and grasped at the tiny grains of sands evaporating under him. But to no avail. The earth melted beneath Narmer sending him hurling into the welcoming grave.

ଔ

Tariq paced back and forth as he watched soldiers push on the plank wedged under the stone that covered the entrance to Kwame's tomb.

"God! Please let us get to Latifa in time," he prayed to Latifa's God a moment before he shouted for the men to work faster.

Using the tools left by those who were digging the new tomb, soldiers continued to hack at the earth beneath the colossal stone. Time seemed to drag by as the soldiers continued their endeavor. The light of the sun dimmed in the sky and the moon's light rose to take its place. Night slowly passed as the work continued. When the moon's light began to fade from the sky, the workers managed to hack enough of the hardened earth in front of the stone so that the rock could finally be rolled away.

Once the open cave was revealed, Tariq pushed the laborers aside and rushed into the tomb. Striding down the narrow ramp, he bolted to the door of the internment chamber. Jabari appeared beside him and using his sword cut the rope that secured the door from the outside. Tariq kicked the door opened. The moment he stepped over the threshold, he stumbled over a heap on the floor. Reacting quick, he managed to remain on his feet.

It took a moment for Tariq's eyes to adjust to the darkness in the burial chamber. Slowly, a sliver of mauve light from the early morning sun seeped down the ramp and through the open door. Guided by the streak of light, he looked to see what had caused him to stumble and saw a petite form lying face down on the floor.

"Oh no!" Tariq exclaimed as he knelt beside the feminine form. Placing his hand on the female's soft shoulder, he turned her body so he could see the female clearly. "Latifa!" he called out when he saw her face.

She stirred weakly.

Gently, Tariq cradled her head in his arms.

Jabari came to stand beside him. "Amun be with us! We've got to get her to a physician!" he exclaimed.

Securing his arms around Latifa, Tariq gathered her into his embrace then rose to his feet. Holding her protectively in his arms, he walked out of the tomb and uttered a prayer that he had not gotten to her too late.

ᘓ

Latifa's eyes fluttered opened. Slowly, they focused on the person looking down at her. She recognized Tariq.

"Thank God," he breathe and tenderly rubbed her cheek.

"Tariq," she whispered.

"Finally, you open your eyes," her father's kind voice sounded.

Recognizing her father's voice, Latifa shifted her gaze and saw he stood at the foot of the bed she was lying in. A worried look showed on his face.

Latifa realized she was laying in Tariq's bed and attempted to raise herself to a sitting position.

Her mother and sister suddenly appeared beside her.

"Baby, let me help you," Akela cooed then took over assisting her to an upright position.

"I am so glad you're all right. Do you remember what happened?" Tanesha inquired.

An image of Narmer flashed in Latifa's mind followed by an image of him throwing her into the tomb. Selma's face flickered in her thoughts even as the memory of the torch light followed by consuming darkness seared her mind. The sound of her own screams echoed in her ears and rattled her brain. Tears crowded in her eyes then spilled down her cheeks.

"Narmer and Selma put me in that tomb. They did it to hurt Tariq and keep me away from him," she revealed.

"They have not succeeded. You shall be my Queen," Tariq assured.

"My daughter cannot stay among such depravity!" Rassom countered.

"Our people know what happen to you, sister. None can abide yet another instance of mistreatment of one of us by the Egyptians," Tanesha stated to Latifa.

"I have lost five years of marriage to my wife because she was in this dreadful land. I shall not lose another day. Neither shall I lose my daughter," Rassom hedged. "We shall leave this god forsaken place. We are all leaving this place as soon as Latifa feels better. We must return to our own home."

"Latifa cannot leave!" Tariq objected.

"It's dangerous for my daughters here. As their father, I have to keep my children safe. They are not safe in Egypt. None of us shall be safe in this land."

"I can protect Latifa!" Tariq insisted.

"Obviously you can't! You may be the King of this wretched place but that doesn't mean you can protect my daughter!" Rassom argued.

"Please stop bickering!" Latifa pleaded.

Everyone fell silent.

Latifa thought about her father's words. Her father was insisting she return to Nubia. But, what of her future with Tariq? She had been able to finally admit her love for him and been set to marry him and make Egypt her home. But, could she live in a place where she did not feel safe? Could she ever feel at home in a place where there was such deception and treachery? And what of her family? They would all return to Nubia. Now that they had been reunited, did she want to live without seeing her father, mother and sister?

"The physician is on his way," Tariq's voice interrupted her thoughts.

"I do not want the physician. I want to be alone," Latifa muttered wearily. "Please," she added when Tariq started to protest.

"A bath has been drawn for you, if you want it," Tariq said before the small group left the room.

Once she was alone, Latifa's mind filled with memories of the suffocating darkness in Kwame's tomb. As she thought of it, that darkness seemed to enter the bedroom and wrap itself around her throat. She gasped for breath because it seemed her very life was slipping from her. Her heart thumped in her chest. Panic and fear rose up to strangle her releasing tears and causing uncontrollable sobs to shake her body.

Latifa cried until all of the tears were drained from her. When she could cry no more, she brushed her tear stained cheeks with her hands. Slowly, she slid her legs over the side of the bed and stood on wobbly feet. She walked to the balcony and looked beyond the palace grounds. The streets were unusually empty. An unmistakable sense of foreboding seemed to hang in the air.

Latifa turned from the sight. Leaving the balcony, she walked to the washroom. For a moment, she stood and watched vapors rise from the water and dissipate in the air.

Finally, she slid out of the grubby garment that was to have been her wedding dress and stepped into the bathing pool. She lowered herself into it and the steaming liquid heated her skin.

Her thoughts immediately turned to the time she was in the tomb. She had been hours away from death. If Tariq had not rescued her, today would have been the last day she drew breath. If the present day had been her last on earth, would she have been happy with the sum of her life? She remembered how her main goal had been to be a great warrior. She had felt no real yearning for love or marriage...and then she met Tariq. She had resisted him in the beginning because she had vowed she would never find enjoyment in the arms of a man. She had made that pledge because she believed to be a great warrior she could not involve herself with a man. But, in the end, she had broken the vow she made and discarded the beliefs she once held because of her attraction to a man. Never could she have imagined the man would be the Pharaoh of Egypt. Once, thoughts of revenge against the Pharaoh filled her mind. Now, she knew the Pharaoh was not her enemy. Instead, her heart ached with love for him and more than anything she wanted to be his wife.

But, did she dare stay in Egypt? Her family would return to Nubia and she would be in Egypt without them. Could she survive in a foreign land without her loved ones by her side? There were so many obstacles against her union with Tariq and too many people dedicated to the destruction of their relationship. She had almost been murdered by Narmer and Selma. Staying in Egypt could mean she risked her life again. Life with the Pharaoh meant a life where plots and intrigue abound. With enemies lurking all around, how long could she survive in Egypt? She was young with her whole life ahead of her. Why should she risk it all just because she had feelings for Tariq that were best described as love? After all, Tariq had yet to say he loved her. He had said he wanted her to be his Queen. More than likely, he wanted her because he enjoyed her body and liked having her at his convenience. With that being the case, the question she had to answer was, was the attraction between them enough to have her ignore all she held dear including her very life?

When Tariq had spoken of love, he had said he was not looking for love…that love made a man weak. He even went so far as to say someone in his position could not accept such folly. Just because he asked her to marry him did not mean he would change his way of thinking. But, at least by marrying her, he was announcing to the world that she was more than a companion who shared his bed. Although that was true, at the banquet he had said a Pharaoh married to seal alliances and establish dynasties. Maybe the marriage proposal had been done out of duty. She had no proof that Tariq's feelings for her rose to a level that had anything to do with love. One thing was for certain, a woman who was truly loved by a man did not have to guess if the man loved her. Tanesha's relationship with Aren was proof of that. With such uncertainty about the depth of Tariq's feelings for her, was living as his wife a life she wanted to live even if she reigned as the Queen of Egypt?

Water rippled around Latifa's body when she straightened herself. As she began to wash her limbs, she once again recalled wanting to be a good warrior. One thing she knew for sure, a good warrior knew when to retreat. Was she going to retreat or was she going to fight for her future and stay in Tariq's life? The truth was, she needed no more time to think. The decision was made. She just needed to inform Tariq. But, at the moment, her heart ached so badly she could not bring herself to exit the bathing pool. Instead, she stayed submerged in the water until all of its heat fled and she could no longer stand the cold.

ᚼ

"You came," Latifa breathed a sigh of relief when she saw Tariq walk into the garden toward her.

"Of course I came," he said after he took her in his arms.

Latifa wrapped her arms around Tariq savoring the feeling of security that cradled her.

When they parted, Tariq took her hand in his and they began to stroll through the garden.

"I am glad to see you are up and out of bed. Do you feel well?" he inquired.

"Because of Narmer what I feel most is afraid."

"Narmer was gravely injured when he fell. He clings to life but it does not seem he'll survive the night. If he succumbs, it'll be his hatred that caused his death."

"And Selma. What of her?" Latifa queried as they walked to the pavilion.

"Her fate is in your hands. Whatever you desire, it shall be done."

Latifa turned from Tariq and covered her face with her hands.

Tariq touched her shoulder. "What is it?" he questioned.

Dropping her hands, Latifa turned to look at the man she loved.

Spying tears in her eyes, Tariq prodded, "Tell me."

"I don't know if I can."

"You at a loss for words? I do not believe it. You are strong and bold, my little lioness. You can do anything."

"Oh Tariq, if only I was as courageous as you say I am then I would not be afraid to spend the rest of my life with you." Latifa shifted her eyes to look at the water cascading in the fountain and then at the leaves of the majestic trees which rustled in the warm breeze.

"You've been through a horrible experience. It's going to take some time for you to feel right again. You have to—"

"I can't marry you," Latifa cut in.

"What?" Tariq put his fingers under her chin and turned her face to his.

"I want to. Believe me. I want to marry you but I just can't." Tears began to run down her face as she looked into Tariq's eyes.

"I know you're upset and you're saying things you don't mean."

"Oh Tariq," Latifa placed her hand on his cheek. "It would never work between us. There are too many obstacles."

"Your sister is freed. Your mother is returned to you. All you have lost has been restored."

"Tariq, please don't make this any harder than it already is. Egypt is not the place for me. It never shall be. No one cares for me here. They don't want me with you."

"I don't care about anyone else's thoughts on the matter."

Latifa reached out and touched his arm. "Not even Jabari's thoughts? He is not only a member of your military he is also your friend. You respect him. He doesn't approve of me. The members of The Council do not approve of me. The High Priest is Selma's father. He does not approve of me. Once Selma is punished, he shall turn the other priests against you if he hasn't already. To affectively lead this nation, you need support. Your people shall not accept a Queen who does not believe in Amun or any of the other Egyptian gods. I am an outsider. I do not believe as Egyptians believe. I believe in the Hebrew God. The God of Abraham. That shall never change."

"Many gods are worshiped in Egypt. What is one more?"

Latifa shook her head. "There is too much between us. The Nubians are preparing to leave the city. I shall leave with them. A horse awaits me just beyond the palace gates. I shall return to my people and my home."

"No! You can't leave. We can make it work."

"I have just been united with my family. Would you separate me from them? Moreover, your brother and Selma tried to kill me. I would never feel safe. If we were to have children what about them? Would I have to worry that some supporter of Narmer might try to kill our children as they did me?"

"Narmer shall pay. Selma shall pay." Tariq's jaw clinched tightly. "Don't walk away from what we share."

"I must."

Resolutely, Tariq pulled Latifa against his chest and hugged her tight. She lifted her face to him and his lips claimed hers. His lips left hers to touch her cheek, nose and forehead.

In that moment, Latifa desperately wanted to hear Tariq say he loved her. Despite everything, she was sure if he told her he loved her she could find the courage to put her fears aside and stay with him.

"Why do you want me to stay?" Latifa prodded hopefully.

"Remember the night we sailed from Aswan and you spoke of leaving. I told you then why I did not want you to leave. The reason has not changed. I do not want you to leave me because I would miss you too much."

Tariq said he would miss her. He had not said he loved her.

With sadness in her voice, Latifa whispered, "You must honor the wager we made. You promised me my freedom. Please let me go."

"Wait a few days longer. We can resolve any issues between us."

Latifa shook her head. "My mind is made up. I am leaving."

"This can't be our final parting."

Latifa tried unsuccessfully to wipe away her tears. "Your life is here. My life is in Nubia. Please know, you shall remain in my heart always."

"Is this how King Solomon and the Queen of Sheba felt when they parted?" Tariq questioned.

Latifa smiled slightly. "Surely it was. I am sure the Queen told Solomon what I tell you and that is my life in Nubia shall not be as it was for my heart is broken and it shall never be whole again."

Their lips met once more in a searing kiss that seemed to bind their souls together for eternity. When their lips parted, it was as if the very life within them left their bodies.

Latifa looked up at Tariq and in that moment she once again waited…hoped…wanted to hear him say he loved her. If he did, she would put her fear and anxiety aside and stay with him despite all that stood between them.

He opened his mouth.

She held her breath and waited for him to speak.

"Go in peace," he murmured.

Upon hearing his words, Latifa stepped from his embrace. Turning slowly, she walked to the side gate in the garden, opened it and stepped out of the garden. She looked at the waning sun then cast one last look at Tariq before she shut the gate and walked away.

Chapter Sixteen

From her place atop a horse, Latifa watched the crowd of Nubians fill the street. In accordance to Tariq's decree, Nubians newly released from slavery added to the count creating a joyous multitude. Lively chatter and cheerful songs filled the air causing Latifa to wish she could feel some of the happiness around her. But, the truth was, all she felt was numb. She was leaving Tariq and there was no joy in her heart. Pulling the reins of her horse, she brought the animal to a stop. Glancing over her shoulder, she looked at the place that was to have been her home.

"Having second thoughts about embarking on the journey home?" a familiar voice sounded in her ear.

Latifa turned and saw her father had ridden his horse next to hers. "I must return home. I must," she muttered.

"You don't look happy about it," he noted.

"I am not," Latifa revealed.

"Let not your heart be troubled. We are returning home where things shall be as planned. Kofi does not know what has transpired in this land. Once I explain things to him, he'll be willing to forgive you for being with the Egyptian. He is a kind man and shall understand the Egyptian is a heathen who made you do things you wouldn't have done unless you were forced to do them. Your wedding to Kofi shall proceed as I intended. You must forget about the Egyptian and your time in Egypt. Once you are married, you shall be like your sister, happy to have a man of your own," her father assured.

"Isn't this wonderful? Our people are returning home," Aleka grinned as she sidled her horse to the pair and brought her steed to a stop beside them. Her grin faded when she looked at her daughter. "Is anything troubling you?" she asked.

Latifa shook her head negatively then spurred her horse forward so her parents would not see the tears crowding in her eyes.

When night fell, Latifa unable to sleep walked to the entrance of the tent that was her resting place. Stepping through the opening, she scanned the encampment. Lulled by the stillness of the night, she looked up at the moon in its place high in the sky. It was the same moon by whose light she and Tariq walked when they were on the trail. On a night such as this, she had come close to making love to him. After which, she had found out their passionate encounter had been viewed by spectators and had fled from the Egyptians' camp. Instead of running away as before, she now wished she could run back into Tariq's arms.

Even as she thought the thought, she knew she could not go back. She did not belong in Tariq's world. Her presence in his life served only to complicate both their lives. She loved him too much to stand in his way and loved herself too much to risk her life again. But, if he truly loved her… If only Tariq had told her he loved her. If only she had told him she loved him. Maybe things could have been different. He treated her with such gentleness and kindness. Maybe that was his way of telling her he loved her. Shouldn't that be all she needed? Why had she let uncertainty get in the way? After the way she fled her life with Tariq, Latifa knew her father had been right. She would not have made a very good warrior. But, should she blame herself? Tariq was a decisive, authoritative leader. If he loved her, he would have taken the lead and told her of his love. She should not have had to wonder if she had a place in his heart.

Her father was sure Kofi would still want her. Since he had never formally called off their betrothal, officially she was duty bound to proceed with the wedding. Even though this was true, just as before, she still did not want to marry Kofi. This time, it was not because she wanted to be a warrior. Nor was it because she did not want to be involved with a man. It was because she had met Tariq. It was because she knew how it felt to be in love. She now wanted to be involved with a man. She did not want to live a life without love. The truth was, in her heart, she knew she would never be happy in Kofi's arms or receiving Kofi's kiss. All she wanted was Tariq.

She lowered her head. She had to stop thinking of Tariq. She had just been reunited with her family and could not leave them. She had decided love was not enough to keep her in Egypt. She would return to Nubia so that she along with her parents and sister could rebuild their lives together as a family.

From his place in bed, Tariq closed his eyes and listened to the quietness of the night. The menacing claws of silence pried his eyes back opened and commanded him out of bed. Exhaling deeply, he donned a robe, walked to the balcony and looked up at the moon. Its apricot colored light splashed against the walls surrounding the palace illuminating the guards who move along the parapets. Shifting his gaze, he looked beyond the walls toward the city. The streets looked as lonely and empty as he felt. Such feelings were preventing his sleep. He realized he had felt a similar heavy heartedness when he thought Latifa was dead. He knew why he felt as he did now. It was because Latifa was gone never to return.

His thoughts turned to their last meeting. Her declaration that they could not be together had been unexpected and shocking. Never had he dreamed he would be unnerved over the loss of a woman. He had thought he could live life without involving his heart with such feelings of... It could not be love, could it? He never expected love...thought he had no use for love. With Latifa, he had been provoked by her fire and courage then ravaged with desire for her body. Had he finally been consumed by love for her? If so, when had it happened? He was not sure.

He would not have guessed he would one day want a wife let alone want Latifa for his wife. Remembering the first day they met, he slipped his fingers under his robe and touched his side where she had cut him. He felt the scar that remained. Their relationship had gotten off to a tumultuous start. But, somehow things had changed. His side had healed but without Latifa in his life his heart would not. During the time he thought she was dead, he realized a truth and that was without her he was not whole.

221

Tariq gritted his teeth. He was a battle hardened warrior. He was Pharaoh. King of all Egypt. Not a love sick boy. He had no time for thoughts of love. He had no time for a woman especially one who rejected him. Latifa rejected him! How dare she reject him! He had power and wealth. Every woman in his kingdom whether slave or free delighted at the chance to catch his eye. Selma had even conspired murder in hopes that he remain hers. He could snap his finger and have his bedroom filled with maidens eager to please him. Since that was true, he needed to move past his confounded feelings over Latifa's departure.

Tariq sat on the wall of the balcony and once again thought about his final conversation with Latifa in the garden. She told him she did not feel safe in Egypt. She had noted that there were a lot of barriers that stood between them. None of those barriers were important to him. What was important was there was only one woman he wanted. The question was what was he going to do about it?

Tariq recalled the news he received from the messenger that the Nubians who left the city were camped near Aswan. He could send word to Latifa in Aswan and command her to return to the palace and be with him. He was Pharaoh after all and his word was law. Tariq smirked at the thought. Not even the words of the Pharaoh could get Latifa to do something she did not want to do. He knew that all too well.

Tariq slapped the palm of his hand against the balcony wall. He had too much pride to grovel to a woman. Instead, he should respect the reasons why she left and just let her go. But, truth be told, he did not want to let her go. The facts were the obstacles that were between them stemmed from his position as Pharaoh. He had never wanted to be Pharaoh. He had never planned on giving up the nomadic life of a warrior and settling for palace life. Life as Pharaoh meant nights alone in the huge palace which never felt like his home. So, what was the solution to his dilemma?

"Tariq!"

Tariq looked down at the person who called his name and saw it was Jabari who hailed him. He noticed mauve light covered Jabari's face and realized the sun was about to rise which meant he had sat on the wall of the balcony all night. He waved to Jabari and shouted out, "I'll meet you in The Great Room!"

Jabari nodded and disappeared inside the palace.

Tariq walked back into his bedroom then made his way to The Great Room where Jabari waited.

"You look ragged," Jabari noted when Tariq entered the room.

"I haven't been to sleep," Tariq revealed as he sank into a chair around one of the tables in the room.

"Regretting letting the Nubians go?" Jabari questioned.

"I am regretting letting one Nubian go."

"Latifa."

Tariq nodded.

Jabari pulled back one of the chairs from the table and sat in it. "The last time we spoke of it, you were content to let her be your concubine. The next thing I know, you asked her to be your wife. What made you change your mind?"

"When I was presented with the option of being with another woman, I realized I wanted Latifa more than I wanted any other woman. I remembered how I felt when I thought she was dead. When I thought she was dead, I wanted just one more moment to talk to her...to see her. I missed her feisty irreverent attitude, her courage and her fire for life. If I did not choose to make her my wife, I would have confined her to a life of scorn and rebuke that comes to a woman who plays the role of concubine. I know Latifa does not deserve to have her reputation disparaged. She deserves much better than that. Just as my mother deserved to have it, Latifa deserves to have the title of wife."

"You haven't admitted it to yourself but it's time you admit you're in love."

Tariq inhaled deeply. "So, this is love? My heart hurts and I feel...miserable at the moment."

Jabari grinned. "I never thought I would see you fall in love especially with a girl who at one point could not stand the sight of you, cut you with a knife and tried to poison you. However, I knew you loved Latifa when I saw the way

223

you reacted when you thought she had departed to the afterlife. I thought Latifa was an improper companion for you. I continue to have my misgivings, especially after she listened to Narmer and tried to poison you. But, to be fair, I listened to him as well."

Tariq's brow wrinkled.

"I was not honest with you during the time you thought Latifa was dead. I went along with Narmer and agreed to tell you she had been killed."

"What?" Tariq abruptly stood to his feet. "You knew Latifa was alive yet you lied to me!"

Jabari nodded.

Tariq clenched his right hand into a fist and rammed it against Jabari's jaw. Unchecked, he clinched his left hand into a fist and smacked Jabari's jaw in a follow through so forceful it sent Jabari tumbling out of his chair.

From his place on the floor, Jabari rubbed his cheek then sheepishly hung his head. "I wanted you to stay focused on the military because I thought it was what was best for Egypt. You've known me for a long time. You know all I want is to serve Egypt."

"You betrayed me! I ought to have you flogged!"

"I promise it shall never happen again. I did it because I felt it was best for you. I now know I was mistaken."

"I never thought you would listen to Narmer but I should have suspected it." Tariq began to pace the room. "There was no way you could have known on your own that Latifa needed a bandage for her leg after the boating mishap near Elephantine Island. Yet you brought bandages along with dry clothes to her." He slammed his fist into his palm. "Everyone I trusted listened to Narmer."

Jabari rose to his feet, straightened the chair he had been knocked from and sat back in it. "I was mistaken to forget the direction of your destiny cannot be assumed...that your path still unfolds before you. Latifa could have told you about my dishonorable actions at any time. But, she did not. For that I esteem her. Since she means that much to you, go after her," Jabari stated.

"A short time ago, you were displeased because you thought she had too much sway over me. Now, you tell me I love Latifa and I should go after her."

"When it comes to love, it may seem unlikely but I know what I'm talking about."

Tariq looked at him skeptically.

Jabari's lips stretched into thin lines as he nodded to the empty chair at the table. "Have a seat," he said in a low voice.

Tariq sank back into his seat.

"Over the years, we've put our lives on the line for each other. We've shared almost everything."

"That is true," Tariq conceded.

"There is something that I never shared with you. Before I joined the military, I was in love. She was my life. I wanted to found a house with her. Her father forbade our union because he was a nobleman and I was the son of a farmer. He said he wanted his daughter to marry someone titled. I listened to him and instead of marrying her as I'd planned, I joined the military. I figured I could advance within the ranks from my station as a foot soldier and earn a title. My love begged me to stay. However, I decided to leave and return to her once I had a title.

"Shortly after I returned from a military campaign, I found out she was going to have my child. I knew it was dishonorable for an unmarried woman to be with child and I did not want to abandon her to such a fate. I decided I would marry her despite her father's objection. But, when I went for her, she and her family were gone. I never saw her again nor did I see my child. Since my love would not be with me, I became devoted to Egypt. I dedicated my life to the military. I think all this time, I've been hoping an enemy's arrow would strike my heart and put me out of my misery."

"That is an incredibly sad story."

Jabari cleared his throat. "Don't make the same mistake I did. Go after Latifa. Tell her how you feel. It is true, I disapproved of Latifa because she swayed your thoughts. But, it was also because she reminded me of my lost love and how I should have listened and let my love

225

sway my thoughts. Don't let your love get away from you as mine did from me. From this day forward, I shall support your relationship with Latifa."

"The crown is what has come between Latifa and I. I took the throne because it is what my father desired and I wanted to please him. But, what has it brought me? I never planned or wanted to be Pharaoh. I am just the bastard son of the Pharaoh. Maybe problems are arising because Narmer is right and I am not the rightful heir to the throne."

"Never speak as if you might give up the crown. To do so would mean future generations would not know your name for your name would be erased from all monuments, official documents and notices. Though his attempt to claim the throne was defeated before, if you were to abandon the throne and Narmer was no longer a threat, Osorkon son of Takelot and Queen Kapes would no doubt seize the chance to ascend to power and rule from Tanis. It would then be Osorkon's name and his lineage that is remembered. You must admit to yourself once and for all if you love Latifa or if it is just lust you feel for her. If it is love heed my advice."

Tariq was quiet for a moment. "I do love Latifa. I shall go after her and try to convince her to live as my Queen. I refuse to return to the palace without her. The crown means nothing to me if I have no one to share it with."

Tariq rose to his feet and called for a servant. When the servant appeared, he ordered a horse readied stating he could travel faster if he did not travel in a royal transport. Jabari insisted he have security travel with him. Tariq reluctantly agreed stating the men were to stay out of sight. Tariq then returned to his room and dressed as a commoner.

When he exited the palace, he found Jabari standing beside his awaiting horse.

"It's uncertain if Latifa shall return to live as my wife. She could maintain the obstacles between us are too much to overcome."

"You have decided fitting solutions to tenuous situations before. The best course of action shall come to you."

226

"Just as I go after Latifa, you must go after your love. Maybe you can find her," Tariq suggested.

"So much time has passed—"

"Just as my destiny is still unfolding so is yours. You are a true friend, Jabari. You have been closer to me than my own brother," Tariq revealed as he adjusted the *klaft* that covered his head.

The two men hugged each other then Tariq climbed on his awaiting horse. Without another word, he spurred the horse toward the palace gate. Exiting the gate, he road swiftly through the city then directed his steed to the banks of the Nile. Once there, he boarded a *felucca* headed for Aswan.

⋈

As she had before, Latifa sat atop her horse and watched as a horde of happy Nubians dressed in brightly colored *kangas* and *kitenges* passed before her. Once again, she told herself she should be like everyone else and be happy to be heading back to Nubia. But, the truth was, now that her people were on the move again she was unhappier than ever. After all, today was to have been her wedding day....the day she became Tariq's wife...the day she became Queen of Egypt. Instead, she was leaving Tariq and Egypt never to see either again.

"I'll ask you once more, is anything troubling you?" her mother's voice interrupted her musing.

Latifa glanced at her mother who sat atop a horse. Instead of answering the inquiry, she lowered her head without speaking a word.

"I am your mother. I would like to know what is troubling you," Aleka explained.

Latifa was silent for many moments. Finally, she said, "I am miserable."

"Why are you miserable?"

"I know what I must do but it is heart wrenching."

"And what is it you must do?"

"I must leave Egypt."

"What is your reason for leaving?"

227

"It is the only option."

"Then you agree with your father and once we are home you'll marry Kofi as planned."

"I can't marry Kofi for I do not love him."

Her mother nodded. "I know, daughter. It is written all over your face. Deep in his heart, your father knows it too. He just wants you to be safe and well taken care of. That's the reason he's insisting on proceeding with your marriage to Kofi. But, it's obvious a marriage to Kofi is ill advised because your heart yearns for the Egyptian."

"I find I don't want to leave him."

"Then do not leave."

Latifa lowered her head. "I am leaving because we belong to two different worlds. He is ruler of all of Egypt. He lives in a land where people do anything for power...including murder. I just wouldn't feel safe."

"And what of your world?"

"My world is my family. We are newly reunited. I could not bear another separation."

"But you can bear to spend the rest of your life with your heart in misery. That is your solution?"

"It is the only way," Latifa mustered a forlorn frown.

"Is it really the only way?" her mother questioned.

The pair fell quiet as they watched the last of the travelers in the retreating group pass in front of them.

Aleka broke the silence. "Look at our people. They travel very well without you as part of the group. If you love Tariq as much as it seems, you should return to him."

"But—"

"Forget the objections. If he loves you as much as you love him...together the two of you should be able to find a way to solve the problems between you. Look at it this way, daughter. Since Tariq is Pharaoh of Egypt, I am sure he can figure out a way to keep you safe and see to it that you see your family."

Latifa's heart began to thump in her chest. Was it truly possible she and Tariq could make a life together? Did she dare believe she would not have to fear for her safety in Egypt? Was it possible she could stay with Tariq and still maintain contact with her family? Though her sense of

228

safety with Tariq had been shattered, maybe it could be restored. If her mother said it was possible, surely it was. With a sliver of renewed hope, she looked at the crowd of Nubians trudging toward the horizon.

"You must make your decision. Do we ride to catch up with our people and head home? Or do I put you on a *felucca* back to Thebes?"

Latifa scanned the mass of people in the distance to see if she could spot her father somewhere in the crowd. "I must speak with Father. He has to approve of the decision I make. He would never forgive me if I made my decision without consulting him."

"Your father is leading the exodus. You must make your choice and not look back. If you choose to return home, we must ride to catch up with the group. If you choose to return to Thebes, leave it to me to make your father understand. I can explain everything to him. He knows what it's like to be separated from the person you love. Our hearts have been hurting since we were torn apart five years ago. Neither one of us want that for you."

Latifa gingerly bit down on her lip. The next decision she made would change the course of her life forever. After she made her choice, there was no going back. Did she ignore her heart, do the reasonable thing and return home? Or, did she follow her heart and risk not seeing her family again? Should she head into an unknown future without knowing if the man she loved loved her in return? Truly, this was the most difficult decision she ever had to make.

"I want to be with Tariq. I do not want the life I'll live without him," the words spilled out of her mouth before she could stop them.

"So, you want to return to Thebes."

Latifa looked at her mother and nodded. "I love Tariq and I want to be with him. But, I turned down his offer of marriage. I don't know if he loves me or shall want me back."

Aleka opened her mouth to speak then promptly closed it.

Latifa watched her mother's gaze shift to a point behind her. She turned to see what had caught her mother's attention.

When she did, she saw a man on a horse riding in a gallop toward them. Her brow wrinkled. Who was the rider and why was he approaching the retreating Nubians with such haste? Sand kicked up by the hooves of the horse swirled in the air obscuring a movement behind the advancing horse. Latifa focused on the movement and realized it was a dog running behind the horse. She blinked in amazement when she recognized the dog was Anubis. If Anubis was near...

Latifa's heart picked up speed. She shifted her eyes to the rider. Could it be?

Suddenly, the rider raised his hand and pulled the headdress from his head.

"Tariq!" Latifa exclaimed the moment she recognized him. In a flash, she prodded her horse into a gallop toward the man she loved.

The pounding of the horses' hooves against the earth matched the fast paced pounding of the lovers' hearts with each movement bringing the couple closer and closer together.

When their horses neared, Latifa saw Tariq slow his steed and jump from his stallion. Latifa followed his lead then called out his name as she sprinted toward him. A few moments later, she was in his arms.

"I don't want to live life without you," he breathe in her ear. "Return to the palace with me. If you do, I shall see to it that you are safe. If you find you can't and it means losing you, I'll leave it all behind."

Latifa blinked in surprise as she stared at Tariq. "I cannot believe what I am hearing."

A dog's bark caused the couple to look and see Anubis wagging her tail as she scampered to the pair.

Latifa knelt and petted the canine. Anubis licked her face causing her to laugh.

"What is Anubis doing here?" she questioned.

"I realized she was following me shortly after I left the palace," Tariq revealed. "It seems she knew I was coming after you and she wanted to make sure you did not get away. She is the reason we discovered you were in Kwame's tomb."

"I am beyond impressed with this dog," Latifa giggled.

"She's just like me. She doesn't want to live without you."

Latifa rose to her feet. "My mother thinks we can come to a solution that allows us to be together. Surely that is true."

"Of course, your mother is right." Tariq rubbed his chin thoughtfully. "I have a solution. If you stay in Thebes, to make you feel safe, I shall banish the High Priest and all of the Councilmen who follow him. Or if you desire, we shall leave Thebes and change the location of the capital from Thebes. Another alternative, since your home was destroyed by Narmer your people have nothing to go back to. Instead of rebuilding, your people should make Aswan the new home of the Nubians. If they stay in Aswan, you can see your family anytime you so desire."

"Oh Tariq. Do you think it's possible my people could stay in Aswan?"

"It is your father's decision. If your father declines the offer to stay in Aswan and your family returns to Nubia, a treaty has been established between Egypt and Nubia to trade gold. There shall be caravans traveling between the territories all the time. You shall be able to see your family as much as you like."

At the mention of her family, Latifa looked around. She saw her mother was riding toward the departing throng. She turned her eyes to Tariq. "I can't believe you are offering such things."

"I make the offer because I am a warrior who fights for what I want. You must reconsider your decision and become my wife."

"Tariq, I am happy you still want me to be your wife. But, I am still not certain why you want to be with me."

Tariq reached out, took her hand and placed it over the small scar on his side. "That first day we met you cut me here. Do you remember?"

Latifa gently ran her fingers over the small scar then nodded.

"Though I was unaware of it, you branded me then and now I am yours. You proved to be a better warrior than me, for you have caused me to surrender to you."

"Oh Tariq, I am no warrior."

"No? Then what are you?"

"I am just a woman who knows you want me to be your wife but does not know exactly how you feel about me."

"I want you to be my wife because I love you, Latifa, with all my heart. Now and forever I'll always love you. I once thought love was foolishness. I thought a warrior had no use for love...that having status in the military would be enough. I was sure love would make me weak and make me lose my focus. I can stand here and say I was wrong to think such things because I love you and want to be with you."

"I am so happy to hear you say those words. I did not think I would ever hear you tell me you love me."

"I do love you. Even Jabari can see that I love you. He told me about his involvement with Narmer. He apologized and said he shall support our relationship. You once said you thought the Pharaoh was deceitful and treacherous. I hope you see I am none of those things. I am just a man who never expected to fall in love."

"I was wrong to assume the worse about you. I was wrong to ever want to cause you harm. You are a good man and I am proud to be with you. When I told you I couldn't stay with you, it was because I was afraid so I retreated. I want you to forgive me for walking away from—"

Tariq placed his finger over Latifa's lips silencing her. "There is nothing to forgive, little lioness," he whispered.

In the next instant, Tariq swept Latifa into his arms. His lips touched her lips in a searing kiss that made Latifa's legs weak and caused her to lean into him just as she had done the first time they kissed. For many moments, there was only the two of them in the world.

When their lips parted, Latifa looked at Tariq then she looked in the direction she had come in time to see her people about to disappear in the distance. As she relaxed in Tariq's embrace, she realized she had no desire to follow her tribesmen. She was exactly where she wanted to be – happily wrapped in Tariq's arms.

As she relished the feel of Tariq's arms around her, she thought back to earlier times and recalled her father telling her she was not the type to be a woman of war. He had told her she should forget that misdirected sentiment and think about getting married. According to him, she would be happiest in a relationship with a man. A smile graced her lips. She would have to tell her father what he wanted had finally happened. She had put away that misdirected sentiment. She no longer wanted to be a warrior. She wanted to be a wife...Tariq's wife.

Her life had turned out so differently than she planned. In the life she planned, there was no finding enjoyment in a man's arms. But things had changed. Now, she could not imagine living the life she once thought she wanted because she now knew how wonderful it felt to love and be loved. She looked forward to her new life. In her new life, there was love. There was marriage. There was safety. And there was honor. She looked forward to her future and it was all because she had been seduced by the Pharaoh.

Author's Note

Thank you for taking time out of your busy schedule to read *Seduced by the Pharaoh*. I really hope you found it to be an enjoyable read. If so, you will probably like the other books I have written. You can find them on my website www.TheWorldsBestBook.com. If you find the other books I have written to be entertaining, please do not forget to tell a friend about them.

Peace and Love,

Sheniqua Waters

Have You Read?

Something to Hide by Sheniqua Waters
Slavery. Seduction. Secrets. – Southern belle Lily lives a life of privilege on her father's tobacco plantation before she marries the man she loves, a rancher named Brock. When Lily's enemies learn the secret of her birth, they enact an insidious ruse to have her abducted into the seedy world of slavery.

After years away, Lily survives the auction block and makes her way home only to find Brock has developed feelings for another woman. Can Lily make her husband remember the love they shared before it is too late? Or will the secrets she holds keep them apart forever?

Slave Girl by Sheniqua Waters
Home. Happiness. Harem. – Laila cannot believe she has been kidnapped from her happy home. When she finds herself sold into a Turkish harem, she is not sure she will ever make it back to those she loves. Once she catches the eye of the handsome yet arrogant palace heir, Kudar al Numan, her days and nights in the harem become much more than she expects.

As Laila fights to deny her feelings for Kudar, their relationship is threatened by the jealousy of another woman. When Laila's nemesis hatches a plan to separate her for Kudar, is there hope for a happy ever after?